SH

A CALCULATED GUESS

A Novel By

SUSAN RANELLE AMARI

 For information, address Bridgehampton Publishing, PO Box 90, Peninsula, OH 44264.

First Printing, 2016

ISBN: 9780692683736
ISBN: 0692683739

For additional copies, or to contact the author, visit *acalculatedguess.com* or address the publisher at PO Box 90, Peninsula, OH, 44264.

Acknowledgements:

Cover design: Julianna Kovach Zingale | Cleveland
Photo by © Scott Pond Studios, LLC
Editing: Ronald O'Keefe

CHAPTER ONE

The Event April 2013

It happened at dusk, at the end of a brightly lit day that offered the assurance that the Ohio winter had reached its long anticipated end. As he drove home, Oliver Warner's mood reflected this annually anticipated triumph of nature, and he allowed himself a moment of accomplishment.

When had he had that last joint? Around 9:00 a.m., he thought.

He had found it under that form he needed to send to Social Security. It had somehow escaped the clean sweep he had conducted three days earlier when he decided to go totally clean. And when he found it, he remembered what the Dalai Lama said about there being no accidents in life.

He tapped his fingers against the steering wheel, scrunched up his slightly bloodshot eyes, and put a hand through his curly, white hair. Maybe it wasn't the Dalai Lama, he thought. Now who said that? Jesus?

No, he countered, Jesus said stuff more along the lines of "if you find an errant joint, share it with someone who doesn't have one."

He gripped the steering wheel. Why couldn't he remember?

He thought for a moment, then felt his body relax. Oh why did he always get stuck on trivialities? What did it matter who exactly said it? The most important thing is someone pretty smart did.

So when he came upon the joint and thought of the quote, he knew it wasn't some random accident, it was something much bigger, like the universe telling him he should stop trying to be someone he wasn't. So he figured what the heck, and smoked it right before breakfast. And then what happened?

Nothing, he thought, leaning back. Not one single thing!

Nothing happened that was any worse or better than the previous three days when he was clean. Nobody irritated him more or less, or said anything unusually stupid or brilliant. And best of all, no one seemed to notice.

He smiled, reached for his *The Big Pink* CD, the one he always chose to mark significant moments of triumph, put it into the slot, and turned up the volume.

It was just so obvious, he thought. He was just one of those people who could smoke an occasional joint, and life would proceed just as usual. And anyway, if there was any time in life you should be able to enjoy a joint, it would be the age of sixty-two. Career for all intents and purposes over; marriage long over; kid raised with a life of her own.

He would just keep it like Ben Franklin or Dr. Oz recommended. Reasonable moderation. Nothing stronger than weed. Two joints a day. One in the morning, one at night. Like an aperitif. Civilized.

So it was now time for his second.

He moved in his seat, felt a slight twinge of uneasiness. There probably wasn't another joint left in his apartment, he thought. He'd have to call someone, pick up something on the way home.

He reached over with his right hand, left hand on the wheel, and rummaged through the CDs, paperback books, and random ATM receipts that covered the passenger seat. Where was that iPhone? It was probably at the bottom of everything, he thought. He leaned more to the right, then looked down.

There it was, black rectangle on the floor. He reached down, and grasped it with his right hand. When his eyes returned to the road, she was there, long flowing hair and wide surprised eyes caught in the headlights. He let the phone drop, slammed on the brakes, and had a momentary hope that disintegrated into a sickening thud.

He pulled off to the side of the road, flung the door open, and ran up to her. He heard his breathing against the exaggerated pounding of his heart.

She was face down and motionless, her blood spattered hair fanned the gray cement. He knelt down and touched her back, then turned her over, put his fingers on her neck and checked for a pulse. Nothing.

A car screeched to a halt. He heard a door open and close, and then a man, holding a cell phone, ran towards him. "Are you OK? Jesus! I called 911, they should be here soon. I was right behind you, saw the whole thing. Is she alive? She can't be alive. Jesus."

Oliver picked up one of her outstretched hands. Long, slender fingers. The fingers of an artist. He felt for a pulse at the wrist, then gently placed the arm down. Her silver bangle bracelets jangled, an ankh ring glimmered in the last of the setting sun. He slumped down next to her, next to the elegant boots set at inelegant angles, and listened to the sound of approaching sirens.

One police car pulled up, then two, followed by an ambulance. The vehicles' lights cast garish flashes, like disco balls from hell.

The man with the phone ran up to one of the police officers, as paramedics went to the body. "I saw everything. She came out of nowhere. Nowhere!" he said.

The officer took out a flashlight, looked at the ground. "Did you see a purse?"

"A purse?" asked the man.

"Identification."

The man called to Oliver. "Did you see a purse?"

Oliver shook his head.

"Probably thrown," the officer replied. "One thing I know for sure. She didn't come from nowhere. Everybody comes from somewhere."

CHAPTER TWO

WHAT CAME BEFORE CATE

She put her fork down, ran a hand through her long, dark hair, then dramatically raised her eyes to the ceiling. "Oh my God! It's just a trip," she said, waving her hands in emphasis. "What is the big deal about a trip to help a sick friend? You went on that golf trip to Scotland, remember? And no one was sick then. It was just 'cause you wanted to."

Craig looked at her over his wire-rimmed glasses. "It's not the same thing and you know it." He shook his head, then returned to his pasta. "Golfing in Scotland! Everyone knows that's a once in a lifetime thing." He speared a piece of pasta with his fork, raised it to his mouth. "And anyway, we weren't even really a couple then, it was at the very beginning."

Cate watched as he chewed, then she leaned forward. "You told me to read a book. When I said a week was so long, you said 'read a book.' I am only going to New Orleans for a weekend, so you can make it a short book."

He put his fork down and took a bite of garlic bread. The melted butter dribbled down his chin. "But it's the weekend of the Ohio State-Purdue game. You knew that! You were going to meet Pat and Lou and their wives. And I've already responded to that alumni tail-gate thing, remember? The thing with Brutus?"

She bit her lip, lifted her napkin to her mouth. "Yes, I know and I feel really bad about that, but what could I do? I couldn't tell him no! Not when he called and asked. Can you imagine how difficult that must have been for him, asking for help? And he's sick, really sick, and we've been friends forever, since college."

"And he—what's his name again?"

"Trey. Well really Antoine Doussan-Fossier III, but everyone calls him Trey."

"So this Trey . . ." he cocked his head, narrowed his eyes. "He doesn't have anyone else to help him out?"

"Well his parents are passed, and he's always been sort of private. He never worked—not that I remember anyway. Had family money, you know, investment stuff."

Craig took a drink. "That's odd. Your being friends with someone like that. I mean, you of all people admiring someone living off of old southern money."

She moved in her seat, reached for a second piece of garlic bread, felt his eyes on her hands. "He's a friend. And he's gay, if that's what you're worried about."

"Oh gay, of course," he said, sitting back in his seat. "Yes, of course, that would negate everything else."

She picked up the piece of bread, fondled it in her hand, then looked at him, and took a large bite. She chewed slowly, deliberately.

He sighed in mock exaggeration. "You aren't punishing me by eating those carbs Cate." Then he leaned forward, lowered his voice.

"You have a very prominent passive-aggressive streak. It's really quite unattractive."

"Well is it attractive to turn down a life-long friend when he asks for help because there's a tailgate party in Columbus?"

"It's not just that," he said, settling back into his chair. "Well maybe a little, but mostly that's just the straw that broke the camel's back."

He lifted his napkin, shook the crumbs on the floor, then put it back on his lap. "We've been seeing each other for what? Three months? Three months and there is always something. The kids, your mother, your job, now a—" he held up his hands in air quotes, " 'sick' friend . . ."

"I hate it when you do that quotation mark stuff."

He rolled his eyes, clasped his hands together. "Can we be adult here? Is it so hard for you to understand? It's not just this trip to New Orleans, it's the fact that there's *always* something else. Come on. Your youngest kid is twenty-three, a year older than mine, and I have a mother, too. I handle the exact same things fine, and always find time for you."

She took a deep breath, then with a hesitation that quickly moved to resignation, pushed her plate forward, placed her napkin on top. "But . . . the truth of it is, you don't handle the exact same things, do you? I mean, you don't really take care of your mother. Your sister takes care of her. You call once a week. Big difference."

She leaned back in her seat, took a glass of water, then smoothed the tablecloth in front of her. "And your kids? Let's get real. Your ex-wife raised your kids, you visited."

He pointed his fork. "Why go there Cate? That personal low blow? I have told you many, many times, I broke my neck to see my kids as much as I could. Never missed one of those weekend visitations!"

She leaned forward. "But you were the one who said we do the exact same things and you can handle it and I can't. I'm just pointing out the difference."

"OK," he said putting his fork down. "OK! You win. You do more! Happy? Now can we please get back to what we were talking about? The fact is that I'm really, really tired of feeling like the last thing on a long list of things you have to do. Pun intended." He held up his hand, motioning to the waiter for the bill.

They avoided eye contact, sat in awkward silence until the waiter returned. Craig signed the receipt with a flourish, then put the pen down. "You know what? Go to New Orleans. And I will do what I need to do, which is find someone who can make a relationship a priority, not a sporadic diversion."

He put the copy of the bill in his pocket, took a drink of water. "And if you ever want a real, adult relationship, you know my number, call."

Cate tilted her head, narrowed her eyes. "You know what I think? When you're at that game, why don't you try to work your magic on one of those cheerleaders, because that's what you want. A twenty-year-old with nothing on her plate but you."

He stood up, walked to her side of the table, and leaned down, close to her face. "Just so you know Cate, that's what every man wants." Then he turned and walked away.

She sat for a moment, then picked up her purse and went to the door, pushing it open. She felt the brisk autumn air on her face.

It was such a beautiful night, still some sun lingering in the sky. People were walking on each side of the cobblestone streets; opera music streamed from a restaurant. She passed a storefront window and stopped. In between the Italian soccer shirts and pictures of Frank Sinatra, she caught her reflection.

Long hair, shapely body, boots. She studied the reflection for a moment, leaning closer. Maybe she could lose five pounds, she thought. Maybe tomorrow she'd start on that new diet. She bit her lip and turned around, almost bumping into an older man heading the opposite way.

"Oh, sorry," she said.

"*La mia fortuna, bella signora.*"

She stopped, then smiled. "*Grazie,*" she replied, tossing her hair. "*Grazie mille!*"

She quickened her pace, listening to the comforting click click click of her boots on the cobblestone street as she headed towards the parking lot. She turned down a side street, got to her car and opened its door.

Oh, she was so uncomfortable, her stomach pressing so tightly against her jeans. She tapped her fingers on the car door. It was all those carbs, she thought. Those carbs mixed with Craig and twenty-year-old cheerleaders. They had combined, creating a large, bitter knot in the pit of her stomach.

She spotted a green space off to the side, closed the car door and walked towards it, passing a young couple walking a dog. She turned and watched as they walked out of sight, then quickly crossed over to the green space, behind a large tree.

She bent over, made herself sick, then wiped her mouth, and walked back to the car. She opened the door and sat down, took a drink from the water bottle on the passenger seat.

Better. Yes, she felt better. Now she could start fresh.

She reached for her CDs, pulling out the one titled *Cate's Favorites*, and put it in the player. She put the key into the ignition and pulled out of the parking lot.

Call when you want a real adult relationship.

What a self-important Neanderthal! He visited his kids twice a month? Called his mother once a week? He had no idea what she had to deal with.

And, anyway, what was the point of that whole dressing-down? Was it to help her, be a partner to her? Basically it could have all been edited down to a "what about me?" Well, she knew exactly where that would lead. Pretty soon, instead of visiting art galleries in New York or Asheville, she'd be off watching him golf in Hilton Head, or wasting fall weekends on tailgating parties with Brutus. She couldn't handle one weekend of that, much less a whole season. Wasn't that the whole reason she came up with that story about Trey in the first place?

She pulled her car onto the on-ramp, merged into the highway traffic.

Trey.

God she hadn't talked to him in long time. She really should give him a call, maybe tonight. It was still early after all.

⅄

Cate opened the apartment door and went straight to the refrigerator, pulling out the unopened, large bottle of Passion Fruit Margarita Light that was sitting next to the soy milk. Her mom had put it in her grocery cart the last time she took her shopping (along with three bottles of white-out, and a jumbo box of tampons). Cate hadn't noticed until they were half-way through check out, and at that point returning things seemed too complicated and time-consuming. Plus her mom had already handed the clerk a dollar off coupon for the tampons, and Cate had learned long ago never, ever to question the purchase of anything if her mother had a dollar off coupon.

Tonight was as good a night as any to see if the Passion Margarita was drinkable, she thought, breaking its seal and pouring the bright pink liquid into the glass. She took a sip, and carried it into her bedroom, heading towards a large gold and black trunk at the foot of her bed.

She opened the lid and started pulling out the top contents, scattering them on the floor—the Mother's Day cards and the kids' Marine Fitness awards, a title to a car she had particularly loved. Half way down were baptismal and communion programs, her divorce decree and newspaper clippings from her first jobs at the paper. By the time she got to the navy blue and white scrapbook with Marietta College on the front, the bedroom floor was almost covered.

She pulled the scrapbook out and went to the bed, opening it to its first pages as she settled back into the pillows. An invitation and photo fell out. She picked up the invitation. In gold embossed lettering it read,

Antoine Doussan-Fossier III requests the honour of your presence
At a night of endless debauchery this Friday evening, 8:00 pm
at the Chateau
(If you require directions, this invitation was extended in error)

Funny she thought. If someone found this, even the kids, they would mistake it for just an ordinary keepsake, a fluke survivor of time.

She touched its worn edges.

It was her first invitation to one of Trey's parties, fall 1972. She had gotten it on an otherwise nondescript day when she had gone into the student union for coffee, and Stretch had handed her the manila envelope stamped with an embossed fleur-de-lis.

She knew when he handed it to her what it was, and more importantly, what it meant. Back then, it was confirmation that she had been deemed interesting. Not just popular, or good looking, or rich, because you could be all those things and never receive an invitation to one of Antoine Doussan-Fossier III's parties.

Trey's parties were nothing like any of the other college or frat house parties where people just showed up with a six pack of beer and some dope. Held at his off campus house which was always referred to as "The Chateau," they were only open to people who presented the hand delivered, fleur-de-lis invitations at the door.

The Chateau was a three story Victorian mansion on Washington Street, the largest boulevard in Marietta, with charming and rambling homes that dated back to the town's 1835 founding. It had a beautiful façade, turreted and stately, and stood in stark contrast to the usual off-campus party settings where cupboard doors hung off hinges, and stray, skinny dogs sniffed beer cans on the front lawns.

Trey, like his parties, was an equal mixture of legend and mystery. He was rarely seen on campus, and no one seemed to know his exact year of matriculation—just that he had been there a long time. He was older, maybe twenty-five, and his parents, who were from a line of Louisiana pirates and/or politicians, gave the school generous donations to ensure his continual enrollment.

Long before the day Cate received the invitation, she had looked him up on his fraternity composite. As she came to his picture, she felt a slight sense of deflation. No, she thought, this can't be right. Looking back at her was someone as unprovocative as one of the Beach Boys—brown, shoulder-length hair swept to the side; soft, prep school features devoid of any of his name or legend's colorful promise. But then she met him, and it was all there, all the things that had escaped the camera's lens. The flamboyance, the difference.

Cate placed the invitation down next to her, and reached for the photo.

There she was on Trey's couch with Stretch and Cindy. Stretch with his always-there sunglasses, arm draped around her shoulders;

Cindy on his lap leaning towards the camera, her smile enhanced by the wide doe eyes and long blonde hair that fell in seductive disarray around her shoulders.

Cindy. Now, that is where the camera got it right.

One look at her confident lean into the lens, and you knew pretty much all you needed to know about Cindy. Homecoming queen of her prestigious Virginia high school, she had come to the small college campus and took it by storm. There was nothing quite as compelling back then as a homecoming queen who opted out.

When Cindy walked into a room, eyes followed—to her face, where blonde innocence played against pouty seduction; and to her willowy, patrician frame that was always softened by a seemingly endless supply of ethereally flowing, hippie-chic clothes.

But the thing that got the eyes to stay was her sureness of attitude, a confidence and charisma that Cate thought surpassed almost every woman, and most of the men, she had met in all the years since.

She put the photo down, pulled on a bedspread thread.

Cindy could have become anything. Head of a corporation, maybe even a TV personality. Or maybe by now she was retired with grandkids. After all, she had married Mark shortly after graduation. Maybe at this very minute she was heading to the golf course wearing a sweatshirt that read "Nana hearts her grandkids."

Cate furrowed her eyes, then laughed. No. That was impossible.

She picked up the photo again.

Oh, yes. Yes. Cindy was probably writing. Writing important stuff, not the marketing slop Cate did for a living. Because—how had Professor Schwartz put it that day? Cindy's writing was ". . . on a different level. You can't teach writing like this."

When he had said that, it had made Cate crazy, knowing Cindy had written the assignment in all of about forty-five minutes while coming down from an acid trip, and Cate had painfully picked over hers for weeks.

She took a long drink from her glass, then went to the kitchen to pour another.

Yeah, that's probably what she is doing, she thought. Has probably left Mark by now and is traveling the world, living some romantic bohemian life, writing articles so impressive people cut them out and post them on refrigerators.

She filled the glass again and took a long drink, set the glass down, and picked up her phone.

"I was just thinking about you," Trey said, answering on the first ring. "I was hoping something in your life had blown up because that seems to be the only time you call. You broke up with someone, right?"

"Well, I guess . . . sort of. But this guy was really—"

"Controlling, I know. Come on Cate, admit it. Break-ups are your thing, that's where you shine. Relationships fuck you up. I didn't even recognize you during your marriage, even your hair was off. You cut it like that ice skater, remember?"

"Dorothy Hamill?"

"God that was terrible. And that marriage ridiculously went on and on and on. "

"Fourteen years, I know."

"I never liked that guy. Every time I talked to him, he'd nod his head and smile, but all the time he'd be scanning the room for someone better to talk to."

Cate walked over to the living room window. "I don't want to talk about that now. You know what I found? An invitation to one of your Chateau parties, and a picture of me, Stretch and Cindy." She looked out at the velvet sky. "What a great time that was. And I knew it then, isn't that funny? I knew it the day I left campus that something important was over, that things were never going to be the same."

"Well Cate, that doesn't exactly make you Jean Dixon. Everyone thinks the same thing when they leave college. And anyway, those years, or in my case, that decade, were happy, but they weren't heaven. You're just giving into that tendency you have towards romantic exaggeration."

"Oh really?" she asked. "What in the world was wrong with them? A million friends to talk to? Yeah, that was terrible. No one dying or getting sick? Yeah, who wouldn't miss that! No taxes to file or business meetings that go on and on till your head feels like it's going to blow up and—"

"OK, OK, point made. But not everything was perfect. Like I couldn't be *out* then."

"Oh sure you could have. No one would have cared."

Trey laughed. "Oh boy, have you forgotten. Back then, most everyone cared, even our friends. It's been forty years Cate. Geez. Forty years. You came to that first party with Cindy when you guys were what? Sophomores?"

"Right. Fall, 1972. Cindy. Do you know what she's doing? Do you think she's still with Mark?"

"Can't imagine that," he said, "but I sort of hope so. And I hope she gained fifty pounds and now plays bingo and wears patchwork sweatshirts and stuff. That would be worth waiting forty years to see. It would make me feel so better about my life, but it's probably too much to ask for."

"I thought about that too, but, no, that could never happen to Cindy."

"Why not Cate? Shit happens in life."

"Not that," she said.

"Why?" he asked. "Cindy's the only one in the world oblivious to time? Time changes everything. Plus, the one thing you can count on with time is crazy shit happens. Crazy shit that you could never see coming. Anyway, you always overestimated her! I honestly don't know what that was about. Self-confidence always seems to throw you off."

"No, I'm just saying she could have changed, but only up to a point. Remember how she always sang that song late at night when everyone was drunk—"

"*Me and Bobby McGee.*"

"Yeah! That's it!" She picked up her glass, took a drink. "Now how could someone like that, someone so pointedly cool, end up in grandma sweatshirts? It just wouldn't make sense. God, I'd love to see her again. And Duke and CK and Stretch. People aren't like that anymore, things are never about fun. Everyone's so, 'Oh, have you had your colonoscopy?' What happened to fun? Do you get your limit at twenty-one and then it's all over?"

"You know what I think? I think you need a vacation. Why don't you take a break, come down and visit?"

"Well now how could I do that? There's my mom and work and the kids—"

"Oh come on, Cate, you're talking to me, not a boyfriend you're keeping at bay. Your kids are out of the house, and I'm not talking about abandoning everything for a lifetime, I'm talking about three days. You're that important you can't take three days off?"

"Yeah but—"

"No buts. Anyway, I'm getting an idea. All you have to do is check flights and settle stuff there. Besides, maybe your family needs a break from you."

"Maybe," she said, standing up. "But this is so odd, I just told this guy tonight—oh never mind, it's a long story. I'll check things out tomorrow. You're still in New Orleans, right?"

"Cate," he said, "where else would I possibly be?"

⅄

After the call, she took a long, hot shower, then got out, and went to her room. She took the towel off her head, shook her hair. She was too tired to clean up now.

She made her way through the mess on the floor, then slumped on the bed. The photo was lying next to the pillow. She picked it up, looked at it, then turned out the light.

The last time she saw Cindy was two days after graduation, 1975. Cate had just finished packing for her return home. The day was oppressively hot, with an unforgiving sun. The campus was almost empty, the dorm rooms bare and quiet. Each box she carried felt heavier and heavier. She hurried with the last one, and it fell over, right outside the dorm hall door.

She sat down next to the spilled contents, the air closing in on her. She found it hard to breathe. After a few moments, she began picking up the items, putting them back in the box. Then she heard the music.

Zeppelin, *Stairway*.

A large blue van, music streaming from the open windows, passed by, then turned around, and stopped. Cindy leaned out the back window. "Last chance," she said.

Cate stood up, raised her hands over her eyes to shield them from the sun. "I can't."

"Just one minute," Cindy said to Mark, sitting next to her, then she opened the van's door, and walked towards her. "You *can*, you just won't," she said.

"Cindy, I can't. I've got no money. My parents want me home, get a job. Blah blah blah."

"You can find a job in D.C. We'll cover for you. I have that job at the newspaper, maybe I can get you one after a while."

"No. I mean, my parents would never get over it. It would be a forever line in the sand, me going somewhere else without a good reason like a fiancé or marriage." She turned around and picked up a box, put it into the trunk. "It's different for you," she said, turning around. "You're going to be with Mark."

Cindy moved closer, blue eyes flashing. "Oh, you're dead wrong on that. I'm not 'going to be with Mark.' He is going to be with me."

Cate squinted. God, the sun was glaring. It captured the gold in Cindy's hair, creating little celestial highlights.

"Come *onnnnn* Cindy, let's get going!" Mark implored, leaning out the van's window.

"I'm coming, relax." She turned to Cate, pulled her close. "Well, if you ever decide to live your own life, give me a call." She let go, then got into the van and reclaimed her seat. Mark leaned towards her, moving her hair to the side as he nuzzled her neck. Someone in the van turned up the already blaring music.

Cate lifted a hand in a tentative wave, and then, after the van had vanished from sight, turned and slammed down the car trunk's lid.

Years later whenever she would think about that day, it was always underscored by the gold in Cindy's hair and Zeppelin lyrics, and the certainty that, compared to Cindy's trip to D.C., her three-hour drive to her parents' Cleveland home was like one long funeral march.

⅄

She moved restlessly in her bed, started to feel queasy. Crazy Margarita crap, she thought. She got up to go to the bathroom. Crossing the room, her foot hit something sharp.

Damn, she thought, turning on the light.

She looked on the floor. There, mixed with all the programs and report cards and certificates was something bright. She bent over, picked it up.

Oh Jesus, she had forgotten.

The ring! The ankh ring Trey had given her and Cindy as graduation gifts.

She held it in her hand, remembering how Cindy had ripped through her wrappings first, lifting the lid off the gift box, squealing with delight as she held up the shiny silver.

"I liked them so much, I bought two," Trey had said.

Cate slipped the ring on her finger, pushing it down. It was snug, but it still fit. After all these years, it still fit.

She wondered if Cindy had hers.

She walked to the front door of her parents' home, knocked once, then pushed the door open. "Mom? Mom?"

"I'm in here," her mother called from her bedroom.

Cate entered, found her sitting on the bed, head tilted down. "You OK?" she asked, walking towards her.

Her mother raised her hand in an unspoken *stop,* then pushed herself up. "Of course, sure. I just got dizzy is all, had to sit down for a moment."

Cate went to the kitchen refrigerator, and pulled out the orange juice. She poured a small glass, then returned, and handed it to her mother. "Drink this."

"Oh for Christ's sake, Cate, I'm fine," her mother said, taking the glass, and setting it on the dresser. "I took my insulin this morning. Why are you always making such a big deal of everything? You never get dizzy?"

"Well, actually I don't," Cate said. "And it *is* a big deal. I mean, if you get dizzy and fall. That is a big deal."

"But I didn't fall, did I?" She ran a brush through her hair, then pointed it at Cate. "I'm not a baby."

"It's not that I think you're a baby, Mom," Cate said, "it's just that you're alone here. You know, maybe you should think about that place Aunt Lisa went to, she loves it. And who knows, you might like it too. They have bingo, crafts and people are always around in case—"

Her mother put the brush down, and picked up a lipstick. "Stop it Caterina. Stop it now." She opened the tube, rolled up the shaft of red, and lifted it to her lips, moving it side to side.

"You look pretty, Mom," Cate said.

"Pretty? Those days are long gone." She placed the lipstick on the dresser, turned and headed towards the kitchen. "Better check the lasagna."

Cate followed behind, passing a large picture of her dad on a hallway wall. She stopped, remembering the Sunday dinner when they were all at the kitchen table, and her dad had touched her mother's cheek and said "Isn't she beautiful?" and Sara had giggled and replied, "Grandpa ahhhhhhh."

"Lasagna's almost done!" her mom called out. "What time will the kids be here?"

"Oh," Cate said, entering the kitchen. "No, I thought I told you. They couldn't come today, they'll be here next week. They each had stuff they had to get done."

"Oh, *oh*. Well, I guess . . . it's just you and me then. Such a waste! But, if everyone has more important things to do, what can you do? Used to be no one missed Sunday dinners. And leftovers?" She held up her hands to the ceiling. "There were no leftovers! I remember when—oh what holiday was it, you must have been ten or so. We had your dad's family over, all those kids! We made five pans of lasagna and ran out! Five pans! Do you remember? And that crazy second cousin of yours, oh what's his name—I can't think of it? You know, the crazy one."

"All those cousins were crazy Mom," Cate said, sitting down at the kitchen table, pouring herself a glass of wine.

"No this one was crazier than the rest." Her mother picked up a knife to cut the lasagna, then put it down, snapped her fingers. "Carlo! You remember him?"

"No."

"Oh, of course you do! He was what? Ten years older than you or something? A nut! Yeah that was it, Carlo. I wonder what ever happened to him. Probably dead now from a motorcycle accident or something. He thought he was a big shot, moved to California." She cut the lasagna, placed a piece on each plate, then carried them over and sat down.

Cate picked up her fork. "Mom, I'm thinking of going out of town in a few weeks, just for a long weekend trip. The kids will be sure to call and come over."

"Trip to where? Niagara Falls?" her mom asked. "That's a nice trip. Your dad and I went there, a long time ago, when was it? Oh right, maybe a year before you were born. Yes, I remember now because—"

"No Mom, not Niagara Falls. New Orleans. I'm going to New Orleans to visit my friend from college, Trey? You remember him?"

"New Orleans? Why would you go to New Orleans? They kill people in New Orleans. I see it all the time on TV. And it's way too far to drive. Niagara Falls, you can drive to Niagara Falls. Go there."

"But Mom," Cate said, "I don't know anyone in Niagara Falls. Trey lives in New Orleans, in a very, very safe part of town. And I'm not driving, I'm flying."

"Flying?" Her mother's fork stopped mid-way to her mouth.

"It's safe Mom."

"Well tell that to those poor people who ran into those buildings in New York, may God have mercy on their souls." She crossed herself, kissed her thumb. "And may the guilty rot in the flames of eternal damnation and may flesh eating bugs and vultures pick at their eyeballs and may Satan's ugly gargoyles vomit bile—"

"Mom, please," Cate said.

"Oh today everybody is so quick to forgive—"

"It's not that Mom," Cate said, "it's just . . . I'm eating." She pushed the lasagna around on her the plate, then put her fork down. "So, besides all that, you're OK with me leaving for a few days, the kids coming over?"

"Me?" her mother asked, raising her eyes. "Me? I'm the least of your worries. I'm safe and happy here. You're the one risking your life to go to a place they kill people for no reason. You're not eating. Eat!"

"Mom, it's not like that, they don't—" Cate stopped, picked up her fork. "So what happened that day with Carlo?"

Her mother's eyes brightened. "Well, we had a whole houseful of people here and that nut Carlo pulls up in his motorcycle with his stupid girlfriend. I didn't even know who she was, and of course nobody ever told me she was coming, even though I was the one doing the cooking. Now that I think of it, I think he ended up marrying her. It didn't last long though. Everyone knew it was doomed."

⅄

Three weeks later, Cate picked up her suitcase and walked out of the New Orleans Louis Armstrong Airport into the beautiful October sun. She reached into her purse for her sunglasses, and scanned the area, looking for the "driver" Trey said would be there.

Tall, middle aged, sunglasses, he had said. He would be holding a sign marked "Trey's Driver."

Coming from anyone else, Cate would have found that offensive, but coming from Trey it was endearing, a confirmation that time couldn't change everything. He had been always fond of over-the-top expressions, like drivers and hand-delivered invitations and extravagant gifts.

Cate smiled, remembering the day of the fraternity dance when the florist delivered sixty long stemmed yellow roses to her dorm room. Trey had organized everything, the roses, the tiara, her election as sweetheart. She had kept the program, her picture on its cover, through all her many moves, carefully placing it in her top dresser drawer as part of her unpacking ritual.

She smoothed down the front of her jeans. But there was something else to that memory, an underside. Oh yes, Cindy. Yes.

The day the flowers arrived, Cindy had walked into her dorm room, pointedly ignoring the impossible-to-ignore floral display. Instead, she went over to Cate's dress that hung from her closet door. She stood back and took a long drag from her cigarette. "Look at you," she said, lifting its purple fabric, then letting it go. "The whole country is falling apart with Watergate, and you're going to a fraternity dance."

Cate shook her head as if to rid herself of that memory, tapped her foot on the pavement. Now where was that driver? She put her suitcase down, and just as she did, a Land Rover screeched to a stop right in front of her. A tall man wearing sunglasses, a Hawaiian shirt and numerous strands of glittering Mardi Gras beads got out and ran over. He stopped at the curb, took his sunglasses off.

"Cate," he said.

She looked up, questioning, then a smile slowly crossed her face. "Stretch!" She said, throwing her arms around him. "Stretch! Oh my God."

He twirled her around. "Wow," he said. "Look at us, forty years later. Look at us! Life must be good Cate. You look great, just great. I pulled up and knew you right away. I was so excited, I left that stupid sign Trey told me I had to hold up. Don't tell him. Do not tell him that! You know how he is about his surprises."

Cate laughed. "But I was surprised. I was *so* surprised."

He picked up her suitcase and threw it in the back seat of the car, then opened the front passenger door. "That surprise—the first of many," he said as she got in.

He went around the car, got into the driver's seat, then leaned over to get a CD from the glove compartment. His long, disheveled grayish-blonde hair fell slightly forward. "We stayed up all night burning this just for your arrival," he said, putting it into the player. He then pressed on the gas pedal, and peeled out of the airport, cutting off a car to their left.

"Ha ha! Welcome back to the '70s, Catie!" he said as the Chambers Brothers and *Time Has Come Today* started playing. "Greatest time in fucking history. And here is the good news. In New Orleans, it might as easily be 1970! Or 1870! Or 1984! It just doesn't fucking matter. Now how long has it been since you've visited?"

"Oh, it's been at least five years. Last time I was here, Trey said you were living in Florida. You still living there?"

"Well I was, but I took an early retirement, sold the house. Since then I have just been hanging around here and there."

"Hanging around here or in Florida?"

"Well for a while I was with this woman in Florida, then that got all messed up, she started bitchin' about this and that, so I thought, who needs that crap, life is too fucking short. So about a year ago, I ended up visiting Trey and I haven't left since."

"Oh, gee. That's great. He didn't tell me."

"Yep, so now I am an official Masker. It's all I do. Wear masks, go to parades. There's one every week. See my T-shirt," he said, as he slowed the car to an almost stop as he unbuttoned his Hawaiian shirt, revealing the shirt underneath.

"*New Orleans. So far behind we're ahead*," Cate read.

The driver behind them honked his horn. Stretch turned his head, and rolled down his window. "This ain't fucking New York, asshole!" he shouted as the car passed.

"Dumb fuck," he said as he rolled up the window, then looked at her. "Oh, sorry."

"It's fine," she said laughing.

"Yeah. Living here is a much better way to live. *Only* way to live. Who needs that other shit?" He turned to her. "You know, Maz died last year."

"Maz? No!"

"Yep. Yep," he said, nodding his head. "Dropped over dead, just like that. After a business meeting. Can you imagine that? Poor fuck. Yeah, that life will kill you. I mean, they said it was his liver, but they always blame shit on livers. It was really his life. And I'll tell you one thing, I am not going out after a fucking business meeting, you can bank your money on that. No way!"

Cate took off her sunglasses, put them in her purse. "So sad. Hm . . ." She looked out the window. "You have kids Stretch?"

"Kids? Yeah. One."

"In Florida?"

"I'm pretty sure he's still there. I mean he's older now, in his twenties."

Cate laughed. "What do you mean, 'you're pretty sure he's still there?'"

"Well he's a man now, doing his thing, you know." He turned off the highway. "Anyway, it was a bad scene with the divorce. Things never got right. His mother turned him against me, so just better if I bowed out. I mean, what can you do about some of this shit? Just make life easy for everybody, that's what I think."

"Right. Right . . . I've got three."

"Three what?"

"Kids."

"Cool."

She turned her gaze to the side window, and felt herself catch her breath. As they made their way towards the Garden District, the ancient southern oaks lining St. Charles Boulevard became higher and fuller, creating a lush green canopy that added to the almost mystical beauty of the defiantly unique mansions. Green ivy crawled; black iron laced; hurricane lamps flickered. Gaudy Mardi Gras beads hung jauntily from random tree branches, breaking the self-importance, providing the perfect juxtaposition.

Cate sighed, leaning back. "Just fucking magical," she said.

"What?"

"The irony. Gaudy beads on serious old oak trees? Perfect."

Stretch lifted an eyebrow as he pulled the car into a driveway overgrown with bougainvillea. He stopped, pulled the key out of the ignition, and turned to her.

"You know what I think when I see beads on trees?" he asked, opening his car door.

"What?"

"Nothing. Absolutely fucking nothing."

Cate laughed and got out of the car, carefully maneuvering her way up the uneven pathway. She got to the front step, looked up.

Now this was a home, she thought. She scanned its pale yellow stucco, the balconies off the second floor windows, the expansive front porch. No, home wasn't exactly right. This was more aptly a mansion, albeit now not in the greatest repair. But even with that, it was still one of those century-old estates that helped create the ambience, evoked the words of Williams and Capote. Its slight disrepair just added the last critical ingredient, the enduring melancholia.

She stepped up to the front entrance as Stretch fumbled with the keys. A green streetcar, just barely visible through the yard's overgrowth, made its way up St. Charles.

Stretch opened the door, and they entered the foyer, a sea of gilded gold set off by deep maroon, dissected by a looming, oak staircase. He put her suitcase down, and picked up an oversized hand bell that sat on an ornate hallway table. He lifted it, and on its first ring, Trey dramatically emerged from a room at the top of the stairs.

His hair seemed darker than when she last saw him, but it was still long and full. His body was slender and well maintained. He wore a black cape, and as he made his way down the steps, it floated behind, so she could see its red underside. When he got to the bottom of the steps, he scooped her up. "How did you like the sign?" he asked, putting her down.

"The sign?"

"The sign I told Stretch to use? 'Trey's Driver?' I told him to hold it over his face, so you'd be even more surprised. Were you surprised?"

"Oh that! Yes! It was amazing, a great surprise! Thank you."

"Just the start," Trey replied. "Do you smell that?"

"What?" asked Cate.

"The gumbo of course!" he said. "The Doussan-Fossier family recipe gumbo! I have been making it all day in anticipation of your welcome to NOLA dinner celebration. Come into the kitchen, I need to check on it."

She followed him into the kitchen, her heels clicking against the black and white checkerboard floor. "Jesus Trey," she said, walking up to the large pot on the stove. "This is enough to feed an army—there's just three of us!"

Trey smiled, twirled his cape, and said, "Well, then. Maybe it is not going to be just the three of us."

⅄

Three hours and many drinks later, Cate got up from the dining room table and went to the kitchen, put her glass on the counter.

An hour after her arrival, there had been a "surprise" knock on the door, which led to another, which led to another. Unbeknownst to Cate, Trey had invited some of the old Chateau regulars for a surprise weekend reunion. So now, sitting at the dining room table were CK and Mary, Hammer and Alice, Diane and Bill, all who had married right after college. Then followed the others, Duke and his pregnant new wife Tiffany, Rossi and his new wife Kristin, and a stream of singles—Jane, Murphy, Crash, and Ronnie.

Cate opened a kitchen cupboard door, then closed it, and opened another.

"Need something?" Trey asked, walking into the room.

"No. Well, actually yes. I was looking for some aspirin."

"Right there," he said, pointing to a large container prominently displayed on the windowsill.

She opened the bottle, pulled out three pills, and filled a glass of water.

"Something wrong?" he asked.

"No," she said, swallowing the pills. She looked at him, noticed a hint of a smile. "No, really! The dinner was awesome. And everyone showing up—CK and Mary and Duke and um, what's her name?"

"Tiffany," he said, nodding his head.

"Yeah, Tiffany. I mean, I expected Nancy, but someone young enough to be his pregnant daughter . . . yeah, it's all good."

"Let's go outside," he said, moving towards the back door. "I need a smoke."

She followed him out, and they sat down on a rusted wrought iron bench that faced the yard's overgrowth. Trey lit a cigarette. "I'm not much for taking care of things," he said.

"What?"

"The yard. You were looking at the yard."

"Oh, no!" she said. "No. I wasn't even thinking about the yard. I was wondering . . ." she looked behind him towards the door, then moved towards his ear. "Didn't you think it was weird the way CK and Mary were talking about . . . you know, that one part about values?"

She sat back. "Are you kidding me? *CK?* Did he forget how he got that damn nickname? Always in that phone booth doing his Clark Kent Superman thing, working a dope deal or lining up a townie. Now he's all value this and value that. And Duke with his teenaged wife? What happened to Nancy? Nancy was great! Now he's got hair plugs and a thirty-year-old pregnant wife named *Tiffany*?"

Trey reached under his cape with his left hand. "Oh Catie, Catie, Catie. You have to lighten up." He pulled out a joint, dropped his cigarette to the ground. "Come on, it's a party, not some pearly gate inquisition." He lit the joint, and took a puff, holding his lips tight. "And anyway, just because CK sold some dope or did a townie when he was nineteen, what does that have to do with anything?" He leaned towards her. "He was always a hypocrite, did you forget that part?"

He handed her the joint, then leaned back, looked at the sky. "Isn't it funny? The past I mean. It's just this huge invisible thing that may have happened the way we remember or maybe didn't. 'Cause it's all selective . . . what we choose to remember, and what we choose to forget.

"Now come on, finish that up. There is one surprise left, and I don't want to be late."

⅄

Cate brushed away the scattered crumbs and stray cigarette ashes from the plastic table cloth, then slumped back in her seat. It was 11:00 p.m., time for her to be in bed. She had told them to go ahead without her, but they wouldn't hear of it, so here she was, in some ramshackle karaoke bar listening to a middle-aged guy sing a painstakingly horrible version of *Dream On.*

Her chair faced the stage; Trey and Murphy were on either side, and Stretch sat across from her. Trey lit a cigarette, its smoke blended into the thick foggy cloud that covered the dimly lit room.

The man finished to drunken applause and left the stage. Cate scrunched up her nose, took a long drink of her beer, and glanced around the crowded room. She noticed a woman at the side of the stage talking to the MC, ready to go on.

She picked up her purse, stood up. "I have to go to the bathroom."

Trey grabbed her hand. "Not now."

"But I've got to—"

"Just hold on."

She sat back down as the woman took the stage, started singing.

"*Busted flat . . . waitin' for a train . . .*"

Stretch stood up applauding, then put his fingers in his mouth and whistled. He turned around and lifted a quizzical eyebrow in her direction.

"Yeah, that's a good song," Cate said, rising.

Trey grabbed her hand, his eyes still on the stage.

"What?" Cate asked. "You wanted me to hear the song. I get it, it's the song Cindy used to sing, *Me and Bobby McGee.* Great, but I really have to go to the bathroom."

"Cate," said Trey, "you don't get it."

"What?"

"That *is* Cindy," he said, pointing to the stage.

She turned her eyes back to the stage as her body dropped back into the chair. "Cindy?"

⅄

It had taken Cate a while to find the Cindy she remembered in the woman on the stage. Familiar pieces emerged one by one, until everything fit together like pieces of a puzzle. There was the obvious confidence, and the hair was reminiscent, only not as lush and golden. The height was right, as was her gauzy blouse's style, but the frame was now thirty pounds away from willowy.

Pieces started to fall into place more rapidly when the song ended and Cindy took a seat at the table. She regaled them with her story, or as she more colorfully put it, "The short, edited version of my past forty years, none of which, I might add, ever lived up to expectations."

She had married and divorced Mark. The marriage didn't work out, or as Cate thought Cindy said, was "di-sastrous." But after Cindy said that, everyone laughed, and no one, Cate knew, would laugh after "di-sastrous," so she decided she must have been mistaken. Maybe she said "de-lusional." That would be more Cindy-like.

It was hard to follow the conversation, what with all the singing, and the day's drinking, so Cate focused on Cindy's face. And that was when things really started to fall into place.

Those same, vivid blue eyes. The way they moved from person to person, the way the lashes fluttered, and especially the way they enhanced the story she was telling—her eyes widening, narrowing, brightening, smoldering, as if they were reacting to the most entertaining and fascinating tale on earth.

Her mannerisms had always been contagious, and people around the table listened intently as she explained that Mark had met a younger woman, who he later married, and she had a short second marriage to a guy named Randy, who was actually a semi-important guitarist with Creedence? No, for a group who *opened for* Creedence, but still . . .

Someone asked if she was retired. She laughed and said, "Retired? Well I guess you could say that! I retired about, let's see, thirty-six years ago, after I left that Washington newspaper. So much bullshit, school board meetings and interviews of little boys who won Boy Scout awards. Not for me."

She had a daughter, Layla, who was now a thirty-five-year-old lawyer. She lived somewhere near Dayton, with her husband and teenaged daughter. Cindy was going there after the weekend for a prolonged stay. Why, she didn't say. Just a general, "her daughter needed her help." She also didn't give many details about where she had come from, outside of the fact that she had most recently lived in Denver.

By the time Cindy got to the Dayton part, everything fit together.

It was Cindy. Of course.

They had a few more drinks, then took taxis back to the house. The married couples went off to their rooms. Stretch put on the stereo, and Cate and Cindy went into the kitchen.

"Does he have anything to eat?" Cindy asked, going into the refrigerator. "I'm starving."

"There's some leftover gumbo."

"Oh it looks awesome," she said, pulling the container out and putting it into the microwave. "You want some?"

"No just getting water."

As they waited for the microwave beep, Cate felt Cindy's eyes on her. Cate shifted uncomfortably, leaned against the counter. "What?" she asked. "Why are you looking at me like that?"

The microwave sounded, Cindy pulled out the container, and poured some into a bowl. "You're thin, as thin as when we were in college."

"No! Are you kidding me? I wish. Three pounds off."

Cindy laughed. "Um, OK, that's sort of weird in itself, your knowing that. The last time I was three pounds off I was probably doing cocaine. That was a long, long time ago, with husband two. That whole marriage was an awesome powdery blur. You know—awesome until it wasn't." She chewed on the gumbo. "You know."

"Well, not exactly," Cate said.

"The '80s? No? Well, now that I think of it, you might be one of those people who just wouldn't know."

Cate turned to the sink, poured her water from the glass. "I'm going to go out there and see what they are up to." She walked into the living room. Trey and Stretch were discussing something in the corner, while Fleetwood Mac's *I Don't Want To Know* played on the stereo. "Where is everyone?" she asked, scanning the room.

"All went to bed," said Trey. "It's just us."

"Oh, I love this song!" Cindy said, entering the room behind Cate. She grabbed Stretch's hands, pulled him out into the middle of the room. Trey and Cate sat down on the couch and watched them dance until the end of the song, then Cate stood up. "I think I'm going to call it a night," she said, kissing Trey on the forehead.

"You OK?"

"Yeah, just tired. Got that headache brewing. Night, you guys."

She turned and went up to her room, got into bed, and turned off the light. She had almost nodded off to sleep when there was a knock on the door.

"You OK?" Cindy asked, leaning her head into the room, then fully entering, taking a seat on the twin bed next to Cate's.

"Yeah, just beat."

Cindy turned on the nightstand light, leaned closer. "We didn't talk about Duke and his teenage pregnant wife! What's up with that? What happened to Nancy?"

Cate sat up. "I know! It's crazy! I guess he divorced her. You know men. It doesn't matter what they look like. We become invisible; they get younger wives. It's nuts. And Nancy was so great, so smart . . ."

"Yeah, *way* smarter than him," Cindy said, leaning back on the bed. "Although, now that I think about it—who's to say he dumped her? Maybe she dumped him and right now, at this very moment, she's living off her divorce settlement, drinking champagne on some European cruise."

"No," said Cate, moving in the bed. "No, not Nancy."

"Well, that's as believable as some thirty-year-old randomly falling head over heels in love with Duke. And what do we really know about Nancy—really? We haven't seen her since college. We'll never find out the real truth anyway. No one tells the whole truth about anything." She leaned forward. "Like I bet you have lied about fifty times since you got here."

"No. Well, I might have told a couple of little lies, but not about anything big or terribly significant."

"Ok. Let's put it this way. Your divorce. If people ask why you got divorced what do you say?"

"Short version, he had an affair," Cate said.

"Yeah but that's not the whole truth, is it?" Cindy asked. "I mean, you even said *short version.* That's leaving a whole lot of other stuff out. And besides that, half the time we don't even understand the truth behind the stuff that we do. So when you think of it, the truth is just—" she waved her right hand in the air as if she was trying to grasp the appropriate words, "it's just basically what we need or want it to be. A self-serving guess."

"Oh come on Cindy," Cate said. "The truth is not a guess, it's the truth."

"Well, the good news is, no one cares anyway, so it's not like it's any big deal." She got up and went to the dresser mirror, fluffed her hair with her fingers. "It's like what Jack Nicholson said in that movie. Oh, you know . . . "

" 'You can't handle the truth?' "

"Yeah, that's it! No one wants to hear the long sad yada yada yada of everyone else's life. We all have our own shit."

She leaned into the mirror, touched the corners of her mouth. "Like take my divorce from Mark. *Maybe* it was because he fell for a younger woman. Or maybe he fell for a younger woman because I had an affair first, unfortunately right around the time I got pregnant with Layla. Now that changes everything doesn't it? One version he's a villain; the other it's a 'serves her right.' And here's the funny thing, both can be true."

"Are you playing with me now or talking for real?" Cate asked.

Cindy turned around, held up her hands. "See. Point made. Who wants to hear every back story detail. No one." She turned back to the mirror. "Stretch looks pretty good doesn't he?"

"Stretch?"

"Yeah. He's sort of cute."

"Cute?" Cate laughed. "Well maybe. I just don't think of him like that I guess."

"Well of course you don't." She walked over to Cate's bed, sat down next to her. "You were always so loyal." She patted her hand, then stopped, lifted it up. "Oh my God, the ring! You're still wearing the ring. See what I mean? Loyal. Mine is packed away somewhere heading for Dayton."

She put Cate's hand down, pushed herself off the bed and walked to the door. "I've got to get some sleep or tomorrow will be shot," she said. "But trust me on this. Nancy? I would put money on the fact that right now Nancy is happy as a fricking clam, saying 'You go Tiffany, with your pregnant bad self. Have at it.'"

⅄

Cate woke up to the ringing of her cell phone. She reached out with her right hand, locating it on the nightstand. "Hello?"

"Oh good! You're up. You made it there? You never bothered to call."

"I texted the kids, Mom. Mike was supposed to tell you when he stopped by yesterday."

"Oh maybe he did. But you *said* you would call. But that's OK, your forgetting I mean. Anyway, I have a problem. You know what happened yesterday? Tony came over, talked about all this stupid stuff, then, real nonchalant asked if I was selling the house, said his goofy son Joey wanted to buy it. Can you believe that?"

"Well that's nothing Mom, probably just conversation," Cate said.

"No, he meant something by it—like I was going to die soon or be put into a home, and there he would be, eating in my kitchen! He was always braggy! Bragging that he had graduated from high school, when everyone knows they gave some special phony diploma just to be rid of him. They do stuff like that to make those people feel better about themselves. And anyway, who does he think he is coming into my home, saying he's going to buy it like *he's* Mr. Moneybags? I could buy and sell him! He probably doesn't have a—"

"Mom," Cate interrupted, "it's not that big of a deal. You don't have to sell the house, so don't worry about it. Look, Sara is coming over today, and I'll be home Sunday night, so just try to just forget about it for now. We'll talk about it when I get home."

"Sara's coming over today? What time?"

"I'm not sure."

"Well I didn't know Sara was coming over! Why doesn't anyone tell me anything? I'm the one cooking!"

"Mom it's seven in the morning," Cate said. "Give it a couple of hours, then call Sara and ask when she'll be over. I'll give you a call as soon as I get home tomorrow night. OK? OK. Love you too. No, I won't forget."

Cate put the phone down, and went into the bathroom to wash her face. No point in trying to go back to sleep, she thought. Might as well go downstairs and make some coffee. She put on her robe and headed to the kitchen, slowing down at the foyer when she saw Tiffany at the kitchen table.

"Oh thank God!" Tiffany called out. "I'm so glad someone is finally up! I can't sleep worth a dime anymore. The baby is always moving around, sticking out an arm or leg here and there. Look . . ." She lifted her blouse, revealing her stomach as it shifted in a rolling movement to the left.

"Oh, yeah . . . that's um—awesome," said Cate, slowly walking to the coffeemaker.

Tiffany pulled the blouse down, patted her stomach. "My doctor says he's going to be big! Like in the highest percentile, nine pounds or so. We think he'll be a quarterback. Do you have kids?" she asked, her blond hair falling in blunt cut perfection to her chin.

"Um, well they aren't really kids anymore. They're all around thirty." Cate poured water through the coffee maker's top. "One of them was a nine pound baby. She's a nurse now. Weighs a hundred ten pounds soaking wet—so don't buy those season tickets just yet."

Cate turned around and leaned against the counter, noticed Tiffany's quick glance away. She pushed her hair away from her face. "You want some coffee?" she offered, as she pulled a mug from a cupboard.

"Oh no, I'm trying to avoid the—"

"Caffeine?" Cate asked, as she poured herself a mug, then took a seat at the table. "I did the same thing. With all three of my kids." She took a sip of the coffee. "Can't believe that was all some thirty years ago. Time does funny things when you have kids. You'll see. When they're little, the days seem endless, but the years? The years go by in a flash."

"What are their names?" Tiffany asked.

"Mike, Jack and Sara."

"Do you have any pictures?"

"Maybe. I might have some up in my purse."

"Oh, I'd like to see them."

"Really?"

"Of course really," Tiffany said, laughing.

"OK," Cate said, getting up, and heading back upstairs. When she got to the top of the stair landing, she saw Cindy outside the bedroom door.

"Hey," Cindy said, turning towards her.

"Good morning. You OK?"

Cindy brushed her bed-hair away from her face. "You got the aspirin?"

"Yeah, I took them from downstairs," Cate said, as she entered the room and picked up the aspirin bottle from the dresser, handing it to Cindy.

"Thanks," Cindy said. "Feel miserable. Did I come to your room last night?"

"Yeah."

"I was pretty high."

"Me too."

"What did we talk about?"

"A little about Duke, the rest is foggy," Cate answered. "You want coffee? There's coffee downstairs. Tiffany is there, she's the only one up."

"Tiffany?" Cindy asked, then laughed. "Um no, I think I'll pass. I'm just going to go back to bed. Catch you later."

She walked out of the room, and Cate went to her purse, pulled out her wallet.

Of course she remembered their talk last night, but what was the point of discussion? They were both drunk, and Cindy had qualified everything with *maybe this* and *maybe that*. And anyway, who ever knew with Cindy! Leave it to her to have some romantic, mysterious back story about the father of her child. If she didn't have one, she'd certainly enjoy making one up.

She pulled out some pictures, and headed back downstairs.

That day, they didn't get moving until early afternoon, when they decided to go to the French Quarter for coffee and beignets. Tiffany declined, said she was going to take an afternoon nap.

They got on the streetcar, and made their way to Jackson Square. When they got off, Cate said, "Hey, go ahead to the cafe, I think I am just going to sit up there for awhile, watch the Mississippi. Come get me when you are done."

"You want anything?" Duke asked.

"Maybe a latte."

She walked up an incline on the opposite side of the square, to a park bench that overlooked the river. It was another beautiful day, bright like summer, but without any of the summer's oppressive heat and humidity. Cate sat down and watched the river, wondering for a moment how it must have felt to watch it rise to its precarious top that August, 2005.

"Here you go," said Duke, coming up and handing her a latte. He took a seat next to her.

"Oh, you didn't have to do that," Cate said. "I mean, I didn't expect you to bring it to me, you should have stayed there, enjoyed the beignets and conversation."

"Hey, I don't need beignets," he said, rubbing his stomach. "Anyway, I wanted to thank you."

"For what?"

"Tiffany said you were nice to her this morning, talked to her about stuff. It made her feel good. I wanted to thank you for that. I know—" he started, "I know it's sort of awkward . . . everyone knew Nancy and all."

"Yeah well. Is she OK?" Cate asked.

"Tiffany?"

"No Nancy. I wondered if she was doing OK. I always liked Nancy."

He shifted in his seat. "The divorce . . . it was complicated."

"Aren't they all?"

He glanced at her, then leaned forward. "No, ours was unusually—let me start again. About four years ago Nancy comes to me, says we've grown apart, which of course I knew. I mean, we had separate bedrooms for years. She never really worked, and didn't really have all that much interest in what I did. She had her friends, her book club and gardening, shit like that."

"Well that doesn't mean she was worthless, not working."

"No, that's not what I meant," he said. "She said she wanted her own space, not necessarily a divorce, but private space to figure some stuff out. And after that—well the bottom line is that she figured it out and asked for a divorce. I met Tiffany a year or so later."

"Oh. So Nancy's still in that apartment in Atlanta?"

"Yes. With her partner. Kathy." He took a sip of his coffee, looked away. "Funny, I swear to God, I never saw that coming. Like I was oblivious to my own life. But anyway, there it was, just one of those frickin' sucker punches in life. And it really didn't get better until I met Tiffany."

He stood up, faced the bustling square, the tourists, artists, voodoo priestesses, and at the forefront, the triumphant statue of the impeached president. "I don't talk about it all that much, just prefer to leave it in the past I guess."

"Sure," Cate said.

"It's amazing isn't it?" he asked, turning to her.

"What?" she asked.

"This," he said, turning back to the square. "When everyone said this place was done. Look at it now. It's really quite amazing."

⅄

The rest of that day and night was a blur of final activities. A shopping trip to Magazine Street; a food fest at Le Petite Grocery; bar hopping in the Quarter. By the time they got home it was past midnight. They all disbursed to their rooms, except for Stretch and Cindy who stayed downstairs, listening to old albums.

Cate went to her room and finished packing. She closed the suitcase, ran a comb through her hair, then went down the hallway to Trey's room, softly knocked on the door. "Trey, you up?"

"Something wrong?" he asked, as he opened the door.

"No, nothing," said Cate. "Not a thing. Everything was wonderful, all that you did getting everyone together, planning the weekend. I just wanted to thank you."

"Anything for you," he said kissing her cheek.

"Oh, I feel sort of bad, we didn't get to talk much really, not alone anyway."

"So, the night is still young." He walked over to his bed, patted the thick, purple comforter. "Come over here then, we can talk as long as you like."

She joined him, lying down, putting her head on his shoulder. "You happy Trey?"

"Me? Sure. Why?"

"We always talk about me. Like my stuff. What about you?" She turned on her side, propped her head up with her elbow. "Do you have someone? You never talk about it."

"Yes."

"You do?" Cate asked, sitting up.

"Yes, of course," he answered, looked at her, then laughed. "Why do you look so surprised? Is the concept so unfathomable?"

"Of course not! It's just that I have never ever heard you admit it, but it makes me happy." She snuggled back into his shoulder. "Would I like him?"

"You do—I mean, would."

"What's he like?"

"Tall, funny . . ."

"Why didn't you bring him around this weekend?"

"Hey," he said pulling away. "Enough." He got up and walked to his dresser, opened a drawer and pulled out a pair of socks. "Feet are cold."

Cate sat up. "I wasn't trying to pry. I just—"

"I know," he said, putting the socks on, pulling them up. "He's just private is all. Like not totally committed . . ."

"To you?"

"To the whole idea of being gay," he said.

"Oh."

"Yeah. I know it's sort of messed up." He returned to the bed. "We're quite a pair, you and me, aren't we? But you know what?"

"What?" she asked.

He leaned closer. "We're still a whole lot better than most of the people here. Cindy—"

"Cindy?"

"Like her back story makes sense?" he asked. "Come on, the thing about her going to her daughter's to help her take care of a granddaughter?"

"But that's true," Cate said. "We're on the same connecting flight to Charlotte."

"Well, yes, she is going there. But to take care of a granddaughter? Does that sound remotely plausible? Like Cindy would be the go-to person on babysitting? And anyway, how come her daughter suddenly needs her now? The kid's what? Fourteen, fifteen?"

"I guess I just never thought of it like that."

"And by the way, what's the granddaughter's name?" he asked.

"I don't know."

"Exactly! Did you ever know a grandmother who didn't mention a grandkid's name? A little odd."

"Hm."

"Hm what?"

"I don't know. I just never heard you talk about Cindy like that," Cate said.

"Like what?"

"I don't know. Critical I guess."

"I'm just saying it doesn't make sense. You're just bowled over by her for some reason, always have been. It's her confidence. Confidence always throws you off. Didn't Janis teach you anything?"

"Janis?"

"Janis Joplin? Janis Joplin was undeniable proof that whenever you see that balls-to-the-wall confidence you know for a fact there's some darkness going on somewhere."

⅄

By the time Cate and Cindy sat down in the rocking chairs in the Charlotte airport, waiting for their final connections home—Cindy to Dayton, Cate to Cleveland—their energy had been spent, and any thoughts of drinks were confined to water, any activity surpassing rocking and remembrance, too much of an effort.

"It was a good time," Cindy said, slowly rocking in the chair. "Well the best time I am going to have anyway for a long, long time."

"Trey really put a lot into it."

"Yeah, well he was always into stuff like that, being the big benefactor party host," Cindy said. "I think he's mad at me though. I got that vibe."

"No."

Cindy laughed. "Um yeah. I definitely got that vibe." She rocked a little harder. "Probably cause Stretch and I hooked up."

"You and Stretch?" Cate stopped rocking, took a long look at Cindy's face.

"Yeah. What? What is so crazy about that? And I'm pretty sure Trey is pissed off about it."

"Well, I mean, it is surprising, but why would it piss him off?" Cate asked.

Cindy turned to her. "You're kidding me right?" She touched her arm, her blue eyes widening. "Come on, you can't possibly not know? That he's in love with Stretch? How could you not know that? What did you think? They were still just living out their college years in New Orleans?" She laughed and turned away.

Cate shifted in her seat. "You don't know that. I mean, not that it matters, but you don't know that."

"Well no one knows anything for sure, like I said that night in your room. The whole truth is a guess thing. But it does make sense, doesn't it? Stretch loses his job, his life goes to hell, and Trey gets his dream."

Cate started to reply, but was interrupted by the ringing of her phone. "Hey, Mom," she said, picking up. "No. I'm just about to go to the gate." She listened for a moment, tapped her foot on the floor. "No, like I said, no one is going to make you sell the house.

"Mom, I'm sorry but I really can't talk now. I'll be home tonight, we'll talk then. Yes. I'll call as soon as I land. Yes. I love you too." She pressed the end button, dropped the phone into her purse.

"Does she do that all the time?" Cindy asked.

"Well, she's eighty-seven."

"You should try not picking up. That's what I do with people I don't want to talk to."

"I never said I didn't want to talk to her."

"Well you never said that but—"

Cate sighed, ran a hand through her hair. "Cindy, you and I . . . we're just different."

Cindy laughed, leaned back into the rocker. "Different? Well of course we're different! Who doesn't know that?" She shook her head, then pushed herself up. "Gee, it's almost two o'clock, I better get to the gate. Talk about crazy relatives, I'm off to the belly of the beast. My daughter runs her house like a humorless Betty Ford Center. I told you that right?"

"You told me you were going to help out with your granddaughter."

"Oh yeah that too, but I mean I won't be able to drink, or eat anything but tofu, or have anything that might remotely be interpreted as 'fun.' I will probably lose twenty pounds the first two weeks, be bored to death." She grabbed her purse. "Hey, we should plan to get together. You're still in Cleveland, right?"

"Well, Akron actually, but same difference. Just thirty minutes away."

"So Dayton isn't that far! We should get together, why not? Give ourselves a break from the crazies." She gave Cate a long hug, then took her hand, and pointed to her ring. "I have to find mine. Remember what Trey said when he gave them to us? Something about eternal life, and . . . something else? Come on, what was it?"

"I don't remember him saying anything except that he liked them so much he bought two."

Cindy lifted her eyes, "No, it was something gay." She looked towards the ceiling, then snapped her finger. "Oh yeah. It was something about a feather. Don't remember what, just remember him going all Elton John emo. You know him. Loves that drama queen stuff." She shifted the purse on her shoulder. "Well, I best get going."

She leaned over and gave Cate a quick kiss on the cheek, then headed off, turning around to wave before she blended into the crowd. Cate returned to the rocker, then, after a moment, reached down into her purse and pulled out her phone.

She punched in "ankh," then clicked on Urban Dictionary.

> *What it means is when a person dies, their heart is weighted on a scale against the feather of truth. If a person's heart isn't too heavy they would pass on, thus creating an eternal life.*

Well, Cindy sort of had it right, Cate thought. The feather and the eternity. She just had missed the poetry.

But who was she to talk? She had forgotten everything.

She put the phone back, then rose to go to the gate.

Now how in the world could she have forgotten something as poetic as *feather of truth*, she thought. Such a beautiful thought. Much more beautiful than *the feather of a guess.*

CHAPTER THREE

CINDY

"Mom, please, can you come here, I am going to be late! Mom!"

Cindy sighed and angrily pushed aside the bedcovers. She reached for her phone on the nightstand and pulled it close to her face. Six frickin' o'clock. Jesus.

She dropped the phone down and reluctantly got out of bed, scooping up her brightly colored kimono from the floor. It was the only thing, she thought, which showed any semblance of life in this monotonous beige and white, nothing to offend, but nothing to inspire, house. She tied the robe around her waist, then went to the dresser mirror, moving closer, turning sideways.

Maybe she should cut her hair, she thought. Not much, just a titch. She lifted her hair off her shoulders to try to visualize a new look, then frowned. No, no, that wasn't any better, that was actually worse! She would look like every other middle-aged woman with a haircut like that.

She leaned closer. No, it wasn't the length of the hair that was off, it was the color. Yes that was it! The color was—

"Mom!" Layla shouted, now frantically knocking at the door.

"Jesus Layla, what is your problem?" Cindy said, opening the door, then returning to the mirror. "I've got something important going on here. Did you notice? The color of my hair? And now that I am really looking at things, it isn't just the hair, it's happening all over."

She turned to her, moving the hair away from her face. "Do you see this? My eyebrows. My skin. I'm turning as fucking beige as everything in this house! Drab Slavic beige. I used to be golden. It's like a light turned off somewhere."

"Really Mom? Really? I don't have time for this now. I'm late, and people depend on me. You can work out your color trauma later." She pulled up her phone, sent a quick text, then looked up. "Now Jana is still sleeping, and this is not going to be another conversation about how she shouldn't be in a Catholic school. I don't have time for that now."

"Oh, that is such nonsense, my granddaughter in a Catholic school of all things," Cindy said. "And you and Luke ruining my welcome home dinner with all of your hand wringing *what will we do*—as if she had been found gang banging some boys in a classroom instead of what she really did which was roll her skirt up and wear some makeup. Just fucking ridiculous. Like we should all head for the vapors on that."

"Stop that Mother, stop. We talked about this and you promised. It was a condition, remember? Our house, our rules. So do not talk like that, 'gang banging, fuck,' " said Layla.

"Oh my God. She's not a baby Layla, she's fifteen! Do you ever listen to the music kids listen to today?"

"Look," Layla said, "we are not getting into this now, and I'm certainly not apologizing for how we choose to raise our daughter." She tightened the belt of her immaculately tailored coat. "It was the deal. You do remember the deal right? *My* rules. If you can't go along with that, you're going to have to find another place to live. Do you want to do that?"

"No, it's just . . . all I am saying Layla is Jana is a young woman, not a baby."

Layla smoothed down her glistening black hair, lifted her eyes. "Do you want to do that?"

"No of course I do not," Cindy said, sitting down on the bed.

"All right then. Jana has this one day home suspension and I cannot take off, so I am going to tell you what she needs to accomplish today, and I am going to trust that it will be done. And don't roll your eyes. It's infantile.

"First. She is to work on her lessons. She has a checklist of everything that needs to be accomplished while she is at home, and I want it done during the day because I have a late meeting tonight, and she has ballet. Oh . . . and she has to turn in an essay on why she got the suspension and how she can improve her behavior in the future. OK?"

"Fine," Cindy replied.

Layla turned, opening the door. "Get her up no later than 7:30. This is not a day off. And if there is extra time, she can practice ballet. Now, I mean it Mom. I am dead serious. No swearing. No 'you don't have to do this' or 'this is stupid.' No giving her the cookies I know you have in your drawer. Sugar encourages her, and she has to be mindful of her weight. And absolutely no *Housewives*."

She left the room, and started down the hallway. Cindy got up off the bed, followed behind. "OK Layla, OK. I'm going to do all that, just like you want, but I have to say one last thing. Just one thing.

"If you ask me Layla, which I know you didn't, but if you did, I think you should be grateful that you have a daughter who doesn't follow nonsensical rules. It shows a strength of spirit, and that's important in a woman. And anyway, come on, it's not 1950. She lifted up a skirt and put on makeup. So what."

Layla stopped and turned around. "First of all, it's *Lee* . . . and, as you said, Mother, I didn't ask you."

⅄

Cindy returned to bed after Layla left, but couldn't sleep, so she ate sugar cookies as she waited for the time to pass 7:30. When it reached 7:43, she finished the last cookie in the row, closed the bag and placed it under the bed.

Opening the door to Jana's room, she saw her nestled in bed, blankets around her chin, her long blonde hair falling across the pillow. She moved closer.

That face. That unblemished, fresh face with the beautiful high cheekbones that flushed rosy pink, and those full, pouty lips. Lips just like hers, she thought, reminiscent of those great '60s beauties—Jeannie Shrimpton, Patti Boyd. God, she would be dynamite with bangs! She gently touched her shoulder. "Baby, you have to wake up."

Jana softly groaned, pulled the blankets higher.

"I'm sorry babe. It's direct orders from your mom. I'm already almost half an hour late getting you up."

Jana's long lashes fluttered, then her eyes reluctantly opened one at a time, revealing their brilliant blue. "Oh God, I hate my life," she said, hitting the pillow.

"Yeah, well this is the good part. Wait till you get to the rest of it. Get up and shower, you'll feel better. Then come in the living room, I have specific instructions on what we have to accomplish today from the SS."

"Oh God," Jana said, slowly lifting her tall body that was just starting to break out into the feminine form. "My mom is a psycho."

"Yeah, well you're not going to get any argument from me on that. But in her defense . . . she's just scared."

"Of what?"

"Come on, let's get going. We'll talk about that later."

⅄

"Put down you *sincerely* apologize for breaking the dress code and it won't happen again," Cindy said.

Jana's blue eyes looked at her defiantly. "I don't have to listen to you."

"Yeah, you do."

"Since when?"

"Since I came here." Cindy moved closer. "It's part of my like—I guess you could call it my job. The deal I made with your mom. And that is why I am sitting here at a table doing this crap when I should be in bed."

Jana leaned back. "The deal you made?"

"Yes, when I came here."

"Oh . . .I thought you were finally just being a grandma. Didn't know it was part of some deal." She turned away and picked up another piece of paper. "Anyway all this should seem funny to you, no? Rolled up skirts? Makeup? I mean compared to the shit you did."

"Just for your information," Cindy said, "when I was your age, I wasn't doing any shit. Nothing. I was straight up with the game plan. So don't talk about stuff you don't know."

"That's not what I heard."

"Oh really?" Cindy stood up. "Really?" She walked into the kitchen and poured a cup of coffee, then came back to the table. "The woman you were named for—my mother, your great grandmother—the one your mother thinks was so saintly? If I was sitting here with her and if I said what you just said to me, I would have been back-handed so hard I would have flown across this room."

"No. You're making that up! Mom said Nana was the kindest woman she ever knew."

"Yeah, well, of course, to your mom! She was totally different with me." Cindy took a sip of coffee. "You'll find that out as you get older—how people have totally different personalities with different people. It's actually quite amazing. Like right now, someone is saying his serial-killer neighbor seemed like a 'really nice guy.' Now, come on, let's get this done. We finish this, we're done before noon and have the rest of the day to ourselves."

Jana put her head on the table. "I'm tired."

"I have cookies in my bedroom."

"The good stuff or the fake ones Mom gets?"

"The good stuff."

Jana sat up, tapped her pen on the table, then slowly began writing. When the page was full, she pushed it towards Cindy.

Cindy read it, then put the paper down. "Perfect. *Sincerely apologize; never happen again;* etcetera etcetera etcetera."

She went to her bedroom, and opened a few dresser drawers, then reached underneath her bed, way to the right. She came back into the dining room holding a half-dozen bags of cookies, and handed them to Jana.

"Have you ever thought of cutting bangs?" she asked.

⅄

Cindy cupped her chin in her hand. "You look amazing. Amazing." She put the scissors down and lifted her up from the toilet to face the mirror. "Look."

Jana gazed at her reflection. "I think I like it."

"Of course you do!" Cindy said, coming from behind to join in the reflection. "Look at you. You look extraordinary."

"Mom is not going to be happy though."

"Why?"

"Ballet. No one has bangs in ballet."

"Now why wouldn't you tell me that before I started cutting! I don't need her mad!" Cindy sat down on the toilet, raised her hands, palms up. "Look Jana, I have to cultivate a general atmosphere here, not go backwards, stir things up over something as insignificant as your bangs. Your mother is just waiting for me to do something stupid. Can you fake it when you go to ballet? Pull them off to the side?"

"Grandma," Jana said, turning to her, "chill. It's OK." She moved her head from side to side.

"It is? But you said—"

"Tonight we'll just have to distract her with something extremely positive . . . like I'll say the teacher singled me out, said I danced better than anyone else. Something like that always gets her off."

Cindy looked at her, then slowly got up from the toilet, moved behind her. "That's good Jana. Good."

Jana smiled. "Look, Grandma. Look at our lips, our noses. They're the same."

"Yep, they most certainly are."

Cindy moved forward, gently nudging Jana out of the way, until she had sole possession of the mirror. "What do you think of my hair Jana?" she asked. "And be truthful, it's important."

"Um, I think . . ." She ran a hand through Cindy's long hair. "I don't really mind the length."

"No. I mean of course you don't, of course that's OK. That's what makes me who I am. Look at Stevie Nicks. No one is telling Stevie Nicks to cut her hair."

"Stevie who?"

Cindy turned. "You know all about ballet, but you don't know who Stevie Nicks is? It's like you're being raised by wolves."

"It's the color Grandma, it's too drab. It doesn't pop your eyes."

"Exactly! That's what I just said this morning. It's too beige, right?"

"Yeah," Jana said. "It needs more strength, like get the gray out, make it more golden, but subdued, not brassy . . . and—oh! You know what else you should do? Oh, this would be great. You should get a Brazilian."

"Brazilian? Come on Jana, we're not talking about *that.*"

"No, Grandma. Gross. A Brazilian Blow-Out—a treatment that makes the hair on your head hair silky smooth! Yeah, do that! Get it colored, a really good trim and a Brazilian—it will make your hair like new! But it will be expensive."

"How expensive?" Cindy asked.

"If you go to Mom's hairdresser, she's the best, over $500?"

"No shit."

"Truly. That is how much it would be."

Cindy said, turning away from the mirror. "OK. So tonight, be sure to tell your mom about the teacher thing. Be sure to do that, because that's good. And say I made you practice for hours." She walked out of the bathroom and headed down the hallway towards the kitchen.

"But do I really have to do that?" asked Jana, following behind.

"What?"

"The practicing for hours?"

"Oh Jesus, Jana, you're smarter than that. I know that now. Of course not."

Jana smiled. "Awesome."

⅄

The days stretched ahead, a week, then a month, until it was almost Thanksgiving.

Layla and Cindy were at the kitchen table finishing their dinner of quinoa and roasted vegetable salad. Luke was at an after-work meeting; Jana at a friend's house.

Cindy took a sip of her water and looked at her plate. Who the fuck likes this stuff, she thought. And it's the same day after day after day. She took a bite of a red pepper and tried to imagine it was a McDonald's cheeseburger.

Layla looked down, then moved in her seat. "I want to say Mom, I am really, really pleased at how this is going and, um—I want you to know I appreciate it. I know it is hard."

Cindy's eyes widened for a moment, then relaxed. She moved the quinoa around on the plate with her fork. "Hard? Yeah, well you always believed the worst of me. Listened to too many of their stories.

"I know they told you I was an addict. An addict . . . so dramatic. I was never an addict! Well, certainly not hard core like they made it sound. It was that thing with Randy that turned my head around. But I was so young, so easily influenced. Not that any of that mattered to them, because once I left, the deal was done. It was war. What I went through, why I left never mattered. From then on, your father and grandmother were on this mission to destroy me, prove me a villain, exaggerate everything I did twenty-five-thousand times over."

Layla put her fork down. "Mom, you have to admit, most of the time—no really, all of the time—you were never around. They didn't exaggerate that. And they were the ones who had to cover."

"As God is my witness Lee," Cindy said, "I tried to come back as much as I could. You don't know how hard they made it! It was so unfair, how they never forgave me. You're older now, you should understand. People always spin things from their own perspectives.

I mean, look at you. You're gone a lot too. People could say—" She stopped, took a drink of water.

Layla's face tightened. "I *work*. That's a big difference."

"Oh, of course. Exactly. That's my point. That it would be unfair if people said that."

"Working is not heading off to Denver to do drugs with a guitarist," Layla said.

Cindy put her fork down, got up and carried her plate to the kitchen sink.

Layla sighed, leaned back. "I didn't—look, I just wanted to acknowledge what a big help you have been with Jana. How much Luke and I appreciate it."

"It's no big deal, Lee really. But I do appreciate the mention." She looked over at Layla's plate. "You done?"

Layla nodded, and Cindy went over, picked up her plate, and placed it in the sink. Then she came back, pulling up the waist of her loose fitting jeans before she sat down. "Oh this is embarrassing," she said. "These hardly fit anymore."

"That's another thing Mom. You've lost so much weight! You look amazing, you really do."

"Fifteen pounds. Ten more and I weigh what I weighed in college," Cindy said. "None of my clothes really fit anymore."

"Does Jana look like she's gained a few pounds?" Layla asked.

"Jana?"

"Yeah. I mean, she's still slender and all, but she has to watch with ballet. A few pounds makes a difference."

"Well no, I certainly haven't noticed that," Cindy said, touching a finger to her nose. "Well since I have been here anyway, her teacher is always stopping me, saying how great she is doing. I mean, she was just picked for the lead in the April end of year performance. That's a huge honor. And I've been careful about her practicing. Hours and hours of practice. She is *so* dedicated . . ." she moved her eyes off to the side, hesitated.

"What?" Layla asked.

"Oh . . .I don't know, it might be me but that teacher, Mrs. Barfield? I find her sort of snooty a little. You know, the type of person who judges the way things look. The last time I picked Jana up, I had on these jeans, and she kept staring at them, in a not so good way. And I kept pulling them up. Just felt so uncomfortable." She took a sip of water.

Layla reached for her purse, removed a credit card from her wallet, and slid it across the table. "Your clothes don't fit, you need to get new ones. Really, on me."

Cindy looked at the card, then at Layla. "Really?"

"Yes, of course. We can't have you going around town in clothes that don't fit."

"Well, I guess that makes sense—for Jana and all." Cindy picked up the card, and put it in her pocket. "I won't buy much, just a few things."

Layla got up from the table and carried her glass to the sink. "Well, just make sure you don't buy—um, no offense, those old-school hippie tops. Buy some quality stuff, like cashmere."

"OK. It's just . . . I mean, I appreciate the clothes offer and all, but, I was wondering . . . do you think I should do something with my hair? Like I'm thinking that may be throwing people off too."

"Oh thank God, yes!" said Layla turning away from the sink. "Yes! I was hoping you would cut your hair. I'll call my hairdresser, make an appointment."

"Well, I mean, I am not certain I will cut it, but—"

"Just something different, more tidy, yes."

"Yeah, something more tidy," Cindy said. "That's exactly what I was thinking. With the holidays coming up and everything. You want to be tidy."

"I'm going to go take a bath," Layla said. "Oh and I forgot. Tomorrow I have a meeting, so can you take Jana to ballet, then out to dinner? And make sure she eats light. I swear she's gained a few pounds."

"No problem," Cindy replied.

⅄

"Oh my God," Jana said, coming out from the dance studio. "Oh my fucking God, I didn't even recognize you!"

Cindy held out her arms and turned around.

Her shoulder length hair, which had been a grey-blonde mix of *I don't care* waves, was now a smoothed-to-perfection shade of lightest brown with carefully placed highlights. And instead of her hippie-style clothes, she wore a black form fitting blouse and skinny legged jeans that were tucked into boots that echoed the color of her hair.

"It's a wonder how a little thing like $2000 can up your game," said Cindy.

"It's not just the clothes and the hair, Grandma, it's your face, your body. Honestly, it's—" Jana stopped as her teacher, Mrs. Barfield, approached from the side.

"Lee?" Mrs. Barfield asked.

"Oh no, I'm Ms. Allen, Jana's grandmother."

"Oh, my! I thought Lee had lightened her hair! Have we met?" she asked, extending her hand.

"Um no, I mean I've picked up Jana before, but maybe you didn't notice. I had longer hair?"

"Oh . . . yes. Blonder and—"

"Gray. Yes."

"Yes. Will Lee be coming tonight?" Mrs. Barfield asked as she disengaged from the handshake, then tucked an errant hair back into her gray topknot.

"Oh no, I am picking Jana up," Cindy said. "Lee has a meeting. Is there something wrong? Because I am in charge of Jana, so if there is something—"

"Well, maybe we could talk in my office? It should only take a few minutes."

She turned. Cindy whispered to Jana, "Five minutes max," then followed her to a pink and cream office where Degas dancers twirled on the walls. "Take a seat," Mrs. Barfield said, closing the door.

"What's this about, Mrs.—"

"Call me Natalie," she said, and sat down at her desk, pushing the chair forward. Her brown eyes crinkled in concern. "It's Jana. She is very gifted."

"Yes," said Cindy, taking a seat in a wisp of pink chair.

"Has the perfect body for dance."

"Yes?"

"Now that is sometimes just in the genes." Natalie raised a long index finger into the air, then let it fall. "But when girls go through puberty, it takes discipline to maintain. Now it isn't yet critical, but I have noticed that Jana may have gained a few pounds or so."

"Jana is 5 feet 8 inches, and she weighs all of about 118 pounds," Cindy said.

"Well yes, but in dance body lines are extremely important. You do know she's been selected for a featured role in our end-of-year performance?"

"Yes, I do know that."

"But that selection was based on things in early fall."

Cindy leaned forward. "Let's cut to the chase, Natalie. What are you saying exactly?"

"Well . . . *what I am saying is* she does have an understudy, Olivia, who is extremely dedicated and disciplined. Now, it seems only fair, if Jana cannot return to her early fall form, that she should be replaced by Olivia."

"Really?"

"Yes. And I know how concerned her mother is about matters like this, so I thought I would just relay this ahead of time. So then . . ." She pushed her chair back, started to rise.

"Uh huh. So let me get this straight . . . " Cindy said, sinking deeper into her chair. "Jana needs to lose um . . . two pounds say? And practice more or you will replace her with—"

"There is much time to avoid all that, Ms. Allen. Months. She is very talented, I just want her to get back on the right track."

"Well, I am sure her mother would thank you for that."

"Well I try to keep lines of communication open—"

"But you're not talking to Jana's mother Natalie, you're talking to me, and I'm a totally different thing." Cindy put a hand to her chin, lifted her eyes. "Let's see. I figure you to be what? About my age? Fifty-nine, sixty? Wow, it's a very hard age to be, isn't it? I mean, just take you . . . I bet you were super talented when you were young. I bet you had a lot of people talking about your promise. And here you are, running some little dance studio in an almost suburb of bofunk Dayton, Ohio."

She turned her eyes to Natalie's. "I mean, that's all well and good, but you and I both know it's not fucking Moscow or New York. Yes, I'm sure I'm not telling you anything you don't know. How at sixty all that stuff, how things fell so far off the mark, tends to weigh on you and you get . . . grumpy. You know, a grumpy old woman."

She touched her forehead, offered a soft laugh. "Oh boy, if anyone understands that, it's me! But gee, in your case, it's a much harder because you're running a small business, and how many dance studios are there, even in this godforsaken place of nowhere Ohio? I bet a lot. So it's sort of important what people say about you, and of course, what they don't say. Especially at places like the Club. I love the Club, don't you?

"And how times have changed! I bet I don't have to remind you of that misfortune! Like today . . . it would not sit well with people today, a story of how a young girl was promised a lead in a recital then was replaced just because she gained two pounds. Lots of people would take offense at that. *Most* people would take offense at that."

Cindy picked up her purse, stood up. "I am really looking forward to seeing Jana in the recital. And I will be sure to mention how communicative you are about everything the next time I'm at the Club."

She walked to the door, then turned. "Have a great evening Natalie."

⅄

Her nights were the worst.

She would toss and turn, then finally get out of bed, and go to the armchair by the bedroom window. And as she gazed out at the darkness, she would go over every step of her life that had returned her to the same place she had left some thirty years ago. By the time the morning light finally broke the darkness, she always came to this.

Her mother, the sainted Jana One. Her curse had won.

How else could this all be explained? Someone like her, someone so different, ending up just like every other divorced grandmother—broke, living in the suburban home of her kid, schlepping around grandchildren with no life of her own?

Some nights she would go to her top dresser drawer, reach under the clothing way in the back, and pull out the letter. She would open the frayed and stained envelope, postmarked 1979, unfold the stationery, and read.

Cynthia,

I would say it was good to hear from you but it is not!!!! IT IS NOT!!! My only peace in this whole thing is that your father did not live to see what you have become.

You think you are so special? Leaving a husband and child to go off with what? A guitarist? That isn't special Cynthia, it is ordinary. Below ordinary. Animals know better.

And after how we raised you, gave you every proper advantage, education, social training! It was all to waste.

I am going to tell you something, and you will not understand it now because you are young and beautiful (which has been a huge curse to you by the way, gave you way too much self-importance and leeway), but there will be a time, and believe me, it will come MUCH QUICKER THAN YOU THINK, *when all of that will fade and you will have to reap what you have sowed with all of your God-given blessings.*

Yes, if you continue on this way, you are bound to end up in a worse state of unhappiness than the unhappiness you have brought others.

You discard a man like Mark, a man of substance, who is by the way, a wonderful provider and father to Lee (we do not call her Layla anymore), for what? A guitarist you met after some concert? You have an affair with him, which was bad enough, but then make it worse by taking off with him to Denver?

Cynthia, besides what you have done to everyone else, think for a moment! Do you think your guitarist is going to stay with you when you are old? Or sick?

Better yet, are you going to want to stay with him when you are thirty-five or forty and he is singing at some sleazy Holiday Inn (where he is bound to end up) and you have to work as a waitress to make ends meet?

Could you be so stupid? Please. It is nonsensical.

Yes, when you are my age, if you continue this way (and somehow make it through alive), you will receive your rightful payback.

And when everything blows up (as it most assuredly will), do not count on our money. Your father and I erred with our past generosity, we were always too quick to subsidize your lifestyle, or believe whatever story of need you concocted. Your father worked his whole life to provide things for you, but unfortunately I think this was one place where good intent led to critical mistake. Our generosity didn't do you any favors. It cultivated laziness, and lack of respect, for yourself and for others. It led you to this place where your life is ruled by momentary whim and desire.

So, just so you know, upon my passing, I have decided to leave the bulk of my estate to Lee. I will leave you a nominal amount, but Lee, who is just starting life, has substantial needs of her own. And I know, even though I try, nothing will ever replace the void you have left as her mother. Money is the one thing I can make right. It will at least be the one thing she will never have to worry about.

I have no hopes that what I have written will move you off the path you are on, but I know, I am certain beyond a doubt, your payback will come just as I have written.

Because, Cynthia, you are not so extraordinary that you can escape time.

Your Mother

PS and I am not an idiot. I know you are using some kind of dope, that is apparent, you are not fooling anyone. I would blame your behavior on that, but unfortunately I can't.

After Cindy read the letter, she would carefully refold it, and replace it in the envelope.

Yes, her mother had cursed her, and all of that hateful energy over what she had done, no check that, all of that hateful energy over *who she was*, was never going to be contained by the grave.

Oh, why hadn't her mother ever listened to her side of the story? She was her daughter! And what had she done that was so unbearably terrible, so unforgivable? Today, people leave spouses every day for every sort of reason. Their parents don't abandon them.

And if there was blame, shouldn't it start at the very beginning, with that ill-fated marriage to Mark? Weren't her mother's hands directing that whole messy mix? If she was guilty of anything, it was acquiescing too quickly to her mother and Mark's desires, giving into the belief that if she just went along, everything would be simplified.

Now she would admit, part of that was based on selfish practicalities. Her parents refused to support her and Mark's live-together lifestyle unless it was formalized by marriage. And yes, Cindy had grown weary of that stupid newspaper job, and the endless bills that always seemed to be overdue, but, what kind of parent *forces* a marriage on a daughter as a condition to receive what was rightfully hers?

Manipulative—that's what it was.

Then her dad got Mark a job in that Dayton bank, and yes, she could leave the boredom of the hated newspaper, but it wasn't for anything better, it was for infinitely worse. Life as a housewife in a subdivision inhabited by women who were nothing like her, waiting each night for Mark to come home, only to find when he did, that he didn't want to do anything but eat and sleep.

She was twenty-three, and that was her life. And if she ventured a complaint to her mother, she always got the same responses. *What's wrong with you? You're so lucky and ungrateful! Pray to Mary for a stronger sense of gratitude.*

Gratitude for what? That she was twenty-three and living the life of her fifty-year-old mother?

So who could blame her for that night at the *Creedence* concert, when Mark cancelled at the last minute, saying he was too tired, and she defiantly decided to go alone? Was that so crazy?

And what twenty-three-year-old would have said no, given the circumstances, when that guy approached her after the concert with an invitation to the after-party? Was her "yes" so unfathomable?

And then she met Randy, all black curly hair, smoldering eyes. She saw him, and from then everything was just a countdown to done.

Of course, it all sounds crazy now. It is almost impossible to remember the strength of that youthful pull. You can't recreate it in the middle-aged mind. But yes, it was there, and that alone would have made everything unavoidable without factoring in everything else.

The headiness of how it felt to be chosen as most desirable. The other girls' envious stares. The cocaine and liquor that fueled the movements and sensory overload when they got to his suite, and he slowly unbuttoned her blouse, telling her, with each button's release, how beautiful she was.

She felt like she had just arrived at a place where things finally made sense, fit the version of her rightful destiny. From that moment on, she knew it was just a matter of time before she would leave Mark, but she also knew she had to be smart, not scare Randy away. So she kept things cool, nonchalant. It worked in her favor, made her more forbidden and desirable. They talked on the phone daily, and had euphoric liaisons when he was close to town, but all of that stopped when Cindy got what she thought was a bad case of the flu, and Mark took her to the doctor.

Now there was another unfortunate price she had to pay for backward times, Cindy thought. The doctor looked at his chart, gave a half smile, then told the nurse to get Mark in the waiting room. When Mark came in, the doctor proudly announced (more to Mark than to her) that Cindy didn't have the flu, she was pregnant. Pregnant! Mark and the doctor shook hands, then Mark kissed her on the cheek.

And just like that, her plans fell apart. Cindy knew she couldn't tell Randy she was pregnant! That would ruin everything. They weren't some Linda and Paul McCartney—*we'll move to a farm with all of our kids*; they were more like Rod Stewart and Britt Ekland—*God, you're so hot, where's the party?* A baby didn't fit in that scene.

So there she was. Stuck. Stuck with Mark, who was overjoyed with this turn of events, not at all sympathetic to how uncomfortable she was with her blown up body and increasing anger and resentments, which he fluffed off to fluctuating hormones.

She backed away from Randy's calls, felt the best she could do was become less available until after the baby was born, when she got her looks back and was more on her game. And then, a while after the birth, after an especially horrible/wonderful day, there it was. She had taken Layla, who was always confoundingly fussy, for a walk in her stroller. And as Cindy walked, she felt the return of men's lingering stares. When she got home—somewhere in between Layla's colicky fussing and Mark's call to say he would be late for dinner—she knew it was time.

She picked up the phone and tracked Randy down. Denver. He was in Denver.

She had never been to Denver, but she figured it was beautiful.

She got a babysitter, wrote a hurried note to Mark, and left. Just like that, as if her previous life had never happened.

Now today, she told herself, people would say she was just being true to her "authentic self." And wasn't that all that it was? Her authentic self! What's so horrible about that? Some people are just not cut out for ordinary lives.

Or maybe she was just too young. Or maybe she had postpartum depression. Who knows? It could have been a million things, all of them forgivable.

But not to her mother.

From that point on, all she ever got from her mother was stony silence, only broken by this letter on eternal damnation.

Sometimes when Cindy looked at the letter, she wondered why this was the one thing she had carefully kept from her past. This horrible little reminder. Was she a masochist set on prolonging her mother's judgment, or did she just keep it as proof?

Proof that her mother was not what everyone thought. A little too ready to swoop in and assume her role as righteous savior, ensuring Cindy's role as monumental, self-consumed fuckup.

Well, either way, Cindy thought, it didn't matter, because the bottom line was everything her mother hoped for came to pass.

Randy the dream quickly became Randy the reality. They married; it sputtered, along with his career. He ended up working at a bar, booking young bands, sometimes singing on Open Mic nights.

There were times Cindy looked at him and couldn't find a remnant of that unavoidable smoldering version. At times he seemed more like a longer haired, less successful Mark.

She ventured home to see Layla a few times when money was available, but was always met with Layla's wariness, and Mark and her mother's *serves you right* self-righteousness. It was too much.

When her marriage to Randy ended, she drifted to Aaron, then David, and finally to Stan.

Stan, again doomed. Who would have thought when she met him—that big, vibrant, larger-than-life man, who took her on trips to Aspen and concerts at Red Rock—who would have foreseen that out-of-the-blue stroke, which basically left him an invalid?

And there she was, in his Canyon Boulevard condo, not a cent to her name (the nominal amount her mother had left her had been spent years ago), and there were his kids, swooping in, acting like what? She was going to take care of him? Take him for wheelchair rides around the condominium green space? Cook him easily digestible dinners?

No, sometimes life boiled down to what you knew you couldn't do. And she couldn't do that.

And Stan would have never expected her to! After all, they weren't married, it wasn't for better or for worse. When you're not married it's taken for granted it's for status quo or better.

So she told his kids that her daughter had called, that there was a family emergency back in Ohio, and she had to immediately return. She would keep in touch, come back when it was resolved. All the necessary niceties that she had no intention of doing.

And she made that humiliating trip to Layla's to ask for a place to stay. Temporary, she had promised, until she could figure some stuff out.

Layla was just as she usually was with her, tight pursed lips, only softening when Cindy inserted the part about Stan's stroke reminding her how swiftly life can change, how she wanted the chance to make things right a little, at least for Jana's sake. And she could be a big help, what with Layla's busy career. She could ease her parenting responsibilities, not the big stuff, but the everyday things like driving Jana here and there, or fixing dinners when she had to work late.

So Layla agreed, with the caveat that if anything disruptive happened, the arrangement would end.

One night, after putting the letter away, Cindy went to the living room desk and got a paper and pen. She carried them back to the bedroom, shut the door and sat down.

How old was her mother when she wrote that letter? She tried to calculate it in her head. She had been twenty-five, so her mother was fifty-one. Seven years younger than she was today.

Well, she thought, sorry to say Mom, it is not over yet.

And she took the pen and wrote at the top of the page, *How I Will Get Out of This,* and started to make a list.

⅄

Jana got into the car. "What?" she asked, feeling Cindy's stare.

"You've got makeup on."

"So?"

"For a girls' sleepover?" Cindy asked. She started the car, backed out of the driveway. "You best not be fucking with me Jana. You best not be telling me you're going one place, and then going another. I am going out on a limb here."

Jana laughed. "You're the one going to a party!"

"I'm fifty-eight."

"It doesn't matter, you didn't tell Mom."

"Your mom is in New York with your dad celebrating their anniversary—they deserve a weekend off. They don't need to know every little detail."

"OK."

"OK what?" Cindy asked.

"Mom would freak if she knew you were going to that Club mixer thing."

"She would not."

"Of course she would!" Jana said.

"Why?"

"You know."

"The liquor?" Cindy asked. "Are you crazy? Have you seen me take a drink in the past two months? Have you? Of course not! No one has seen me drink! And they certainly aren't taking drugs at Woodside Country Club events."

"That wouldn't stop Mom."

"Well, good try with all that deflection Jana, but let's get back to you. A girls' party at Morgan's right?"

"Yeah."

"And her parents are going to be there?"

"Sure."

"That sounds shady."

Jana rolled her eyes. "How could 'sure' sound shady?"

"You should have said 'yes,'" Cindy said, glancing at her out of the corner of her eyes, then shaking her head. "Who do you think you're dealing with? I have forgotten more about shady than you'll ever know. So tell me . . . how come I called Morgan's mother with the number you gave me, and she never called me back. How come?"

"How would I know why old people do what they do? I guess she's busy or something." Jana stomped a foot on the car floor. "Why doesn't anyone in this family believe me on anything?"

"OK, I will believe you . . . but you have to swear—"

"I am not a baby!" Jana said looking out of the window. "I'm almost fifteen for God's sake."

"I know that."

"And it's a *sleepover*, everyone goes to them! Everyone! And I do everything she asks me to! Ballet. Grades. Stupid Catholic school. Jesus. It's a fricking sleepover on a Saturday night."

Cindy turned in the driveway of Morgan's house, then parked. "Maybe I should stop in and talk to her parents."

"Oh my God," said Jana, opening the car door.

Cindy started to undo her seat belt, then stopped. "Ok. If you *swear* . . ."

"Thank you," said Jana.

"You better not let me down."

"I won't."

"So I pick you up here at what? Ten tomorrow morning?" Cindy asked.

"Yeah," said Jana. "Thanks Grandma!"

And then she shut the car door, and ran to the front of the rambling house.

⅄

Cindy pulled into the parking lot and shut off the car.

This was it, she thought.

She had seen the notice for the holiday mixer in the last newsletter Layla had left on the kitchen table. Of course, under usual situations, country club mixers would not be her thing. But these were not usual conditions.

She pulled down the car visor to check her hair and makeup, then smoothed down her new Max Mara coat. Everything was as good as it could get, she thought. She opened the car door and walked to the entrance, then into the grand hallway foyer which sparkled with holiday lights and smelled of evergreen trim. "You can check your coat here," said an overly eager woman with flashing Christmas tree earrings that dangled down to her shoulders.

"Oh, OK," said Cindy, taking off the coat, and then adjusting her black cashmere sweater that fell to the hips of her new black cigarette pants. "Thank you."

She made her way back to the main dining room. A woman dressed in red was seated at an entrance table. "Your name?" she asked.

"Cindy Allen."

The woman looked through her list. "Um . . ."

"Oh . . . the membership is under Robinson. Luke and Lee Robinson. I am Lee's mother, Cindy Allen."

"Oh . . . you're Lee's mother!" the woman said, looking up, holding out her hand. "Lee and I are great friends. She didn't tell me you were visiting, but what a treat! And how nice that you can be here with Jana while they are off to New York!" She tilted her head. "Such a nice romantic thing to do for their anniversary! I told her to take one of those buggy rides in Central Park. You know, soooo romantic! *Maybe* you'll get another grandchild!" she added with a wink.

Cindy shook her hand. "Oh yes, and wouldn't that be something?"

The woman took a marker, wrote *Cindy* on the nametag, and dotted the *i* with a little red heart. "There you go," she said, handing it to her, "now *you* have a romantic time too!" She crossed her fingers, then waved them back and forth like a preschool chorus leader.

"Oh, um, thank you," Cindy said, putting the nametag on her sweater, quickly backing away. She turned towards the small bar set up in the corner of the room, and surveyed the crowd.

Nondescript men in tan pants and button down shirts. Overly animated middle-aged women in holiday sweaters. She moved to the bar, and as she took her place in line, two men directly in front of her turned around.

"Can I get you something um . . . Cindy?" one of them asked, leaning over to take a closer look at her nametag.

She hesitated, moved her feet. "Sure," she started, glancing at his nametag, "Jeff. How about just a soda and lemon?"

"Oh come on, it's a party!" said the second one, Bobby.

"No, that is good for right now."

He ordered the drink, then handed it to her. "I haven't seen you around, are you new?"

"Um, not new." She took a small sip. "I mean, I'm not a member, my daughter and her husband belong. I'm just visiting."

"Yes, should have figured that because I would have remembered you. Do you golf?"

She shook her head. "Ah, no. Not a golfer. I don't really get into sports much, just skiing maybe—"

"Well golf is great, you should try it," Bobby ventured. "I could teach you when the weather clears. That would be like in what? July? Will you be here in July?"

A man came over to their group, draped his arm around Bobby, but kept his eyes on Cindy. "Bob . . . Bobby, how the hell are you? Haven't seen you in forever!" He leaned forward, offered her his hand. "I'm Gregg." His stomach bulged against the buttons of his blue oxford cloth shirt. "And you're Cindy with—what's that? Oh, a little heart. Cindy with the little heart!"

"Um yes. Well not the little heart part but—"

"Well Cindy, here's a clue," he drew closer. "You do not want to take golf lessons from Bobby. No way! That's like Obama teaching doctors about health care! That's what that is."

Cindy put her drink down on a table. "You know . . . I am going to have to excuse myself for a moment. I'm sorry, I have to go to the rest room."

"We'll save you a seat!"

She turned and walked out. Entering the rest room, she passed a large gilded mirror.

What the fuck, she thought, as she stopped and looked at her reflection. What was on my mind, thinking I could find anyone in this godforsaken place? Jesus! I've worked so hard for this? *Stretch* was preferable to this!

Well it couldn't be clearer, nothing good was happening tonight. Better throw in the towel, go home and regroup. Tomorrow something else would come to mind.

She turned to walk to coat check as an unlikely song popped into her mind.

Great, she thought, first golf, now Broadway tunes about optimistic orphans.

Her footsteps slowed as she passed the Club bar.

Well, the night was still young, wasn't it? And who would ever know if she just had one drink? She turned back, and tentatively entered the room, took a seat on the closest barstool. "Manhattan, up," she said to the bartender.

"Haven't heard of that drink in awhile," said a man a few seats down.

"Yeah, well—" Cindy began, then turned to look at him.

Dark curly hair, scattered with gray. Longish. Not set in its place like Mark's or the men in the dining room. Flannel shirt and jeans. A great, easy smile that seemed vaguely familiar. "Have we met before?" she asked.

"I don't think so," the man replied laughing. He moved towards her and held out his hand, "I'm Seamus. Seamus Callahan. May I join you?"

"Sure," she said. She took his hand, looked at the liquid in his glass. A rich amber color. Scotch? He sat down next to her.

"I'm Cindy," she said.

"I know . . . it's on the nametag."

"Oh!" she said, looking down, then peeling the nametag from her sweater, crumpling it up into a tiny white ball. "What a nightmare."

"The mixer?"

"Yeah."

"Did you talk about golf?"

"That was a problem. I don't play, and I really don't want to learn. God, is there anything sadder than middle-aged mixers at a country club?"

He smiled. "Only thing I can think of is *holiday* middle-aged mixers at a country club." He raised his glass took a drink, then set it down on the bar. "I'm a widower," he said.

"Excuse me?"

"Oh, I thought I noticed a glance. Totally appropriate, by the way. You never know at a bar, even a country club bar. Maybe especially a country club bar. My wife, she died three years ago."

"Oh. I'm sorry," she said.

"Thanks. It's OK. She hated this place. Wasn't her style. She was a professor, thought country clubs were for the self-important. She's probably rolling over in her grave right now knowing I joined."

"So why did you?" Cindy asked.

"I guess the short answer is it helps with my business, the connections. But the more truthful answer is, a lot of times I'm bored, and it's just a place to go."

Cindy nodded. "Isn't it funny how sometimes life just boils down to that? A place to go, I mean. Most of the time you end up somewhere for no other reason then, at the time, you couldn't think of anywhere better."

"That's actually quite profound," he said.

She laughed. "It's true. Forty years ago, I might have burned this place down, but here I am talking about golf with a guy who hates Obama . . . yeah, here's to all the things we end up doing that we swore we'd never do." She raised her glass, then took a sip. "So, what *is* your business, and how did you end up in Dayton, Ohio?"

"Well, first question, I'm a psychologist." He leaned towards her, lowered his voice. "This Club is a gold mine. As for settling here? My wife and I met our first year at Antioch College, then later, she was offered a professorship, and we returned. Sometimes I would try to pry her out of here, but she wouldn't have it. So that's how I ended up here, now what about you?"

"Me? Oh my daughter lives here, with her husband and my granddaughter. I'm just visiting, helping out," she answered.

"Oh. You're only here for the holidays then?"

"Well maybe longer than that. Semi-permanent. I mean, I'm retired, flexible now, so when she needed my help, I just thought why not? Came out from Den—"

"Hey Cindy, there you are! Everyone is sitting down, we're going to eat!" said Gregg, coming up from behind her.

"Oh, I'm just . . . I'm sorry. I'm not feeling well, I think I am going to have to pass."

"Yeah, she just stopped by when she saw me to say hello," said Seamus, getting off the barstool. "I'm going to walk her to her car."

Gregg stepped back. "Oh, OK Doc." He turned to Cindy. "Remember, if you ever want help with that golf game—"

"Yes, I'll remember . . ." said Cindy, picking up her purse, feeling Seamus's hand on her elbow, guiding her out.

"I think I owe you for that," she said, leaning towards him.

"OK. Then maybe you can repay me by joining me for dinner some night?"

"I'd love to, but dinner?" she stopped, as he opened the Club's front door. "Dinner might be difficult. How about lunch? Lunch would be better."

"Lunch it is then. I'll call, if that's OK," he said.

She gave him her number, and as she watched him walk back into the Club, she thought, *Lord.*

A psychologist. A good looking psychologist in an aging hippie way. A widowed good looking psychologist in an aging hippie way. A drinking widowed good looking psychologist in an aging hippie way.

God damn.

It was almost like hitting the lottery.

CHAPTER FOUR

JANA

This is unbearably *awkward, writing in a journal, but since you* REQUIRED *me to do it, and since I obviously have* NO FREEDOM OF MY OWN, *even in a free country like the United States of America (huge joke!) I will answer your stupid questions.*

You asked me at my appointment if I had anger against my mother, and I said "If you are asking me if I am going to get out an ice pick and kill her in the middle of the night . . . um, probably not."

And I delayed that "probably not" too long.

So what happened? Now I have to continue seeing you and write in this journal and since I'm basically on home arrest (refer back to LACK OF FREEDOM*), it is what it is and I have to do what I have to do.*

So . . . this whole thing started, well a long, long time ago, probably at my birth if you want to know the truth. It did not just start when the police broke into Morgan's party cause a neighbor had called and they unfortunately found a whole bunch of liquor and under-aged kids and more unfortunately, me and Christopher in Morgan's parents' bedroom, and most most unfortunately, he had his pants off and was holding a joint.

This is the way I look at that. First. No one PROVED anything happened in that bedroom, it was all assumption this assumption that. You know why? CAUSE NO ONE IN THIS TOWN HAS A LIFE!!!

That's right! Not one thing better to do but talk about some teenage party where kids drank and partied, just like the adults did the same very night, a few miles down the road at the Club.

And I am going to point out here, how is it that our party was this BIG SIGN that we were all troubled or (in my case) had (dramatic) mental problems (due to freakish mother), when the adult party down the street was a sign that people were festive, and social and important parts of the community? How the fuck is that?

I mean, if you ask me (which of course no one does, cause I'm basically one step away from what do they call those headpieces women have to wear in the Middle East? Berkas? Yeah, berkas), if I had teenagers, I would be THANKING MY LUCKY STARS, they were doing normal shit like having parties when parents are gone rather than sitting in a room making a bomb or on the computer falling in love with a fifty-year-old bald man who promises to pick them up at a bus station in Psycho Adult Village, Indiana.

Yeah, having an ADULT lecture you that somehow you're the most disappointing thing since Adolf Fucking Hitler cause you had a beer and some fun, is hysterical proof they have NO FUCKING IDEA WHAT TO GET UPSET ABOUT.

Our party didn't mean anything except Morgan's parents were gone and we could have it. There's nothing psychotic about that, it's normal!

You said write in a journal from my perspective what happened (like I'm some forty-year-old Oprah watcher), so Ok here it is.

Crazy Gma C was watching me that weekend, and I knew she was a little distracted. Yes, I will admit that. I knew that she would not be Nazi SS sleuth of the year like my mom as to the details of the party, so I waited till after my parents left and just snuck the whole thing in drone-like, saying I was going to Morgan's for a sleepover.

In her defense, she did ask some questions, but she was pretty easily satisfied. Morgan's parents were gone for the night, and the older guys came, including Christopher. They had gotten liquor and some dope, and that, pretty much, is the whole story.

Except for the pants off part with Christopher. But really, there is no story there, because nothing actually happened! I mean nothing in terms of my precious vaginal virginity, and that is the truth! Obviously we were doing shit, but it's not like Christopher was some random choice. I like him a lot. He understands me. And that doesn't happen much, someone understanding me. That night we were talking, and it was so loud in the living room and kitchen, we went to the bedroom just to be able to hear. Christopher spilled a drink on his pants, so he took them off to let them dry, and we were just sort of relaxing, when the cops come busting in and after that . . . well after that, no one really cared to hear our side of the story, everything stopped with "pants off," "joint," and their dirty, little imaginations.

So, really, I don't have anything to feel guilty about, because I didn't do anything. The only part I do feel bad about is sort of lying, or rather, leaving out the whole truth to Grandma C. Cause after this happened, Mom was all over her shit for not knowing, for it happening on her watch.

And it didn't stay there, it escalated to loud arguments between my mother and her about other stuff. I couldn't hear everything since I have pretty much been confined to my room, but I did hear parts, like Mom saying stuff like "I should have known not to trust you," which seemed to set things in a heated, different direction where quite honestly it did not seem to be about me or the party at all.

Which is when I really tried to listen, because for all of my life I have felt I have missed an important under story that would explain a whole lot of things in my family, like when the air seems to be filled with combustible tension two seconds away from exploding.

As long as I can remember, our lives have been full of those moments . . . when people are talking, usually my mom and dad, but sometimes Grandpa Mark too, and I come into the room, and the air is like Important. And then all the talk stops.

Now, I am not an idiot. It's like having a puzzle, and someone is hiding the most important piece that will let you see the whole picture.

So I am telling you all that because you also wanted me to write about my FEELINGS towards my family, as if that was ridiculously somehow connected to just wanting a beer, and a night without parents around.

(Well, on second thought maybe, but regardless, my family . . .)

My mother . . .

I have never seen her messy. Never. Not even first thing in the morning.

She has lists on lists on lists of how things are supposed to proceed. Everything. From her job at the law firm, to my progress in ballet, to the foods we should eat or not eat. It's actually quite alarming, but basically I am pretty sure my mom thinks a well-thought-out list has the power to make time her personal bitch.

I have never written a list in my life, and even if I did, I would certainly misplace it (like any normal person who knows shit happens!!!!).

She is beautiful, but sort of in an untouchable way. Like a piece of fine china, admired but easily cracked.

We are nothing alike, and it shows even in pictures of us when I was a baby. I always looked a little messy, and the camera always seemed to catch my mom in the process of correction—smoothing down my unruly hair or fixing a bow I had defiantly tried to take off my head.

My dad. Oh geez. I think he is awesome, but I also think he got himself into this thing with Mom, sort of like a hurricane, and it just got too much for him, so he decided the easiest way to deal was just to go along, and now, he usually doesn't say much.

Although he did start to defend me about the party and the bedroom situation with Christopher when Mom was going ballistic. He ventured a "Lee, really, let's get a perspective," but then she gave him a look, got perfect forming tears in her eyes and he left to go to the Club or something, and that was the end of that.

My dad works as a consultant now, whatever that is. He used to work at a bank, like Grandpa Mark. They are sort of a lot alike.

Crazy Gma C? She is sort of mysterious, as in she disappears here and there, and I mean disappears for years.

Like we hadn't seen her for maybe five years—no calls, no cards, nothing. But that's not even the crazy part—the crazy part is when she's gone, her existence isn't even acknowledged. Like no one goes, gee, it's a beautiful day, I wonder what Grandma C is doing today? Or gee, we got a postcard, Grandma C is in Panama! Nothing.

So she's gone for five years, then, out of the blue, one day, a week or so before she came here to live, she is at the front door. Came from Denver I think, usually that seems to be where she is most of the time. So she comes, and Mom is simmering, Anglo style, her mouth all tight around the edges. And they go into the living room, real private, French doors closed. I couldn't hear anything that night, but the next morning I think Mom was on the phone with Grandpa M and I heard her say, "She has nowhere else, so . . . she seems to be OK. I'll try. I know I don't owe her anything but . . . it might be good to have someone help with Jana when I'm working late, things at the firm are crazy."

And then a week or so later she moves in. Just like that! And not cause oh she loves us or we love her, or she's just a fucking grandma and that's what happens but it's EXPLAINED like it's some high level deal. And I am part of it.

Gma is coming to "help out with Jana," that's what is said.

Like I am some baby who they can't leave alone and who is the sole reason something has to happen that NOBODY wants.

Gma didn't look too happy to be here (props to her), and I think her coming was the LAST thing my mom wanted, even with all the "extra help" crap.

Things in the family got way worse when she came, my mom is wired tighter than an Alabama cheerleader when she is in the same room, and it's obvious our issues are nothing compared to what's going on with them!

I think Mom is pissed off cause Gma C was never around when she was younger, or maybe it's cause Gma left/hurt Grandpa Mark, or maybe it's cause Mom thinks, or is certain, all of that means Gma doesn't love her the way a mother should love her daughter.

All of that, plus the fact that Gma C is as different from Mom as you can possibly get. Where Mom is guarded and controlled, Gma C is the opposite.

I mean, I don't know what shit Gma C got into back in the day, but I do know that has to be part of the story, cause Mom is way too concerned and worried about what she is doing (example: all the liquor in the house disappeared about a week before Gma C came to stay, and NOT because Mom and Dad drank it cause I found all the bottles, most of them half full, in the trash).

In Gma C's defense, she can't buy a break with this woman! Mom is always sort of watching her, and you get the idea Mom thinks if she takes her guard down for one moment, Gma C will end up smack dab in a gutter.

It makes me feel sort of sorry for her. It's not an easy thing, knowing someone doesn't believe in you and if anyone understands that, it is me!

It makes me want to hug her.

I never do, probably because I'm not sure how she would react cause really, who knows with her? She's just not your typical huggable Grandma, that's for sure.

I did feel bad about lying to her about the party, handing Mom the opportunity to come down on her. I tried to apologize, I went into her room one night after one of their especially loud arguments, and I started to say "I'm sorry," but she stopped me at "I'm sor—" and said, "Jana, don't ever do that. Don't ever apologize for being young. It's annoying. Young is for making mistakes. Now I'm tired and I want to go to bed." And when I turned around to leave, she added, "Promise me something."

Which was an odd thing for her to say, the "promise" part.

So I said what? And she said, "You can fuck up a lot of stuff, but promise me you won't ever fuck up going to a college in a really interesting place full of really interesting people, which would mean it would be very far away from here."

"Uh, OK."

"I mean that," she said. "Don't wimp out on me."

"I won't," I said.

"And then . . . after you graduate, get a God damned career, a high paying one, so you don't have to ever depend on anyone for anything. Then if you want to, you can tell whoever you want to fuck off."

"OK," I said.

"No, promise," she said.

"I promise. But—"

"But nothing. I'm tired now. I want to go to sleep."

I thought it was the strangest advice, especially with the "promise" part. "Promise" is way too Disney for Gma C. Plus, I had never figured her as someone overly concerned with careers. She just isn't that type. Mom is that type. Gma is just . . . well . . . she's really just a hippie is what she is. Like the ones you read about at Woodstock. You know, peace, love, rock and roll. Only to be accurate, you'd have to leave out the peace part.

But that's really who she is, even with this whole new look of hers, where she sort of creepily resembles Mom. It's just so obvious that it is all temporary, just a matter of time before everything blows, and the wild unstraightened hair and loose, gauzy hippie tops return, and she gives everyone the finger and goes back to who knows where.

Because no matter what she wears or how she looks it all boils down to her favorite saying.

"You can do a lot of things, but you can't make a flying monkey an elephant."

I thought when she said that the first time, it was just some silly saying old people say when they want to sound mysterious and wise, but the more she said it (about ballet teachers, room mothers, random Club members and various Republicans), the more I began to think it perfectly explains a whole lot of stuff in my life without (thank God) having to get into it.

Gma and Mom; me and Mom.

You can't make a flying monkey an elephant.

Even though, it seems, everyone breaks their necks trying.

CHAPTER FIVE

SEAMUS

There was a soft knock on his office door.

"Your eleven o'clock is here," Nancy, his receptionist said, entering the room.

"OK," he replied, closing the small notebook, and putting it back into the file on his desk. "You can let him in."

"You want a bottle of water or anything? You look sort of pale."

"Do I? No . . . I'm fine, just a little tired is all."

He put the file into a desk drawer, got a pad of paper, and took a seat on the chair by the couch.

"Hey Doc, how ya doin'?"

"No complaints Oliver. Well maybe a few, but nothing major. How are you?"

"Good," he said, taking a seat on the couch. He glanced around the office, his eyes settling on a picture of Seamus's late wife Lisa on a side table. "Wow," he said, "she was such a beauty. In every way, I mean, not just in how she looked. Well, I'm not telling you anything you don't know. I just loved working with her, always smiling. I miss that."

"Me too," said Seamus, then glanced at his notes. "So um last time . . . last time you said you were having a hard time—with *time* I guess is the best way to put it. How you could structure it better. We discussed setting up a daily routine. How's that going?"

"I set up a schedule. Yeah."

"And?"

"Well, the schedule I set up was like you suggested, similar to the one I had when I taught. Get up around 7:00, start painting around 8:00. Then after a few hours, go to the gallery, come home about 5:30 or 6:00. So basically 8:00 to 5:00, same hours."

"So how'd that work last week?"

"Last week?" Oliver asked.

"Yeah."

"Um . . . well for sure Monday it did." He raised his eyes. "Tuesday . . . Tuesday I got sidetracked."

"With what?" Seamus asked.

"I ended up going down to the *Dayton Times* office. Spent a lot of time there, so Tuesday was a wash. And then Wednesday I was sort of still upset about Tuesday, so things were thrown off."

"Wait. Go back. Why did you go to the *Times* office?"

"That? Oh that is a good one! You'll love it." Oliver leaned forward, clasped his hands. "You read that young punk's column? That Andrew—oh what's his name? Andrew . . ."

"Sampson?"

"Yeah, that's it!" he said, leaning back. "Piece of shit that guy is. His column last week was titled, 'From the Greatest to the Grooviest: Did the Baby Boomers Ruin America?' You read it?"

"Actually, yes. I think I did."

"Horrible shit. Outrageous. Anyway, I get up and am starting my schedule, but I had an hour, it was only 7:00 a.m. or something, so I pick up the paper and the title of that column catches my eye. Then I read it, and after that, there was no way around it, I had to go down to the office and talk to him."

"You couldn't just send him an email?"

"Email? No!" Oliver shook his head. "I had to see him, face to face, tell him what I thought."

"And?"

"Well I go to the office and had to wait a long time, got a lot of funny looks. Eventually he came out. And can you believe? He had on khakis and a polo shirt! Stupid preppy fuck. Oh sorry, but that sort of captures it. Anyway, I told him 'Dude, if it wasn't for us, you would still have to wear a suit to work. You're welcome for that.' "

"So you talked to him and then what happened?" Seamus asked.

"Well I mean by the time that was over, the day was shot and I went home."

"Got high?"

"Well I was generally wound up, so—"

"So you got high. And then the next day, you were still wound up so you get high again?"

"Well, just a little, maybe. Like I said. The whole thing fucked up my routine."

Seamus tapped his pen on the pad of paper. "Oliver look, we've sort of been struggling with this, how your retirement and unstructured time present challenges you didn't have when you were teaching. And how keeping to a schedule is a way for you to get a handle on that, a sense of purpose and control. It also takes away a lot of unstructured time when stuff is apt to happen that you said you didn't want to happen."

"Yeah, but I mean it's not that big. Just a few joints is all," Oliver said.

"But you were the one who said you'd rather that not happen."

"And it wouldn't have happened if I hadn't read that piece of shit column!"

"OK," Seamus said leaning forward, clasping his hands, "this is a problem. *You* need to be in charge of your life—what happens and what doesn't happen. You can't hand that over to some columnist you don't even know. And to be honest, I'm getting a little frustrated here. These things keep coming up week after week, and they keep you in the same place. Is that what you want? Because a good case can be made that you are *finding* reasons to stay in that place, looking for excuses to get high."

Oliver shook his head, then looked at the ceiling. "No, no, no, this isn't on me." He brought his eyes back to Seamus. "He wrote—he used the word *groovy* to make us all look like idiots, like what we did was insignificant. Like we were insignificant . . ."

"So are we?"

"No! I mean everything, civil rights, the draft, women's issues, gay issues . . . everything changed because of us."

"OK. You know that and I know that. Why isn't that enough?"

"I don't like being trivialized," Oliver said. "People died. I mean just because it wasn't fricking Normandy, doesn't make it nothing. People *did* die."

"Yes they did. But let's try this. Do you agree there are assholes in life?" Seamus asked. "Like there are just some people who will always be assholes and no matter what you say, what proof you offer them on this or that being wrong, you can't change that?"

"Oh," Oliver said, eyes widening. "I never thought of that! Yeah, like they just have an asshole destiny. Yeah," he said, nodding, "I would agree with that."

"OK. So let's start there. Out of one hundred percent of people, what percentage do you think are assholes?"

"Today? As in now?"

"Yes, today," Seamus said.

"Oh geez, the number has to be way up there. Like I would say what? Eighty-three percent. But then . . . I mean, it might also vary as to geography. Like say in Washington D.C. it might be what? Ninety-eight percent? Maybe someplace like Berkeley it's—"

"Let's not get bogged down by geography," said Seamus. "Here's the point. There are a whole lot of assholes out there that no matter what, will never be persuaded to be anything different, right?"

"Right."

"So isn't it illogical, if that is what you believe, to allow the course of your day—and really, your life—to be determined by assholes? Think about that Oliver. If there is just this huge group of people with asshole destinies that no one can change, why even bother? What does it matter what they think about us? You and I both know that what we did and who we are *is* significant, so what does it matter what anyone else thinks? You do believe in your significance, don't you?"

"Well . . ." Oliver started, "when I was teaching at the college . . . I still get emails from some of the students. Five, ten, twenty years later. So yeah, that was significant."

"What else?"

"Well Moira of course. I know I'm significant to her. I told you she's going to have a baby this summer, right? My first grandkid."

"Yes. That's great. Anything else?" Seamus asked.

"Heather I guess. We've been together what? Almost five years. But you know it's as up and down as much as my marriage to Doris was. I think it's because she's almost thirty years younger than me, just in a different place. I end it, she ends it. But then a week later we're back together." He ran a hand through his silver hair. "I just think things seem easier when . . . well you know . . . even if they aren't perfect, it just helps when there is someone to—"

"Love?"

"Yeah, exactly."

"So you are significant to her," Seamus said.

"Sure. I mean, I assume that I am."

"Anything else?"

"Nope. That probably covers it."

"What about your paintings?" Seamus asked.

Oliver laughed.

"Why laugh?" Seamus asked. "You've had pretty good success with them, they sell well in the gallery."

"Yeah, well to tourists."

"What's that mean?"

Oliver shook his head. "Well, it just means the people who buy them don't know much about art."

Seamus lifted his shoulders. "How could you know that?"

" 'Cause I know . . . Well, maybe I don't know that for sure."

"No you don't," Seamus said.

"I just—I don't know," Oliver started, "I just thought, and I know this sounds crazy, but I just thought they'd amount to more. Not in money or anything, but you get what I mean. When I was young and busy with the job and marriage and kid, I had all these built-in excuses for why things were sort of falling short. Kept telling myself, boy, when I have the time, I'm going to do the most kick-ass paintings."

He laughed, shook his head. "And now I have the time, and I'm painting pictures of Main Street and happy dogs."

"So, if you don't like that, paint something else," Seamus said.

"Like what?"

"You're the artist. Something that will make *you* happy. Take a week away from the gallery, try to do that."

"But what if I can't think of anything better?" Oliver asked.

"Well, then, I guess you'll know that. But you'll never know if you keep on painting happy dogs."

⅄

At the end of the hour, Seamus went back to his desk, and pulled out the small notebook from the file. He opened it up, turned to the entry where he had left off. When he finished reading, he leaned back in his chair, his eyes settling on Lisa's picture.

There was a soft knock on the door. "You're 1:00 is here," Nancy said.

CHAPTER SIX

CINDY

She checked her email, then turned off the computer.

No, she was not imagining it, something was definitely off. He hadn't called or emailed in what? Four days? Before Christmas, it was every day.

She went into the living room and sat down on the couch. The house was silent. Jana was at school; Layla and Luke at work.

Now what could it be?

It definitely wasn't the way she looked, she thought. She looked better than she had in what—twenty years? She had maintained the twenty-five pound weight loss for almost a month. Her clothes? Well they weren't her inherent style of course, what with all of the mind-numbing blacks, creams and grays, and just an allowable small "pop of color" (as if too much color would implode someone's head), but she understood it was a totally different time, and she had to project a certain image. So she religiously stuck to her plan, even though all the drabness reminded her of Lara in *Dr. Zhivago*—and not the young, foxy Lara, but the beaten down, mature one at the end of the movie, trudging off in twenty feet of communist snow while Zhivago had a heart attack on a bus.

But what could you do? No one was interested anymore in pop art or Mary Quant or psychedelic T-shirts whose patterns resembled something from a bad acid trip.

And anyway, if she understood anything, she understood men. And men, almost always were attracted to the same type of woman.

One afternoon, when she was at his home, she discovered a picture of saintly Lisa on a book shelf in his study. She had wandered in while Seamus was making her lunch. She picked up the picture and carefully noted the hair, the clothes, the jewelry.

She was pretty enough, Cindy decided, but not stunning. Stunning would have implied a sensuality that just wasn't there.

No, Lisa was pretty in an understated, well-bred type of way. In the picture, she smiled full-face into the camera, straight, gleaming teeth, no hint of underlying sarcasm or edginess, no jewelry or overdone hair detracting from the well-bred Katherine Hepburn-y feeling face.

She looked like the type of woman who had a lot of friends who thought she was wise; who gardened, ate yogurt and hiked. Actually it looked like she might have been hiking in the picture.

Cindy had been very careful, not only with her clothes, but also with her personality, to replicate the vibe of the picture, toning down the volume of what she said and how she said it, bringing things down to what she thought would be his comfortable place. She remembered to retain a wit, but avoid the sarcasm. Have one glass of wine, but drop the whiskey. Confine makeup to that ridiculous place where men think you aren't wearing any makeup at all.

And at first it seemed to work. He called or emailed daily. They met for lunch, and sometimes for dinner if Jana and Layla and Luke weren't around, or if she could find a reasonable explanation for her absence.

She wanted to avoid Layla's finding out about the relationship until it was on stronger ground. Her antennae would go up, and it didn't make sense to risk that now, especially since that whole Morgan/party fiasco had already put her on dangerous ice.

Layla had gone crazy ballistic after that, using it as an opportunity to rehash every failing Cindy had as a mother and person over the past thirty-some years. And for the most part, Cindy let her vent, taking refuge in her room like she was the teenager being punished.

She tried valiantly to keep most of her thoughts to herself. She didn't want to encourage confrontations, which, in the end, only worsened her increasingly unbearable itch to leave. And she had only faltered once, throwing gasoline on a smoldering fire, when she unfortunately walked into the kitchen to get a drink of water, and overheard Luke and Layla in a heated discussion about whether or not Jana should see a shrink.

She got her water, took a sip. She couldn't avoid hearing, they were at the kitchen table! She put the glass down, tapped her fingers on the counter, tried very hard to suppress the urge to comment, let the moment pass. But in the end, she couldn't. She turned around and faced them.

"What?" asked Layla, "What?"

"Um," Cindy said, shifting her weight. "I think Luke is right Lee. Jana does not need to see a psychologist."

"Well, I think she does," Layla answered, moving her eyes back to Luke's.

"Why, Lee?" Cindy asked, moving forwards towards the table. " 'Cause she went to a party and did some stuff like every other teenager in the country? She's already being punished for that, she's basically on house arrest. Come on. It was a party and she's a great kid, does everything you want her to do. Gets good grades. Goes to ballet, even though that teacher is a horrible woman, psycho nuts. She just made a mistake is all. She is not mentally ill."

"Yeah, well, you're not her mother and you don't know," Layla said, locking her eyes with Cindy's.

Luke looked out the window; Cindy looked at him and took a step forward. "Well Luke is her father and he says—"

Layla put up her hands. "Stop right there. You have no idea what it's like today. Jana's facing bigger things at fifteen than you faced, not so successfully I might add, at twenty-one. It's not like it was back in your day, someone has a beer, a joint, what's the big deal? Everything you did at twenty-one is now available to preteens. That's a big difference. And the way she looks, one mistake, that's her life. Anyway . . ." she twisted in her seat, turned her eyes back to Luke, "this is between Luke and me. You had your chance to parent. You passed, remember?"

Cindy looked at her for a long moment, then turned and went to her room.

She later assumed Layla won that battle, because there were nights she and Jana left for unexplained stretches of time. But after the argument, Cindy resolved to stay out of it. And anyway, that confrontation only reinforced the importance of her keeping focused on Seamus and her plan, which seemed to be unraveling for some unknown and mystifying reason.

She had been so certain it was just a matter of time before things between them would develop, immediately resolving her whole living arrangement dilemma. They were moving (albeit a little too ploddingly) to intimacy. And she was certain once that was accomplished, the deal would be done.

Didn't she know that about men? Of course she did! You throw that on the table, they keep coming back. Not brain surgery.

But Seamus was a funny one, acting as if that wasn't all that important. He certainly was nothing like Randy, who was all fire, or even Stan, who was all earth, or any other man in between. With all of them, their desire was overt, flattering, and impossible to ignore—the way things were supposed to be. Not moving at some glacier-paced tempo where it took a week to hold hands, a week to kiss, another week to blah blah blah. So much fricking time! Enough time, she thought, to second guess everything, including the attractiveness of the person in front of you.

It had taken him so long to move things from holding hands to kissing, that she considered the possibility he might be gay. But she quickly dismissed that idea because she was certain she saw the desire in his eyes, it was just that when it appeared, it was always negated with an opposing physical reaction, a shake of his head, or movement away.

She figured it all had to do with the toxic mix of his cerebral ways and that dead asexual wife of his. There was no way she had been into sensuality! He probably had been sexually frustrated for decades.

Now this whole glacier-paced scenario certainly wasn't her preference, but she was sure she could change it around. She'd just have to do it slowly, in a refined way, so as not to scare him to death. But she was certain that, once that was done, there would be no going back, and he'd be eternally grateful. He just needed a push was all. Not even a push, a nudge.

So one day, when he had invited her over for lunch, she figured it was time.

She thought out every detail. The ivory colored blouse she wore with the plunging neck that showed off just the right amount of cleavage. The *Poppy* perfume she sprayed at the back of her neck because its notes were supposed to be especially compelling to men. And the switch up of her hair, from straightened control to a hint of earthy abandon, thanks to an overpriced hair product that was supposed to mimic the effects of a sultry day at the beach.

She brushed against him when he was cooking, the softness of her breasts grazing the hardness of his shoulders. "Can I help?" she had asked.

Then, she picked up a piece of carrot from the salad on the counter. Put it in her mouth slowly. He backed away slightly, but she could tell she was winning, so she continued to play as they sat down to eat.

"Gee, doesn't this weather just make you lazy? Like you just want to stay in bed all day?" she asked, casually shaking her head, glancing outside the window, as the light icy rain turned to snow.

He got up, came towards her, "Yes, it does. It does," he said.

He picked up her hands, she rose, and he led her to his bedroom. As they entered, he turned to her, kissing her uncharacteristically hard, lingering at her neck. "Are you OK with—" he started.

She let go of his hand, got on the bed, and lifted off her blouse, revealing the translucent lace of the pale pink bra and the skin underneath. She kept her eyes on his face, opened her mouth slightly, nodded.

She felt the drab softness of the flannel grey bedspread under her body, moved it a little to expose the sheets underneath. Cotton.

Lord, she thought, if any man ever needed her, this was the guy.

He was trying hard to avoid it, she knew, but his eyes kept coming back to her breasts. "Come here," she said, holding out her hand.

He took her hand and sat on the edge of the bed, went to take off her bra, and fumbled. She unhooked it with her hands, threw it on the beige carpet, then lightly touched her breasts with her long fingers. She stopped, rose up and kissed him, slightly biting his lip.

And that got things moving.

Finally, she thought! Jesus. The whole play had taken forever. By the time they had all their clothes off, and he was moving down on her stomach, kissing her navel, she looked over and saw the red flashing numbers on the digital clock next to the bed.

3:15. Oh shit, she thought. Shit. She had to leave now or she would be late to pick up Jana. Oh Lord, Layla would freak. Her hands touched his head. Could she possibly stop him now? "Seamus?" she asked. "Seamus?"

He lifted his head.

"Oh God, I am so sorry, but I just . . . the time? Do you know what time it is? I can't be late to pick up my granddaughter. I'm sorry, so sorry."

He sat up, looked at the clock. "Oh, it's quarter after three."

She sat up, kissed him. "I wouldn't go but . . . I have to pick up Jana."

"Jana?" he asked, shaking his head, pushing himself up. "Jana?"

"Yes," she said, picking up her bra off the floor. "My granddaughter."

"Oh, of course. I didn't know, I don't think you ever mentioned her name before." He slowly picked up his pants, then came back and sat next to her. "I'm really—"

She stopped dressing, and touched his cheek. "No. Things just got away from us, is all. I should have been more aware of the time." She slipped on her blouse, ran her hands through her hair. "Next time."

"Yes," he said. "Right."

Afterwards, she thought the whole interruption might unwittingly work in her favor. Now, all of the awkwardness was out of the way, further intimacy would be expected. And anyway, delayed gratification always worked with people like him. It upped the ante, didn't it?

Especially when it was due to some noble pursuit, like taking care of a granddaughter.

But instead of things heating up, they suddenly, inexplicably went backwards. His emails became less frequent, and the one or two times they did get together, it was in a public place, for lunch or coffee. Most disturbingly, there was a total lack of physicality, no matter what she wore, or what she said, or how untamed she wore her hair.

Their conversations now had a stilted feel. He seemed less in the moment, less relaxed. He began asking questions that were more reminiscent of a job interview.

Like why she had retired so early.

Now that took her off guard, but she quickly rebounded, sloughed it off with a casual, "Oh, it just got to the point that I could. So I figured why not? Why not spend some time with the family?"

But he wanted to know more, what she had done, where she worked.

She told him she taught English literature at a prep school in Denver. When he asked which one, she offered The Colorado Day School, because one of Stan's acquaintances had grandkids that went there.

"Oh," he said, "I have heard of it. A great school."

She was a little worried about that, offering a specific school because she knew it could be easily verified, but then he quickly moved to other questions.

How long did she think she was going to live with Lee? Would she get a place of her own, maybe a condo? And didn't she miss her old friends, or colleagues from work? Would any of them be coming up for a visit?

She tried to bat each of the questions away as best she could.

Yes, she would probably look for a condo, or better yet, maybe a small house, one with character. Maybe she would do that in the spring.

And yes, she missed her old friends, but then again, family was the most important thing, didn't he think? And her work friends were great, but not like her best friend Cate. They have been friends since college, forty years, can you imagine? Wonderful woman, three grown kids, works in marketing, a good—no *gifted*—writer. Super accomplished. She lives in Akron, would probably take a trip down soon. He could meet her!

Cindy was baffled by his sudden change in attitude. He had been so understanding that day . . . unless . . . oh, of course—yes, this had to be it! Unless she had mistaken understanding for *relieved.*

Oh my God, that was it!

He was scared of completing the intimacy, worried about his performance. That's why he had been so cautious, taken so long with everything. Of course! He had probably never been with a woman other than Saint Lisa.

And, on top of that, maybe she worsened his already tentative state with her abrupt, horribly timed leaving that day. Maybe he felt she used Jana as an excuse to avoid the intimacy with *him*! After all, what woman stops everything in bed to pick up a fifteen-year-old? Fifteen-year-olds can wait a half an hour, can't they?

Yes, his ego was spooked and now he was rethinking everything.

God, cerebral men were complicated, she thought. Jesus. There was a reason she had never been with one before. Well now she'd just have to find a way to make him more trustful, more assured of her feelings.

If she could just arrange it so . . . like if he met a friend or family member, that would reignite a feeling of intimacy. Like that idea about Cate coming down? That might be a perfect! Cate would be a living, breathing personal reference, especially valuable because of the way she had described her—that whole sensitive but dependable, "three kids, gifted writer" routine. After all, everyone knows friends reflect friends! And getting them together would further entangle him in her life, and more importantly, relieve his insecurities.

Yes, that was clearly what she needed to do. That would solve this sudden stalling. Then they could move on to the inevitable.

She had seen his eyes on that pink lace. And if there was anything she knew about men, it was in the end, pink lace always wins.

⅄

Cindy opened the front door of the house. "Jana, come on, we're going to be late, we have to get going! I don't want you to get another tardy slip."

She walked to the car and opened the door, sat down and put the key into the ignition. "Come on, come on!" she said, honking the horn.

Jana came out of the house running, holding her backpack, papers and books spilling out. She stooped down to retrieve them, then finally, breathlessly, entered the car. "What time is it?" she asked, pushing the papers back into her backpack.

"8:03, we have just enough time."

Cindy turned her head, backed out of the driveway, then started down the street. Jana rummaged through her papers and books, then raised her hands up, and sat back. "Oh shit."

"What?"

"Oh, I guess nothing." She zipped the backpack up. "I'll just tell him I'll bring it next time."

"You forgot something for school? We can turn around."

"No, not school, for afterwards. The journal. I have an appointment with Doc."

"Doc?" Cindy glanced towards her. "Your mom didn't say anything about me taking you to a doctor appointment. You sick?"

Jana shook her head. "Not sick or anything, you know . . . he's a shrink type of doctor. Oh yeah, I forgot to tell you," she bent down, tied a lace on her right boot. "You don't have to pick me up today, Mom is going to. I usually go at nights, but he switched it this week."

"Oh, OK. I wasn't sure you were doing that."

"Yeah, it's OK though." Jana turned and looked out the window. "He's cool. You would like him. He's got an old hippie vibe."

Cindy leaned back in the driver seat. "An old hippie vibe?"

"Yeah. Longer hair, you know." She reached for the radio dial.

Cindy tapped her hand. "Don't touch that. This doctor with the old hippie vibe, what's his name?"

"Doc Callahan, but I call him Doc."

Cindy raised her foot off the gas pedal. She looked at Jana out of the corner of her eyes. "Callahan? *Seamus* Callahan?"

"Maybe. Why? You know him? Come on Grandma, we need to get going." She turned back to the window, then nodded her head. "Yeah, maybe it is Seamus. I sort of remember that now. Thought it was odd. What kind of name is that?"

"You write in a journal and give it to this guy?"

"He's a doctor Grandma, not just some guy."

Cindy turned into the school parking lot, pulled the car into the drop off lane. She turned and faced Jana. "What do you write in the journal?"

Jana looked at the car clock, put her hand on the door handle. "I'm just going to make it. Pull up Grandma, the guard is telling you to pull up, I've got to get going."

Cindy pulled the car up, and Jana quickly opened the car door and jumped out, headed to the school's entrance.

The car pool guard frantically motioned Cindy on. Cindy held up her index finger and rolled down her window. "Jana?"

Jana turned around. "What? I'm going to be late!" A young girl ran up to her, said something in her ear. Jana laughed, then called back to Cindy. "I'll tell you tonight. Remember, don't pick me up!" Then she turned away.

A car behind Cindy honked; the guard put her hands on her hips, started walking towards her car. "Is there something about 'Move on' you don't understand?" she asked.

"Fuck you," said Cindy, and rolled up the window, then banged her hand against the steering wheel.

CHAPTER SEVEN

Cate

She checked the balance in her checking account ($440), then slowly went to the computer. The balance reflected her mood, that seasonal state of hopelessness that envelops everyone in Northeastern Ohio by early March, when the sun hasn't been seen since late October.

The winter had been especially brutal, and making it worse, her jobs had slowed to a trickle. So when her old employer Hartford Prep called to offer a well-paying project, she did something she vowed she never would do.

She said yes.

The project was to write the press releases, speeches, and publications surrounding the dedication of a multi-million dollar addition made possible by a prominent family's donation. The donation, made in the name of the late family patriarch, was from his children, who, Cate knew from the very first meeting, had very specific ideas about the approach.

"What we really want," said Family Heir Number One, "is—do you know that Frank Sinatra song, *My Way*? Can we work that in, make it the overall theme? That was his favorite song."

"You mean work in the actual song or just the overall *feel* of it?" Cate asked.

Amber, the school's director of strategic marketing, glanced at Cate, then smiled. "Yes, of course we can Henry! That's a great idea. We can put the song in the video, work the lyrics into the narrative."

Henry sat back. "Oh that would be great! Yes, that would make us very, very happy."

After they left, Amber closed her laptop and turned to Cate. "So work on something for next week," she said, standing up and moving towards the door. "The dedication speech, a press release, a feature for the alumni magazine."

"Sure, but—" Cate started.

"What?" Amber asked, turning around.

Cate stood up. "It's just, Amber—*My Way*? I mean, that's fine for the dedication program at the school, but for the press releases? Editors and reporters are just . . . well they're just sort of naturally surly, sort of sarcastic people. A press release that includes . . . you know, the lyrics of *My Way*, that might not work."

Amber put her hand on the doorknob. "Let's just keep this simple and give them what they want. We have another capital campaign this fall." She lifted an eyebrow. "OK?"

So the following week Cate wrote drafts of a press release, an alumni magazine article, and the dedication publication copy, all within what she hoped would meet the general *My Way* parameters. She emailed the drafts to Amber.

"It's a good start," Amber quickly responded, "but it needs to be ratcheted up."

Cate read her reply, slumped back in her chair, and ran a hand through her hair.

Bourbon might help, she thought, and walked to the kitchen cupboard she reserved for the fun stuff. She opened its door, moved the few items on the shelf. No bourbon, no chocolate, no cookies. Just a bottle of leftover vermouth. She sighed and pulled it out, poured some of the liquid into a glass, then went back to the computer and stared at the screen.

How bad would it be to insert a few words, she thought. She clicked on the curser, and inserted *ground breaking* in front of career, then changed career to *legacy. Ground breaking legacy.*

She sat back and narrowed her eyes.

Exclamation points! That was what she needed, more exclamation points. And what was that favorite term Amber used all the time now? She looked up, then snapped her fingers. *Change agent,* that was it. She returned to the keyboard, put in the words and the excitable punctuation, then leaned back and read.

Close, but not enough, she thought. She was avoiding the inevitable, those lyrics.

She shook her head, leaned forward. Oh, who did she think she was anyway? Was she F. Scott Fitzgerald working on *Gatsby*? If they wanted those stupid lyrics, then that's what they'd get. Simple. Why did she have to make everything so hard?

She googled *lyrics of My Way*, then sat back and read.

Now how could she capture that whole testosterone-driven phrase of spitting obstacles out without using the word spit?

Her phone rang. She looked at the screen. Her mom.

She hesitated. She couldn't stop now, she was in a flow. She'd let the call go to voice mail, then call her back as soon as she got done.

Just this once.

She hit *Ignore,* then turned the phone off and turned her attention back to the computer.

⅄

Four hours later, Cate took a last look at the drafts, then got up and went to the kitchen sink. She got a glass of water, leaned against the counter.

She knew they would love them, the writing was just that bad. But this was a job, not art, she told herself, and she had to focus on pay, not some high-horsed vision of—what? What constituted a good press release? No one even read newspapers anymore.

She put the glass down, went back to the desk and sent the revisions to Amber. Then she sat back.

If they were happy with her work, maybe they would give her the job on the upcoming capital campaign. That would be even better pay. Maybe enough to take a real, bona fide vacation, somewhere warm. Maybe it wouldn't even have to be somewhere predictable like Florida. Maybe she could go somewhere exotic like Tahiti . . . or Fiji?

Well no, probably not, she thought, although who knows, she might luck into a sale. She sat up straighter, turned back to the keyboard and googled *bargain vacations to Tahiti*, when there was a knock on the door.

"Michael? What are you doing here in the middle of the day?" she asked, opening the door, then going back to the computer. "Guess what? I think maybe I might be going on a long weekend tri—"

"Your phone is off."

"Oh, yeah. I was finishing up a job. I had to get it done."

"We've been trying to get a hold of you," he said.

She heard something in the tone of his voice, drew her eyes up to his face.

It's amazing how much you can tell by the tone of a voice, and the look on a face, Cate thought. Tells you everything without speaking one word. Makes you wonder how important words could be if at the biggest moments in life they are totally unneeded.

Michael walked over to her, picked up her hand.

"It's Grandma.

"Tony said he went over to drop off a piece of mail, and no one answered the door, so he went in." He knelt down. "She was in the bedroom. They said it was quick, immediate. Her heart."

Cate nodded.

"She lived a good life Mom. Eighty-seven, still in her home, didn't ever have to leave. She would have hated that. She lived the exact life that she wanted."

"Yes."

⅄

She looked at the phone, picked it up in her hand. That one glaring icon, the voice mail.

All day she had avoided listening. All day.

She wanted to be alone when she listened. She wanted to listen at night. She wanted to be in her apartment. She wanted to be sitting on the couch.

She wanted to hear it, but she was terrified to hear it, so everything had to be right. Because what if her mom had said, "Oh I am not feeling well, can you come over?" What then?

Cate picked up the phone.

Maybe she shouldn't listen. Maybe it was a bad idea, knowing. After all, what good would it do now?

She put the phone down.

But, that voice. She really wanted to hear her voice.

She hesitated, then picked the phone back up, clicked on the message icon, and closed her eyes.

"Cate? Cate? This is your mother. When you get this you need to call me because I am not sure what time you are picking me up tomorrow. You didn't say. And I have stuff I have to do so I need to know the time. So when you get un-busy with whatever important stuff you are doing, call me and let me know. OK? Oh . . . and I love you."

The voice mail prompt came on. "Please enter one for replay, seven for delete, nine for save."

She entered one.

"Cate? Cate? This is your mother. When you get this . . ."

⅄

Kelly came into the office, shutting the door behind her. She glanced at Cate on the couch, noted the perfectly groomed hair and freshly manicured fingernails. "You seem better today," she said, picking up a yellow pad and pen, pushing her long curly hair away from her face as she settled into an armchair. "A little perkier."

Cate smiled. "I do? Well maybe. Yes. The sun is shining a little."

"Good." Kelly put on her glasses, and turned to the legal pad. "Did you fill that Ambien prescription I gave you last week? Is that helping?"

"Oh that. Yes. That is helping a lot. I've been taking it for a few days now, yes. Finally I can get some sleep."

"Good, but remember it's temporary, one month, six weeks at the most. Just to get you through for a while."

"Right."

"So last time . . ." Kelly said, flipping through the pages, "we were talking about your mom's passing, your feeling of disconnection, the lethargy and forgetfulness. Has that gotten better?"

"Well yes," Cate said. "I have been going out, trying to keep busy. I'm still a little disconnected, like caught in my own little world, but I think it's getting better."

"So you're going out? Good. With friends or . . . let's see, you mentioned you had reconnected with an old boyfriend at your mom's funeral?"

"Yes . . ." Cate said, shifting in her seat. "Daniel."

Kelly tapped her pen on the pad. "Wait. Is this 'Daniel' *Danny*? The one you broke up with a couple of years ago?"

"Um, gee, yeah, I guess so. Maybe I did mention him to you before. But that was a long time ago. I mean, I hadn't seen him until he came to the funeral. It's been years, like you said."

"Uh huh." Kelly looked at her pad. "And you're seeing him a lot?"

"Well not a lot, three, four times is all. Maybe five. I mean, it's not terrible is it? It perks me up, gives me something to do. You yourself said I looked better."

"I said you looked perkier," Kelly said. "But as I remember, and I do remember, last time around with, um, Danny or Daniel, he had that addiction problem."

Cate held up her hand. "Oh that. Is that what you're thinking? Oh no he's sober, not using now. And anyway, he was never using much, just a little, here and there. Maybe a little of a party guy is all. But he always was able to hold a good job, it was never anything really serious."

"Uh huh. But the way you described him then . . . even when he was sober, he had that addict personality. Needy. Controlling," Kelly said. "And you know all that so I'm wondering . . . why go there again? Could it be with your mom's passing, you need someone to take care of? Or . . ." she tilted her head, "he's not offering you an opportunity to get a pick-me-up here and there is he? Because that would be dangerous Cate, especially with the Ambien. You can't even mix Ambien with liquor, you have to be very careful."

Cate leaned back into the couch. "Oh my God, no. No, of course, I know that. He just showed up at my mom's funeral, and that was nice and I guess I'm lonely. I am lonely and he is there. End of story.

Anyway, why does he have to be the most appropriate person in the world? I'm not going to marry him for God's sake."

"Right. But what I am wondering about is your tendency to gravitate to men like him, ones you know have built-in flaws. We both already know how Daniel is going to play out, it's happened before. And before that there was Craig, who really didn't want a woman like you, and before that—"

"Now that one's not fair," Cate protested. "I didn't even know he was married."

"But you found out, and then did nothing for months. The point I am making is—why these men? You're a smart woman Cate. Why are you choosing men who you know from the beginning, the relationship is doomed?"

Cate put her elbow on the sofa's arm rest, rested her face in the palm of her hand. "Well first of all, there aren't hordes of men to choose from, so there's that. But besides . . . my mom just died. Is it so incomprehensible that I would want to be with someone? Anyone? It's not some major mystery, is it?"

"Maybe, but this started long before your mother died." Kelly leaned to the side, tapped her pen against the pad. "Tell me . . . what was Tommy like? Because you have talked about many men and you have never offered one thing about Tommy. You were married to him for what? Fourteen years?"

"Tommy?" Cate put her arm down, shifted in her seat. "Why talk about Tommy? The divorce is twenty years over, the kids are raised, he's been remarried for decades. It's over and done. History."

"Then just humor me," Kelly said.

"Well, what do you want to know?"

"What was he like?"

Cate sat back, eyes defiant. "Tommy?" She held up her index finger. "Ok, this will prove you wrong.

"Tommy was . . . well he *was* different than me, I will give you that. Lighter, a fun guy. Overall, just a harmless joker. But dependable, straight arrow. I mean, not anyone who would strike you, or me anyway, as a liar, or player. The type of guy you'd feel safe with."

"So when you found out . . ."

Cate leaned back in the couch, kept her gaze. "So when I found out—what do you think? Three kids, no job, and you find out someone you banked your whole life on was not the way that you thought? Upside-down not the way that you thought?"

"Good." Kelly leaned forward. "Good. So maybe it's easier to find someone whose flaws are up front."

Cate looked at her, shook her head. "I'm sorry, this is just too much psychobabble for me."

"Because you don't want to get your hopes up," Kelly continued. "If you know up front that you can't, it takes it right off the table. You're terrified of—"

Cate looked at her, laughed. "Oh come on! All of this because I've seen Daniel a few times? Daniel? I can leave him in two seconds!"

"Exactly. That is exactly my point," Kelly said. "And it's not anything about Daniel, or Craig, or even Tommy."

"Oh, really? Then tell me, what is it about?" Cate asked.

"You, Cate. It's about you."

⅄

WTF, Cate thought as she got in the car.

WTF! It was almost like an inquisition, not a therapy session.

Oh, don't see Daniel! Oh you look perkier—and by the fucking way, what does that mean? *Perky*? Was that a slam? She even hated the word, only used it when she was trying to be sarcastic. She had never felt perky one day in her whole God damned life.

And all that stuff about Tommy. Like she needed to go over that again? As if every day for the past twenty years wasn't enough, she had to now bury her mother and what? Sit in a shrink's office and talk about Tommy?

She turned the key, started the car, and pulled out of the parking lot.

Jesus. Why did she have to tell her about Daniel? She should have figured Kelly would have remembered. If she wanted to talk about him, how hard would it have been to come up with a completely different name? There were a million other names she could have used. Andrew, Steve, Lebron . . .

Her cell phone rang. She reached into her purse for the phone, glanced at the number.

Danny.

Well he would have to wait. She dropped it back into the purse, and right as she did, she heard a siren.

Great, she thought, looking in the rear view mirror. First Kelly, now a cop.

She pulled off to the side of the road, rolled down her window, and waited as the policeman approached.

"Registration and license?" he asked.

"Sure." She reached in her purse for her wallet, picked out her license and handed it to him.

"Registration?"

"Registration?" She opened the glove compartment, sifted through some of the items, then closed it, sat back. "I'm not sure where it is. I've been confused lately. Disorganized. Not myself. I'm usually very organized. My mom . . . my mom just passed."

He looked at the license, then at her. "You were going 50 in a 35."

"Oh geez, I'm sorry. I didn't realize that."

"Well," he said, "I need to check this out, I'll be right back." He went to the police car, and Cate reached over to return the wallet to her purse. She stuffed it inside, and as she did, it hit against something. She lifted the purse, looked into it.

Oh sweet Lord Jesus, she thought. Why had she left that in her purse? Why?

There, inside her purse was that plastic bag of cocaine Danny had left after one of her especially down nights. On the side was a sticky note where he had written, *just in case you need it, hate to see you so unhappy*.

She looked in the rearview mirror. The policeman was walking back towards her car. She zipped the purse up, put it on the car floor, then turned to the open window. "I am really sorry," she said.

He handed her the license. "I'll let it go this time," he said, "but you need to be more cautious."

"I know. I will. I really appreciate this."

"OK. Oh, and I am sorry about your mom, her passing."

"Oh yes, thank you. Yes."

⅄

Two weeks after her session with Kelly and the near-miss with the cop, Cate had stopped picking up Danny's calls. He had eventually stopped calling, and now the only remnant of the relationship was the plastic bag souvenir.

When he had originally placed it in her purse at the end of an extremely down night, she knew they had taken the first step to done.

It was proof they had reached the exact same place they were at years ago, even though for a while she had let herself grasp onto the small hope that this time things might be different. Danny had been careful to portray a sobriety, but the bag was proof that nothing had changed.

That had all happened before her meeting with Kelly, but at that point she wasn't quite ready for the final let-go. Their relationship was still precariously balanced by the simple fact that he was always there, with his daily *how are you today?* expressions of care. And that was a powerful thing. It helped preserve the balance, until things reached the final tipping point when something else was placed on the scale.

Sex.

At the beginning, their sex was not earth-moving, but nice, a feeling of warmth and connection. But then it quickly changed. The feeling of connection was lost, replaced with a level of disappointment reserved for things that start with high expectations.

Their interludes increasingly seemed all about him. His quickness, his desire, his sweaty huffing and puffing and then, his blissful after-euphoria questions . . . *Was it good? Was it the best?* which led to her increasing inability to find anything else to say other than *please can we never do that again.*

Oh, she was well aware she held some of the blame. After all, she could have stopped him, been more truthful, said, *um gee, can you slow things down a little,* or *can you do this?* or maybe even, *can we put on some music?*

They tell you to do that in magazines. Communicate, own your sexuality.

Yes, she understood all that, and she also knew it was not the first time she had felt this way. She felt it with Craig, and Tommy, so yes, she was aware it was something about her, but still—were they all deaf and blind? Was it too much to ask that just one of them would know, or sense, or at least seem concerned, about how things were going before the post-coital interview?

So it was ultimately the sex, and the whole awkward quagmire it presented, that finally tipped the scale, took Danny off the table, and now she had a general sense of nothingness, in her relationships and her work, and an ever-increasing lack of purpose and direction.

Her days were spent in a lethargic routine of watching television, and making and cancelling appointments. Today she had cancelled a second appointment with Kelly and an upcoming dinner with a friend. She thought about all of the things she should do, clean the house, call a client, organize her purse—but HGTV always won out. She put it on as soon as she got out of bed.

It was now 3:00 p.m. Cate watched as the onscreen couple told their realtor they wanted an "open concept" home, with granite countertops and stainless steel appliances. Like she's never heard that before, Cate thought, and reached for the *Discover Asheville* magazine on the floor. She began flipping through its pages, stopping at a picture of a mountain surrounded by fog.

Now that would be something to see, she thought. She turned the page, then went back.

Wait. Hadn't she just told Cindy she would come down to visit? When she took her off guard with that condolence call and invitation, saying she wouldn't take *no* for an answer. Why couldn't she make that a first stop on a road trip to Asheville?

A road trip. She had never taken a road trip before.

Her thoughts were interrupted by the ringing of her phone. She looked down. Rob, Sara's boyfriend.

"Hey Rob," she said, pulling the phone to one ear.

"Me? Today? Nothing. I mean, working a little, but nothing important. Why?

"Oh sure. Of course. I'll be here, not going anywhere. Stop by. There's nothing wrong is there? Oh, OK. Yes. Sure. An hour."

She put the phone down, put the magazine on the coffee table and turned off the TV. She picked up some items that littered the living room floor, a blanket, some dishes. Then she quickly ran back to the bathroom to take a shower.

⅄

"Hey," she said, opening the door. "To what do I owe this surprise?"

He kissed her on the cheek; she smelled the scent of his cologne. "I made you a CD. Your favorite Stevie Nicks stuff," he said.

"You did? How nice! Did you include *Stand Back?"*

"Of course."

"See, you've been around me too long." Cate turned and went into the kitchen, placed the CD on the counter. "Well I can't wait to listen to it." She opened a cupboard door. "You want something to drink? Some coffee?"

"No. No not really." He stood off to the side, shifted nervously. "It wasn't just that. Um, can we go into thc living room?"

Cate turned, noticed his unease. "Sure. Oh sure," she said, closing the cabinet door, wiping her hands on her jeans. She headed into the living room. He followed and took a seat on the couch.

Cate was about to sit down when she noticed an errant dish on the floor. "Oh I'm sorry, the place is a mess. I've just been so busy with work and stuff, haven't had time to clean." She picked up the dish and carried it into the kitchen, then came back and sat down.

"Your house is always clean enough," he said.

"You think?" she asked. "Well that's not true but it's nice—" She stopped, noticed his hands folding and closing, that unusually tentative look in his eyes. "What is it Rob?" she asked.

"Um," he leaned forward. "You know I love Sara very much."

"Yes, I do. I do know that."

"I just . . . I know this is sort of unusually old school, my coming to you, but you've been—I know how close you and Sara are. I just wanted you to be the first to know. I'm going to ask Sara to marry me."

Cate's eyes widened. She tilted her head. "Marry. Marry? I guess . . . well you certainly don't have to get married for *me*! You're as committed as any married couple I know. And a lot of people don't even get married today. It's not like it used to be when I—"

"No, no no, it's not for you or anyone else," he said, outstretching his hands. "It's just—it's come up in discussions between Sara and me, and both of us I think—no, I *know*—we both want a formal commitment. It means something to us."

She started to say "But," then noticed how his shoulders had deflated. Instead, she got up, moved towards him.

"Oh, my God, what's wrong with me?" she asked, bending down, pulling him close. "Of course you want a commitment. Of course. I just wanted to be sure you didn't think you had to do it for me!" She let go, sat next to him. "I couldn't ask for anyone better for Sara, Rob, really. Not that anything is up to me, this is all for you two to decide. But I have always thought she was very lucky to have you. And you to have her. Yes, I've always thought that."

He pushed his hair away from his face, and turned to her with a look that was somewhere between serious and grave. "I just want you to know, you don't ever have to worry . . . I will never do anything to hurt her."

Cate turned away, jumped up from the couch. "Oh, of course I know that! Of course! We should have a drink to celebrate. What do you want? Of course I know I can trust you."

⅄

She watched as his car pulled out of the driveway, then went to the couch to lie down. Now what in the world is wrong with me, she thought, stretching out.

Sara is marrying a wonderful guy, a guy I have known for six, seven years, who has never shown any reason, not one at all, to keep me from the happiness I felt for Michael and Jack when they told me they were getting married.

But there was something he said—oh yes, the "I will never hurt" part.

Now how in the world could he know that? And hadn't Tommy told her the exact same thing? That and a whole lot of other stuff like "love, protect and always be there," all the things that turned out to be bullshit when she was left holding the family bag like the dumbest, least prepared person on earth.

She stared at the ceiling.

Stop, she told herself.

Sara isn't you, and Rob isn't Tommy. They know each other really well, haven't confined things to dates like back in the day. And even if life delivers the same worst case scenario to Sara, she can deal with it. Didn't she raise her for that? Sara was so much smarter, stronger, more sure of herself than she had ever been. Her world was carefully underpinned, it would not disintegrate.

She shook her head, and pushed herself up, returned to the Asheville magazine.

Yes, people get married every day, and half of them get their ever-afters. She flipped through the magazine's pages, then stopped at a picture.

Like some of these homes on that mountain. Half of those homes were happy. Why couldn't Sara be in that half, she asked herself, as she slowly turned the page.

Somebody has to! It might as well be Sara.

CHAPTER EIGHT

SEAMUS

He handed her the journal, then sat down on the chair next to the couch.

"So your mom says things are going well in school and ballet? She thinks we're rounding the bend here." He flipped through his notes, then put them down on his lap. "So how do you think things are going at home?"

She shrugged her shoulders. "I mean . . . it's nothing I am not used to.

"Grandma wants to get an apartment or something. I wish Mom was the one getting an apartment. At least Grandma sometimes listens to me. My mom . . . no matter what I do there's just something about me, about the way that I am, that disappoints her, pisses her off."

"Oh, I am not sure that is right Jana," he said shaking his head. "I think, no I know, your mom loves you very much, is proud of you, it's just—"

"Well you don't live in my home, so you don't really know, do you?"

"No, I don't *really* know. All I'm suggesting is that maybe you are misinterpreting things. Maybe you are oversensitive to her criticism, don't really understand her concerns." He leaned towards her. "You have made some not so great choices Jana. It's natural for a parent to react to that, because sometimes a world can blow apart with one bad decision. And it drives parents crazy knowing how fragile life can be. So maybe your mom's criticism is just an expression of that. And that comes from a place of deep, deep love."

Jana looked away, laughed. "OK. I don't even know why I am talking about this with you. Have you read my journal? Because if you really read my journal you would understand.

"I don't live in a normal family! I went to a party that got busted just like twenty other kids in this town, but I was the only one who had to go to a shrink. And you know why? Because every other parent except for my mom could see it for what it was . . . just a stupid teenage party. My mom? To her it was proof that I am incapable of making anything but a bad choice, and I am heading down the road of her enemy—*her* mother. And that's the whole thing. I'm paying for everything she thinks my grandma did back in the day. And I don't tell people that because it sounds crazy, but I gave you the journal, you should know. For all of the good that it did me.

"So it doesn't matter what I do, what grades I get, how good I am in ballet, or any of that—it is what it is and I'm really sort of over it. But please, save the *deep deep love* stuff. Please."

He looked at her, she looked away. The clock ticked. She moved on the couch, he looked at his pad of paper.

"I think you are wrong Jana," he finally ventured, bringing his eyes back to hers. "You know, it's not unusual for mothers and daughters to have testy periods during the daughter's teenage years. Some mothers do hold on too tight. That could be the case here, and yes, maybe in your case it is made worse by the complications, the history behind your mother's relationship with your grandmother, but I'm going to be totally honest . . . I've talked to your mother and I've never picked up even a hint of her linking you and your grandmother in a negative way. All I have heard is her concern. Maybe too much concern, but concern. And really, she has a very deep sense of pride in being your mother. She just told me—" he looked at his paper, "here . . . she said she is very proud of how you are doing in your schoolwork and especially at ballet."

Jana laughed, shook her head.

"What?" Seamus asked.

"Nothing."

"What?"

"For a moment I thought you might say she was proud of me just 'cause," she said.

Seamus put the pad of paper on the side table. "Jana . . . are you sure you are ready to be done with this? Maybe we still have some things to go over. Are you sleeping and eating OK?"

"Sure, why?"

"I'm just asking, it's just . . . I know I'm not good at this stuff, but it looks like you might have lost a few pounds."

"Oh Jesus, I'm done," she said, standing up.

"Wait—"

"No. I cannot win! I cannot." She picked up her backpack. "I gain or lose two pounds, everyone's on my shit. Jesus. Why am I the only one in this country where two pounds mean anything? You practice ballet for two, three hours a day, see what happens to you."

She started to walk to the door, then turned around and went back, picked up the journal on the couch. "So it's done and we're done and I'm fine, with five full minutes to spare." She slid the journal into her backpack, then tossed her hair. Later," she said, and walked out.

⅄

After she left, he went back to his desk, shook his head.

Wow. Something was off. He tapped his pen on his desk, sat back.

But what did he actually have? In reality, he had many other teenage patients in much worse shape than Jana. Yes, she had lost some weight, but it wasn't a horrible amount, just enough to notice. And that anger? The stuff in her journal? It could all just be textbook teenage angst and or rebellion. And anyway, it was light years better than someone who wouldn't share their emotions at all, or left them to dangerously simmer, or worse yet, disengaged entirely.

Her grades were good, her social life was good, she was a high achiever at ballet, and she carried everything out without any need for meds. Her mother thought things were fine, and she certainly wasn't crying over the ending of their sessions, so in the end, what was it?

She had mother issues. What teenage girl doesn't? And what teenager thinks her family is normal? None of that was anything unusual.

Jana was just a little more feisty or vocal than the average young woman, sometimes bordering on the unpleasant. But that wasn't a mental disease. Matter of fact, a case could be made it was just a healthy breaking away from an overprotective mother. Lee seemed fine to him, but maybe she was overly critical and protective. She did, like Jana said, make her go into counseling over something that was pretty darn common, an underage drinking party. Not many mothers did that.

He turned on his computer, clicked on his email account. Maybe he was overreacting to the whole situation because—

Oh Lord, she had written again.

He sat back in his desk chair. She wanted to get together for dinner or something. Wanted to introduce him to a friend who was coming down for a visit.

Now what had he gotten himself into? Things with Cindy had started out so hopeful. She was, after all, a beautiful woman, and interesting, well read. They had a lot of fun, shared similar interests. At the beginning, it had given him a lot of hopeful energy, made him think things were possible, like he could actually be a part of a couple again. He hadn't felt that way since Lisa.

But then, things started to turn. First there was that afternoon in his bedroom when he realized Jana was Cindy's granddaughter. Up to the moment Cindy said "Jana," he had never pieced that together. Their surnames were different, and Cindy rarely, if ever, talked about her family, and if she did, outside of that day, she had never referred to family members with proper names, it was always daughter this or granddaughter that.

And Jana's journal? The only references were Crazy Grandma C, or Gma C, or Crazy C. How in the world could he have known?

It wasn't that it was such a blatant conflict of interest, but it did carry a tinge of discomfort, a sense of impropriety that gave him the initial pause. And it threw in an additional complexity, an inability to figure out if his feelings, or change of feelings, were being influenced by what he had read in the journal.

Though what was the worst Jana had written? That Cindy partied a lot in her youth (who didn't?), possibly was not the best mother (mother-daughter relationships were the most notoriously complicated under the best of conditions). And what else?

Oh yes. For someone in and out of the picture, Cindy held a hell of a lot of influence.

Now that did give him pause. Even factoring in it was coming from a teenage perspective. It confirmed a notion that he had felt weeks before, that had held him back, made him cautious—until of course that day in the bedroom, when he told himself what the hell? She's a beautiful woman, get on with it.

But after that day's interruption, when he put things together, he felt the journal confirmed something he previously thought had no tangible point of origin outside of his own wary nature.

It confirmed his idea that somehow, for some unknown reason, Cindy was sitting on her personality. That she was in fact, an alpha woman, one who could say more with the lift of an eyebrow than other women could say in twenty perfectly formed sentences.

Now there wasn't anything intrinsically wrong with that, Lisa was an alpha woman, after all. But there was the rub. He didn't want Lisa 2.

Yes, he had loved Lisa very much. Very, very much. Stayed loyal to the very end. But her strength had defined everything in his life. Everything.

She didn't want children, so they hadn't. She didn't want to leave Yellow Springs, so he turned down that San Francisco offer. Their world reflected her needs and wants more than it did his, and that was the truth.

He leaned back in his chair.

He was lonely, yes, and Cindy was beautiful, oh yes . . . and all of that bedroom stuff was really, really compelling—the lace, her sensuality. Yes, yes, yes.

But he had decided to slightly back off, keep it a little more above board, almost professional. Get to know her better. Not throw the whole thing away, but take a step back, and observe.

And when he did, his uneasiness increased. She seemed so perfect, and at the same time, so perfectly not for him.

He leaned forward in his chair, ran his hands through his hair, then read the email again.

Really, all she was asking was for him to join her and a friend for dinner. That was pretty benign. Maybe she was just being friendly. Maybe she was lonely. Who knows.

He had to stop ruminating, reading so much into things! Jesus. He was becoming a doddering old man. He would keep it light, stop being presumptuous. After all, asking him to dinner to meet a friend, wasn't "Marry me or I'll kill myself."

Yes, he should just relax, and go. Jana wasn't his patient anymore, and really, what the hell else was he doing?

He leaned forward, put his hands on the keyboard.

Hi Cindy!

That sounds good, let me know when she is in town. Have a great day!

And then he hit send.

⅄

Seamus was waiting in line at Marcella's to pick up his dinner take-out, when he was nudged from behind. "Oliver!" he said, turning around. "How are you? I haven't seen you in a while."

"Hey Doc, no complaints really." Oliver nervously shifted his feet, moved his hands to his pockets. "You're like me I guess, dinner takeout. The plight of living alone."

"True in my case, but—"

"Yeah well mine too. Heather and I split about a month ago."

"Oh, I'm sorry to hear that," Seamus said. "Hey, you want to have them here?"

"What? The dinners?"

"Sure, why not? It's better than eating alone in front of a television, no?"

"Well I would," Oliver said, taking a hand out of his pocket, running it through his disheveled hair, "but I need to be somewhere in an hour."

"An hour? We'll probably be done in fifteen minutes! Go on, get a table. I'll just ask them to plate them up," Seamus said.

Oliver nodded, then slowly walked to a booth. He took a seat, and picked up the salt shaker, moved it around in his hands.

"They're going to bring them over," Seamus said, joining him. "So . . . other than Heather, how is everything else going?"

"Well, OK, I guess," said Oliver, nervously tapping the shaker against the red tablecloth.

"Good," said Seamus, watching Oliver's hands. "I haven't seen you in awhile. Seems like a long time anyway . . ."

"Yeah," Oliver said. "I think I missed a couple of appointments maybe. Stuff kept coming up. But, I started that idea . . . you know, the painting for me?"

"You did?" Seamus asked. "Good. So how's that going?"

"Well," said Oliver, "to be honest not so great. I'm struggling with it a little. I do a painting, go to bed thinking it's great. Get up, look at it, and think, what a fucking piece of shit. How in the world could I have mistaken that for great? Throw it on an ever-growing heap of canvases on the studio floor. Then the next morning, I start it all over again, like an endless *Groundhog Day*. Drove Heather crazy."

The waitress put the bread and butter on the table. Oliver's bloodshot eyes moved to the loaf. He reached forward, tore off a slice. "Oh good, it's warm," he said, putting some butter on it, watching as it began to melt. "Sort of driving me crazy too, to tell you the truth. The painting I mean. Yeah, sunny streets and happy dogs are much easier."

"Oh, well maybe you just need to give it some time. Maybe it's harder now because you're alone," said Seamus. "There's bound to be an adjustment period, you were with Heather for a long time."

"Yeah Doc, but really, there was always something with her! Always. I think it just boiled down to she wanted all the things I was done with thirty years ago. Marriage, kids, a house."

The waitress placed their food on the table, Seamus picked up his fork. "Yes, but still difficult."

"I guess, but lets get real," Oliver said. "Am I going to go looking for lawn mowers and baby monitors now? Shit. You can only do that stuff when you have no idea how it all turns out." He ate in silence for a moment, then continued, "You know, it's ironic when you think of it."

"What?" Seamus asked.

Oliver raised his hand to the waitress, calling her over. "Can you get me a glass of red wine?" he asked. "A hearty one. A chianti or something. You want one Doc?"

"No, I'm good."

"What was I saying?" Oliver lifted his eyes. "Oh yeah, see this is the thing. You're with a younger woman, and it's like you're younger too. Only better now because there's no next house to buy, or job promotion to get, or kid crying in the middle of the night. But just when you're settling in . . . it's like the nightmare starts all over again. And you don't feel younger, you feel older." He took a bite of his lasagna. "It's just like those people on TV who win the lottery and then wish they were poor. Exactly like that."

"I'll remember that," said Seamus.

"You dating anyone Doc?"

"Me? Um no. Well maybe. I'm seeing someone here and there. It's not serious though."

"She younger?"

"No. I mean, a little younger than me, late fifties."

"Good," Oliver said finishing the glass of chianti, motioning to the waitress for a second. "Only rock stars like Jagger and Clapton can do that shit. They have people to tend to the details, so basically they just get the upside."

"Yeah."

The waitress came over with Oliver's fresh glass of wine. "You guys done with your dinners?"

"Yes," said Seamus.

"Want any dessert?"

Oliver shook his head.

"I guess we're done then, I'll just take the check," Seamus said to the waitress, then turned to Oliver. "This one's on me. You saved me from eating alone." He reached into his pocket for his wallet. "You know Oliver," he started, "maybe you should lighten up on the art for awhile. I don't mean stop doing it, but just sort of lighten the expectations. Make it fun. It doesn't have to be perfect."

"Fun?" asked Oliver.

"Yeah."

Oliver wiped his mouth, put his napkin on the table. "Hm, fun." He sat back, then suddenly, his red-streaked eyes brightened. "Oh my God, how did I never think of this before?"

"What?" asked Seamus.

"Art!" he said, raising his hands. "Art is exactly like being with a younger woman. First, there's that whole 'wonderful until it turns into a nightmare' scenario, and then . . ." He put his hands down, leaned across the table. "You can't really get into it with an older spirit," he said triumphantly, as if he had just explained the Mystery of Life. "Yes, that's it exactly. You need to have either the hope or the obliviousness of youth. One or the other."

⅄

Seamus paid the bill, and they walked outside.

"Wow, it's almost feeling like the beginning of spring," Oliver said. "I thought this winter would never end. Every year it seems to get worse. Can't figure out if it's the winters or me."

"Hey, Oliver . . . I can drop you off at your apartment, I'm going right by," Seamus said.

"No, my truck is right here."

"It's no problem."

Oliver turned to him. "Hey, I'm fine. Two glasses of chianti is all."

"Ok . . . then I'll just see you at your next appointment? I think it's next week?"

"Sure thing," Oliver said, opening the truck door. "Oh and thanks for the dinner Doc. Next one is on me."

Seamus waved and started to turn away, but then quickly turned back, and watched until the truck was lost in the night.

CHAPTER NINE

CINDY

She stared at the ceiling, it was early Sunday morning. She had heard Luke leave to go to the gym; then Layla's bedroom door opened, followed by her footsteps to the kitchen.

It was probably around 7:00 a.m. Jana would sleep for at least another three hours.

Time to get on with it, she thought. Today.

She got up and smoothed the covers of the bed, then went to the chair by the window, sat down.

OK, let's start with the obvious, she thought. Everything in her original plan had turned to shit. Everything—starting with that journal. God! Just her luck that her granddaughter was spilling her guts to the one person in town who could save her from this mess. And just when everything had started to jell! Then Layla goes bat shit crazy over that party, demanding Jana needs counseling, and Jana starts writing who knows what in that journal, and then what happens? A screeching halt.

Well not exactly a screeching halt, there was still some correspondence and that upcoming dinner, but it had definitely stalled, and was nowhere near a *hey, let's live together* declaration.

She had noticed a shift in his attention before the parking lot conversation that clarified everything. And by that time, what could she do? Who knew what Jana could have written? Yes, there was a possibility she could have kept things on her mother, but that possibility was remote, nothing she could bank her future on.

And besides all that, she knew Seamus well enough to know he was the type of person spooked by any hint of impropriety. He wasn't a guy who could play loose with life's rules, so if he found out he was dating a relative of one of his patients, that would be an issue, maybe an insurmountable one, and he would do exactly what he had done—not necessarily break it off, but keep it at friendly, asexual. Maybe forever.

She tried her best to salvage something from the whole situation.

The night after she found out Seamus was Jana's psychologist, she went to Jana's room. She sat next to her on the bed, asked her how things were going at school, etc. All the needed bullshit she had to get out of the way. Then she got up, really nonchalant, and went to her makeup mirror, turned on its lights, and sat down. She moved the mirror so she could see Jana's reflection. "So how do you like this doctor . . . um what's his name?" she asked.

"Doc Callahan? Seamus Callahan."

"Yeah, Seamus." Cindy opened a jar of lip gloss. "Now this is an awesome color," she said, putting a dab on her lips. "I do think I know him."

"You do?"

"I think. Maybe I met him at the Club. Does he have curly hair, brown with a touch of gray?"

"Yeah."

"Yeah. I think I did meet him." Cindy turned around. "You like this on me?"

"Maybe a little too light. Did you like him? I thought he would be the type of person you would like," Jana said. "An old hippie type."

"Um. He talked a little too much I thought. I mean for my taste."

"Talked too much? He's not like . . . maybe you have the wrong person."

"Maybe." Cindy opened the top desk drawer. "Ooooo. You have eye makeup. Your mom wouldn't like that." She took a pot of eye shadow out of the drawer, turned it over. "*Mighty Mushroom.* Catchy." She put some on one eyelid. "The thing of it is Jana. First off, you don't have to go to a doctor. You're not sick, your mom overreacted to what? A party? That's ridiculous. If I had to go to a doctor every time I went to a party and did something dumb, right now I'd be institutionalized and how stupid would that be?"

"It's not just—"

"But besides all that nonsense, Jana, bottom line is this is a small town. That's what I tried to warn you about before. Small towns like this, people have nothing better to do than talk. Especially women. And someone as young and pretty and talented as you . . . you're fair game. So you don't want all your shit out there . . ."

Jana twisted in her bed. "He's a doctor Gma."

"Yeah . . . but he's human, and what I am saying is this is still a small town, and who knows how he interprets the things that you write? Maybe you write something when you're really mad and then that mood passes for you, but for him, those words are there forever, cold on the page. And then maybe he goes to the Club and something is repeated, not maliciously, just to add to a boring conversation—God knows those are the only types that happen in this town—and then that person exaggerates it and gets repeated to someone else, and so on and so on."

"He doesn't seem like that," Jana said.

"No, he doesn't, but I guess I always work with worst case scenarios," Cindy said. "Like that guy you like, what is his name?"

"Christopher?"

"Yeah, Christopher. His parents are big deals at the Club no? And they seem a little um image conscious, uptight?" Cindy turned around. "Am I wrong about that?"

"Well . . . no."

Cindy returned to the mirror. "So who knows with people like that what will set them off? I mean, just getting wind of your seeing a psychologist might be enough." She finished putting the eye shadow on the second eye, leaned back, then turned around. "You like this?"

"No."

"Maybe it's too dark," Cindy said, getting a Kleenex, wiping the shadow off. "Just something to think about. And, now that I am thinking about it, you know what would be the easiest thing to do with this whole situation?" She stood up, walked to the bed. "You know your mother. Just show her a few good test scores, brag about ballet, point out each and every thing you may have done that might impress her, and *voila*! She'll let you off the hook. No problems with Christopher. No mandatory doctor visits. Back to business as usual."

"Maybe," Jana offered.

"Well," Cindy said, "that's what I would do anyway." Then she leaned over, and kissed her on the forehead.

A couple of weeks later, Cindy noticed the private Layla-Jana trips had stopped, so she knew her suggestions had worked. But that certainly didn't seem to have any effect on Seamus's lessening interest. His emails and calls came to an almost complete stop. Outside of his two sentence reply to the invitation for Cate's dinner, there was nothing. She considered addressing the whole thing head-on, but what could she say?

Hey Seamus, I think my granddaughter Jana was a patient of yours! Small world. Hey listen. She may (I am not sure of it, but may) have told you some incorrect information about me due to the fact she's troubled and everything (which is why she was seeing you in the first place! LOL)

No, of course, she couldn't do that.

She also knew his acceptance of the invitation probably meant nothing outside of the fact that he would find it impossible to turn down. Wasn't that why she extended it in the first place? It was guaranteed acceptance, no-fail genius. A turn down would make him look like a prick, something men like him went to great lengths to avoid.

And the dinner idea had seemed almost celestially ordained, what with her randomly calling Trey one night when she was bored, and finding out Cate's mother had died! How perfect was that? It gave her the whole set up for the call and invitation.

Cindy looked out the bedroom window, heard the dripping of the coffee in the kitchen. But now there were too many things in the mix to bank on Seamus as savior. He wasn't a Randy or Stan who threw caution to the wind. One sign of trouble, this guy rethinks everything. So she had to adjust, revise, like generals do in war. And she had to do it now, because she could no longer continue with this setup, being confined to a bedroom, Layla taking the place of her mother with all of her serious, "take this here, pick up there, we're having tofu for dinner" commands.

It was making her crazy, kept her pacing at night, longing for anything that would calm, or soothe, or salve her increasing itchiness.

So over the past weeks, she had started setting the stage for Exit Plan Two. She threw out some trial balloons to soften things up.

"Oh, someone I know is renting one of those older houses in Yellow Springs, and I couldn't believe how cheap it was," she offered in a random conversation with Layla.

And then she got more pointed. "I met this grandmother at the Club, and her kids just set her up in an apartment, and it is working so much better than their living together!"

With Jana, she was more overt.

"What would you think if I moved to an apartment or one of those small houses closer to town? I'd make sure it wasn't far, just something so I could have some private space. And then you could come and visit, maybe even walk over when you wanted to get away from your mom. Wouldn't that be great? I could make you dinners . . . better yet, I could take you to McDonald's and we'd bring it home, eat it in the living room while we watch *Housewives*."

All that was now done, it was time to get on with the rest.

She pushed herself up off the chair, and opened the bedroom door, walked into the kitchen.

Layla was at the table eating her oatmeal as she read *The New York Times*.

Cindy sat down. "Good morning."

"Oh good, you're up early," Layla said looking up. "I need to talk to you about next week's schedule. I have to work late on Wednesday."

"Yes, of course, but first . . . I need to talk to you."

Layla closed the paper, neatly folded it in fourths.

"I just—" Cindy started. "I need to talk to you about something."

"You said that already."

"Yes." Cindy moved uncomfortably in the chair, then stopped. "Oh God, Lee, why is it so hard to talk to you? I always feel like I am approaching a head nun asking permission to do this or that." She shook her head. "OK, I'm just going to say it."

She squared her shoulders, looked into Layla's eyes. "I want an apartment, a place of my own. I promise I will still do everything, everything, just the way I am doing now, just as we agreed. But I can't take this setup anymore, this sort of upside down arrangement, where I am living like a sixteen-year-old under my own daughter's roof. It's like I'm a servant, Lee, that's what it's like, with all the endless lists and instructions. It's demeaning."

Layla stared at her for a moment, then replied, "I should have figured this wouldn't last." She picked up her mug and went to the coffeemaker.

"No no no Lee, listen. Please listen. I said I will do everything the same, and I will. I just need some private space. Is that so hard to understand? And it's for you too. You have your own family. You need privacy too."

Layla leaned against the kitchen counter. "I make lists for you because I know if I don't, if it isn't spelled out, nothing will happen as it should."

Cindy held up her hands. "Oh the lists are not the main point, and I understand how you think you have to spell stuff out, but do you have to do it with all caps and stars and underlines and exclamation points? I *am* your mother."

Layla took another sip of coffee, locked her eyes with Cindy's. "The lists, the notes, that is what good mothers do. They make sure things are done correctly."

Cindy's eyes widened. "That's your idea of what a good mother does? *Makes sure things are done correctly?*"

"Well. . ." said Layla, putting her coffee mug down on the counter. "Let's hear your idea of a good mother. I've been waiting to hear your thoughts on that for thirty-five years."

Cindy stood up. "Look Layla, I'm done apologizing for the past. This is now. And I need a place of my own. Nothing extravagant, just a private space. And you have the money to do that. You don't even have to spend any of your money, take it out of the trust."

"That *is* my money," Layla said.

"But it should have been mine."

"If you had gotten the money, you'd still be in the same place today. Needing more."

"How could you possibly know that?" Cindy asked.

"I know what you do when you are on your own," Layla said, lifting her mug, taking a sip. "I am not having you take care of Jana drunk, high or who knows what."

"Jesus, Lee! What do you think?" Cindy asked, moving towards her. "I want an apartment to start using? Are you kidding me? If you don't trust me, you can trust Jana, she is not a baby, she has eyes. She would tell you."

Layla laughed. "Like that would ever happen, like Jana would say anything negative about you. You're her comrade, she idolizes you." She went to the sink, turned on the faucet, and ran some water into her empty mug. "She's just like you. I see it."

Cindy opened a cupboard door and pulled out a mug. Poured coffee to the brim, then took a long sip.

"That may be true Lee. Yes it may. But isn't it funny how you see the similarities between Jana and me, but you don't see the ones between us?"

Layla placed her mug on the kitchen counter. "I'm nothing like you."

"Really?" Cindy asked, moving closer. "Well we don't look alike that's for sure, but we do share one thing in common. Like I said a while ago. You're too busy with your own life to actually take care of your daughter. Now who does that remind me of?" She looked at the ceiling and clicked her finger. "Oh yes, me! That's exactly who it reminds me of. Fancy that. You're ending up just like me."

Layla pushed Cindy's hand, sent her mug flying, then shattering on the kitchen floor. Pools of coffee settled and seeped.

"Don't you ever, *ever,* say that to me again," Layla said.

"It's true Layla. I partied. You work. But it's all the same result, gone. Now I want an apartment. And I want it by April."

Cindy turned and started to her room.

"Where were you when I was twenty and scared to death when I found out I was pregnant?" Layla asked, following behind. "Where were you? Somewhere in Denver or who knows where?"

"You handled it fine."

"Did I?"

Cindy stopped, turned towards her. "You were twenty Layla, not a baby. You got married, handled it fine. You were still able to finish college, go to law school, all on your grandmother's dime. Yeah, *you* escaped all of her judgmental wrath. So you got your career, free and clear, and Grandma watched the baby. Sounds good to me.

"What could I have possibly added to that? Your grandmother and father made it perfectly clear how much I wasn't needed, how I was just some unfortunate complication. Perfectly clear! You have no idea how they repeated time and time again, how much better it was when I was out of your life."

She turned, shook her head. "You got everything . . . the money, the career, the husband, the whole American dream."

Layla grabbed her by her shoulders, turned her around. "Perfect? Are you kidding me? Why do you think I work so hard? Why? You don't find it odd Luke is never around?"

Cindy narrowed her eyes. "He's afraid of you. He avoids you because you have to control everything."

Layla stepped back. "Oh really? *Really*? That's how much you know!

"He's never around because he's been seeing some woman for the past five years. And he didn't leave the bank, he was fired. And *consulting*? I haven't seen a consulting paycheck for a good half year, so whoever he's consulting, she's getting it for free."

"Why didn't you tell—"

"Like you'd understand what it's like to have a family on your shoulders?" Layla asked. "You? Everything was done for you. Everything. You never had to worry about life. That was something other people took care of for you. A detail."

"So leave him Layla! Leave him for God's sake. It's 2013, not 1978. What is he bringing to the table? You'll have more than enough money without him."

"I could never do that to Jana."

"Jana? Jana will get over it."

"You don't under—"

Jana's bedroom door opened. "What will I get over?" she asked, standing in the door frame.

"Um," Cindy started, glancing at Layla, "oh nothing really honey. Just a little thing. We've been thinking of maybe I would get an apartment, like we were talking about the other day, remember? Something close. It will make no difference in anything really, except I'll have my own space at night, everything else will proceed as usual.

"That's all. I just told your mother you wouldn't think it was any big deal. You're fifteen now, have your own life, you'd understand how everyone needs their own space."

Jana looked at her mother.

"Yes. We were talking about that," Layla said.

Jana walked past them into the kitchen, then turned around. "A mug broke. I heard it."

"Slipped out of my hands," said Cindy.

Jana picked a piece of the shattered mug from the floor, and threw it into the waste basket. She went into a kitchen cupboard and pulled out a cereal box. Layla got a paper towel and started to wipe the spilt coffee.

Cindy went into her room, closed the door, and collapsed on the bed.

Jesus, she thought. She needed a drink.

⅄

She turned the steering wheel, glanced at Jana. "Your mom is going to be late tonight, so I thought we could swing by my house and drop some stuff off? Is that OK?" She waited, then shook her head. "Jana?"

"Yeah, whatever," said Jana, looking out the car window. "That's fine."

"Things OK at school?"

"They're never OK, they're always stupid. So when are you moving?"

"This week. I was so lucky to find an available house so close! And it's perfect, you'll love it. It's only a little down the road really, you can walk there if you want to."

"I don't like walking."

"Oh my God, you're so negative."

"All I said was I don't like walking," Jana said.

"Since when? You walk to the park all the time to do who knows what, and now you don't like walking?" Cindy narrowed her eyes at the passing street signs. "Now, here . . . I have to pay attention, I always get lost. You'd think I was in New York or something. I never had a good sense of direction, too artistic."

She turned down a street, then up the driveway of a white clapboard house. "There," she said, stopping the car. "Now isn't this charming?" She opened the car door, pulled out two bags and a large picture from the back seat.

"It's small," said Jana, picking up a bag, then following her up the walkway to the porch. "And old. It's old."

Cindy put the key into the front door lock. "Jana honestly. Old is charming, it has a history, not something some construction company slapped together in two weeks with pretentious phony pillars in the dining room." She opened the door, and went into the foyer.

Jana passed by, putting the bag down, then entering the living room. Her shoes clicked against the hardwood floors. "The wood is nice," she said, as she headed towards the kitchen.

"Nice? Look at this beautiful black walnut! It's amazing."

"Seriously Gma?" Jana called out.

"What?"

"White appliances? And the stove is electric. And where is the dishwasher?"

"Oh my God," said Cindy, picking up the picture and carrying it into the living room. She carefully placed it on the fireplace mantle, then stepped back. "Jana, come here and look at this. What do you think?" She crossed her arms as she surveyed the image of the smiling woman with outstretched arms and feathered boa.

Jana came in, took a place at her side. "Um . . . I guess . . ."

"Now what's wrong with this picture, for God's sake?" Cindy asked.

"I don't know. It's probably more for your bedroom, or something. Not somewhere where it's the first thing you see."

"It's Janis Joplin."

"Exactly Grandma. She's been dead for like a hundred years or something. Its creepy to have a dead person's picture in the living room, first thing you see."

Cindy turned, went to the kitchen. "I don't know what's wrong with you today."

"It's just my opinion, I don't have to agree with everything you say." Jana plopped down on the floor, picked at her fingernails. "How long are we going to be here anyway?"

"As long as I need to."

She sighed, put her hands down, then gazed up at the picture. "Mom says she was a drug addict who ended up killing herself, and then became some romantic hippie icon cause people are stupid."

"Does she now?"

"But she's right about that, isn't she?" She pushed herself up, looked closer at the picture, then turned away. "She sure wasn't pretty."

Cindy returned to the room. "Give me your phone."

"Why?"

"Just do what I ask."

Jana reached into her pocket, pulled out the phone and handed it to her.

Cindy punched in a few things, then handed the phone back to her. "Hit that video, *Little Girl Blue.* Then you tell me how important pretty is. Go on." She turned, and went back to the kitchen.

Jana sighed, sat back down on the floor, and pressed the arrow. A man with black curly hair and an open necked shirt gave an introduction. The *legendary* Janis Joplin, he said. Then an unassuming frame tentatively approached the microphone, hands nervously grasped together. No boa, no smile.

Jana returned to her fingernails.

The first notes, the first line, the second.

Jana's eyes moved back to the phone right at the moment the woman closed hers.

When the song ended, Jana pushed herself up, and went to the kitchen. "I don't get it," she said. "She didn't seem so rock and roll party girl there. She seemed sad. Sad and scared."

"Exactly," Cindy said, placing a glass on a cupboard shelf. "Remember that when you make judgments based on what someone else says. And the heart of Janis wasn't rock and roll. It was the blues. The blues." She closed the cupboard door. "And just so you know, 'pretty' is nothing to be especially proud of. There's nothing special about pretty, it's a fluke of youth and genetics is all. Millions of women can be pretty for a nanosecond. Unique? Now unique is something different. That's what lasts. That's what makes someone memorable." She slowly wiped her hands on her jeans, then looked up. "What?"

"I don't know Gma . . . I just . . . I know you need space and everything, but I really don't want you to move."

Cindy walked over to her, tousled her hair. "Now don't get all dramatic on me, it's not like I'm dying, I got a house is all. And nothing will change, nothing. Just that I will sleep here." She looked into her eyes, stepped back. "Come on, lighten up. I promise, straight up. Things will be better. Everybody needs a space of their own! And I have never had that before, not really, so I'm due don't you think?"

Jana looked at her, then out the kitchen window. "It *is* pretty here, lots of trees."

"Yes."

"I wish I would have lived then."

"When?"

"Back when you were young," Jana said. "The '60s, '70s. It seems so fun. Oh— I almost forgot, the end-of-year ballet recital. It's next Saturday afternoon. You'll be there, right?"

"Next Saturday afternoon?" Cindy asked.

"Oh gee, let me think. No, it will be fine. It's just—I have that friend of mine from college coming down Friday. But Saturday afternoon? Sure, I'll figure out something else for her to do."

"There's a lot of stuff to do in town," Jana said.

"Right. Yes, of course. I will be at the recital." Cindy walked to the kitchen sink. "I need to wash my hands up, they're all dirty from this stuff. Jana, look in the other bag, and see if it has the hand soap."

"Got it," she said.

Cindy took off her rings and placed them on the counter, then took the soap from Jana and lathered her hands. "Yuck."

Jana looked at the jewelry. "Some of these rings are so cool. Can I wear some for a while?"

"Sure," Cindy said, turning off the faucet, then drying her hands on a towel. "Just not that ring."

"Oh, that's my favorite . . . what is it?"

"An ankh. An Egyptian symbol meaning eternal life or something. Used to be everywhere in the '60s. I can't let you have it though because a friend gave it to me a long time ago. You know Trey, my friend? The queen from New Orleans? Sort of has sentimental value, even though God knows I hate sentiment. It just sort of reminds me of . . . look, if you like it, we'll go downtown to one of those hippie stores, I bet they have stuff just like it. I'll get you one to celebrate your recital."

"Really?"

"Sure. Now, let's go pick something up for dinner. Tomorrow will be an early day, I have some furniture being delivered."

⅄

Cindy looked around the room. Perfect. It was perfect.

She sat down on the gold velvet couch, sank back into the soft cushions and listened to the silence.

Nobody walking down the hall. Nobody slamming doors. No Layla saying remember this or that, or Stan asking what was for dinner, or Randy handing her his favorite jeans that needed to be washed, or Mark ruining her day with a call to say he was going to be late.

There was no one. No one!

She was fifty-eight and she had finally vanquished compromise.

She touched the purple fringe on the lampshade next to the couch. In all the homes she had ever lived in, she had never felt so blissful.

It was Monday night, the second night she had slept in the home. She stayed true to her word, picking up Jana early in the morning to take her to school; returning to take her to ballet, staying until Layla or Luke got home.

She didn't mind that part, not at all. She actually looked forward to it.

Jana was different, unique, with a natural warmness, and an artist's sensitivity and curiosity. Sensitive, but not sappy, and thank God for that, Cindy thought. And she had a personal strength, a street-smart sophistication, a sense of adventure.

Cindy patted the pillow.

And who did she get that from? Not being egotistical or anything, just keeping it real. She obviously got it from her.

She had to admit it was sort of weird how personal qualities sometimes skipped generations, but that's what had obviously happened. Cindy and Jana; Layla and her mother.

She tapped her fingers on the arm of the couch.

Layla really had to be Mark's daughter. She could tell herself or anyone else that maybe Layla was Randy's, but truly, she had to admit it seemed highly unlikely, based on disposition alone.

Layla had no sense of adventure, she was all pursed lips and balance sheets. A God's little helper, keeping guard on everyone else's transgressions. Just like Mark; just like her mother.

Cindy walked to the gilded hallway mirror. She looked at her reflection, turned sideways.

She loved the new blouse she was wearing. It was unlike any of the other stuff she had worn over the past six months. She had bought it at the women's store *Karma* downtown, when she and Jana had stopped there that night after dinner. The sleeves flowed, the coral color was pulsating.

She turned back, faced the mirror.

Her hair was a little too in place, she thought. Too middle-aged-housewife perfect. She shook her head, looked at her reflection. Yes, that was better. Messy.

Now Jana . . . Jana had unbelievable hair. Like hers when she was younger, a wildness in the thick, golden curls.

She walked back to the couch. How funny, she thought. When she first came back to Layla's, she had never, not once, anticipated this. The house had changed everything.

And that was something she could have never foreseen! How wonderful it would feel to be totally on her own. After all, it was only a short month ago that she believed her only shot at happiness was a life with Seamus. Seamus!

She must have some sort of angel watching over her, she thought, because none of this would have ever happened if that original plan hadn't blown up. And if that hadn't happened, she could have lived her whole life without knowing *this*!

She glanced at the picture above the mantle, pulled on the billowy arms of her top. Yes, she had lucked into something much better.

She got up and went to the kitchen. It was 8:00 p.m., early. She could walk to town, see what was going on. She grabbed her purse off the counter, then decided it wasn't right, its color too drab, and headed upstairs to her closet. She pulled out the bright aqua purse Stan had gotten for her right before he got sick, and headed downstairs.

Cate would be in on Friday, they would meet Seamus for dinner, and all of that would be fine, she thought, as she opened the front door. But it would also be perfectly ordinary.

Ordinary.

What a perfectly horrible word. Almost like giving up.

CHAPTER TEN

JANA

So crazy Grandma C is gone, she got herself one of those old houses in town. Not too far away, by the park. I can walk there if I want.

So that part's OK, and I can't really blame her for wanting a place of her own. I still see her every day, she takes me to school, picks me up. Sometimes after ballet we have dinner, go shopping, talk. But I will admit, her leaving is still, what would she call it? A bummer. Because when she left, it seemed all of the color and interest left the house, leaving me with the same, predictably boring shit. For all of her craziness, or maybe because of it, that is exactly how it feels.

No one is deciding to cut my bangs, or talking about mushroom eye shadow, or making me listen to videos of old rock stars back in the day.

Sometimes, it just seems like a huge deafening silence, so big it almost makes me wish for the times her and Mom went at it, the way they do, like professional wrestlers, except they don't need any moves or even words, they do their take downs with a look.

But the good news is I still get to see her, and that helps because at least with Gma, she is not watching me like Mom, with those perpetually freaked-out eyes that look like she thinks if she lets her guard down for a moment something horrible will happen.

Gma is never like that, things are usually lighter with her, even when you factor in that one awkward conversation we had about Doc the night she came into my room. She tried to act all nonchalant, but I got the message she really wanted me to stop seeing him. I'm not exactly sure why, but it didn't matter anyway, because I had already decided I was wasting my time with him, so I just took her (good) advice and got out of that.

I made sure Mom knew of every good grade I had gotten at school, and I spent a lot of time bragging about how great I was doing in rehearsals. Stuff like that.

And all of that can work beyond getting me out of appointments with Doc, if I play my cards right. Because if I play my cards right, and say my recital solo is kick-ass, right after Mom has received all her accolades from all the other lame parents, that will be the perfect time (or as close to perfect as I will ever find) to tell her that I want to quit ballet and start going to that hip hop place Gma took me to.

How I ended up going there in the first place was, in itself, the result of an odd string of events.

Gma and I had stopped at her favorite coffee shop, and she was taking so long with her nonfat milk, whipped cream and touch of cinnamon instructions. So I wandered off to the side and saw this poster for a new dance studio that opened up downtown, Marcel's Hop. They don't do ballet, they do other stuff, jazz, modern, hip hop, krump. The poster had little coupons attached for one free class.

I was reading it, touching a coupon, when Gma came over with her coffee, and looked at the poster and said, "You should go there, it looks fun."

And I said, "Yeah right, Mom would never let me go there."

And then she pulled a coupon off the poster and said, "Then we just won't tell her."

So one night, when Mom had to work late, Grandma C took me there, and it was unbelievable. No uptight old Mrs. Barfield standing there with a yardstick, telling me to breathe through my core, or worried about my turnout, or if I might have gained two pounds, or the positioning of my right leg in a jete.

Nothing like that. There, the dance was all from the beat and the feel of the music. And it didn't matter if my hair was held tightly in the bun at the top of my head, matter of fact, I let my hair down, completely free and no one, not even the teacher complained.

I had never felt so good in a dance class, ever. I didn't think it was possible.

After the class, the teacher came up to me. He wanted me to join their company. He gave me his card, and I told him I would call him after the recital.

So now I just have to tell Mom and Dad. Dad, it won't matter. Mom?

Well that will be harder. Much harder. And Crazy G can't offer any help, because as soon as she would open her mouth, Mom would push back harder, and then there would be no hope.

And it is difficult enough without that whole Mom and Gma complication because Mom likes, no loves, ballet because . . . well it's orderly like her, with everything having a specific, correct way. Oh yes, and it's pretty. Very, very, pretty.

Now isn't that funny, that pretty part? Cause in ballet, yeah, it's pretty to look at, but underneath is all this stuff that is really quite grotesque. The feet that bleed; the unnatural way the legs turn in opposing directions; the fact that, to get that oh-so-pretty-line, you cannot eat normal meals like everyone else.

Yes, ironic.

Me? I'd rather just dance.

CHAPTER ELEVEN

Cate

When she was about forty-five minutes from Yellow Springs, Cate started to second-guess herself, which led to nausea, which led to the feeling that she must be the dumbest woman in the world.

What the heck was she doing taking a road trip to Asheville, by way of Yellow Springs, which, by the way, wasn't on the way at all? She didn't *need* to go either place, she could have stayed safe at home, she thought.

Safe at home?

She sat back in her seat, hands on the wheel, and tried some purposeful breathing. Inhaled from her core, exhaled through her nose.

Stay safe at home. Her mother had said that as a prelude to conversations that always ended in generational impasse.

Cate leaned back in her seat, internally countering the still lingering argument.

Home. Home didn't feel all that safe anymore, what with its indifferent quiet, its left-over spaces from peoples' past exits. Cate took another deep breath, reminded herself of all the things she had previously sorted out.

This trip was going to be her line of demarcation, her important step forward. It was just this stay at Cindy's that was tripping her up, reigniting the anxiety. Because truthfully, Cindy had been well, more than a little annoying in New Orleans. There was her dismissive attitude towards Trey, her off-the-wall liaison with Stretch, the baffling *maybe she is his daughter, maybe she's not* provocation, and that dissertation about truth equals guess.

Of course, all of that softened with Cindy's unexpected condolence call and invitation to visit—so thoughtful and nice! It made Cate think she had been overly sensitive and judgmental. Hadn't Trey basically told her that exact thing when they talked about CK in his back yard? *Lighten up,* he had said.

So yes, she had already sorted this out, told herself nobody died from provocation, and anyway, worst case scenario, if things at Cindy's got too annoying, she could always give an excuse, leave early. No need to cancel a trip.

Exactly, she reminded herself. Nothing could happen that she couldn't get out of. If Cindy irritated her, she would just lea—

She tilted her head, reached over and turned down the volume on the CD player. She was sure she had heard an odd click, click, click.

One minute passed, then two. Then, there it was again.

Click, click, click.

She tried to remember the last time she had taken the car in for maintenance. She looked at the dashboard—no warning lights lit—and then out the window.

The landscape was eerie, a sort of *Children in the Corn* eerie. Flat land, for as far as the eye could see, spotted with scattered, ramshackle farmhouses. A pickup truck with an *Impeach Obama* bumper sticker sped by.

Forget Cindy, she thought. What if her car broke down? She didn't know one thing about cars, not one thing. And she wasn't twenty or thirty or even forty years old. She was almost sixty! Vulnerable. A little old lady, really.

If something did happen to her, people would think, serves her right. They would read the newspaper article about her demise and insert their own thoughts, and it would all fit into the comfortable notion that bad things happen in very predictable ways.

> *A close to sixty-year-old woman (possibly senile) on a (ridiculous) road trip (?) to Asheville by way of Yellow Springs (obviously no sense of direction) was engulfed in flames as her car blew up due to her arrogant neglect of routine car maintenance (karma!). She is survived by three children (who hopefully are much smarter than her).*

Nothing about her death would seem especially tragic. People would read it and think, *had it coming.* Her mother would have thought that.

She tapped her fingers on the steering wheel, then stopped.

Quiet. It was now quiet. The clicking sound had ended.

She felt herself relax. See, she thought, nothing was wrong. Nothing. She was just nervous, letting her imagination get away from her. She reached for a new CD, pushed the eject button, and put it in the player, ran a hand through her hair.

Yes, everything would be fine.

Cate pulled up the driveway, then rechecked the address. Yes, this was it. She got out of the car, walked to the front door and knocked.

"Hi! You're Cate? Come on in!" said a woman, opening the door.

Cate hesitated, unable to move.

"Oh, I'm Jana, Cindy's granddaughter. She's upstairs in the bathroom. She'll be right down."

"Oh," said Cate. "Oh." She walked into the foyer, then turned back. "Honestly, I thought I had crossed some sort of time travel thing. I am telling you the truth. Like a Rod Serling *Twilight Zone* type of thing."

Jana gave a blank stare.

"Oh that was a show like a lifetime ago . . . I just mean—Lord you look like your grandmother. It took my breath away how much you look like her back in the day."

Cindy came bounding down the stairs. "You're here!" she said, putting her arms around her, swinging her around.

"Cindy?" Cate replied, taking her hands, standing back. "Oh my gosh, look at you! You look amazing! You've lost weight, how much? And your hair!"

Cindy stood back, twirled around. Her blouse's long chiffon sleeves billowed. "I know! I swear. I mean, I look at myself in the mirror and I almost fall in love!"

"It wasn't that you ever looked bad, you always looked great, but now you look amazing. And this one . . ." Cate turned to Jana, "oh boy, this one is you. Really you! I mean, I walked in, and I thought I had time-traveled. She is you at seventeen."

"I know," said Cindy. "You like her bangs? I cut her bangs! I just looked at her and knew. She has that Patti Boyd '70s vibe going on, no? Come on, come on into the living room, we'll get you situated later."

Cate entered the room, all velvets and tapestries, fringed lamp-shades and pillows. She turned, facing Cindy. "It's beautiful. If I walked into this home without knowing it was yours, it would not take me long to figure it out. It's *you*." She stopped in front of the fire-place, looked up at the picture over the mantle, the smiling woman with the feather boa.

Cindy sat on the couch. "I know! I have never had a place of my own, isn't that crazy? Never had something I could make exactly the way I wanted it. "

Cate turned around, then sat down next to her. "Well, you did that here, that's for sure."

"And the town," Cindy said, "you will love the town! It's this little island of hippie-ness right smack dab in the middle of nowhere. I mean, it would make sense if it was outside San Francisco, or Austin or somewhere, but not here in nowhere Ohio. Galleries, cool clothes, handmade jewelry—even head shops for God's sake. You can check them out tomorrow, it's just a short walk. So what's your schedule?'

"Schedule?"

"When do you have to get back on the road?"

"Oh, I am thinking Sunday morning probably, Asheville is about seven hours from here, my reservation starts Sunday."

"Oh, OK. Well gee, that doesn't give us a heck of a lot of time, and something came up for tomorrow afternoon. Jana was picked as a lead in her dance recital tomorrow and I promised—"

"Oh, don't worry about it, go," Cate said.

"Yeah, well I figured you could walk down to the village, look around. We'll hook up afterwards, then go out somewhere . . . tonight we're going to meet a guy for dinner in town."

"A guy?" Cate asked.

Jana walked into the room, sat down in an arm chair by the front window.

"Jana, can you imagine," Cindy said, getting up, "I have been friends with this woman for forty years. Forty years! Cate, you want some tea? I have some good stuff I bought downtown. Jasmine or something like that."

"Sure," Cate said, turning to Jana. "So you're a dancer?"

"I guess . . . I dance."

"She's a great dancer! An artist!" Cindy called from the kitchen.

"What kind of dance?"

"Um, ballet now."

"Stevie Nicks was a ballet dancer," Cindy said, coming back into the room, heading to the stereo. She pulled out an album, put it on the old school turntable, then carefully placed the stylus down. The first notes of *Rhiannon* came on. "Can you imagine, Cate, Jana didn't even know who Stevie Nicks was until I came here.

"See Jana, you use ballet, like she did. It gives you power, that imposing lift of the chin, the graceful sweep of a hand. It'll get you out of a hell of a lot of situations, much more than worthless things like algebra or geography. But you know all that already.

"She's going to start other classes soon, like free form stuff, hip hop, krump."

She went back into the kitchen, then returned holding two cups of tea. She handed one to Cate, then turned to Jana. "Can you take her stuff up to the first bedroom? Oh, and my purse too, it's there, at the bottom of the stairs."

"Oh she doesn't have to, I can do that," Cate said.

"I've got them," said Jana, going into the foyer, and scooping everything up, then bounding up the stairs.

Cindy cocked her head until the sound of Jana's footsteps dimmed, then turned to Cate. "So tonight . . . tonight we're going to meet this guy for dinner. His name is Seamus."

" 'This guy?' What does that mean? Is he your guy?"

"Well, I don't know. I mean, he's into me and everything, but I'm not sure. He's smart though, a psychologist. Might be just a little too boring for me." She took a sip of tea. "You'd like him."

"Oh," Cate said, laughing.

"Are you seeing anyone?" Cindy asked.

"Me? Oh no. No, not really."

"How come? You always had one guy or another. Like I always figured you would be the type to get married right away after the divorce."

"Me?" Cate asked, shaking her head. "Oh no. I don't think . . . I'm not sure I could ever do that again."

"Wow," Cindy said, moving closer. "Now see, I am just really starting to understand that whole concept, never having to marry or live with someone. I mean, if you can swing things alone, what *would* be the point of going back to all that?"

"Swing things alone?"

"The money," Cindy answered. "What else could I mean?"

"Oh, I thought you meant the loneliness. Or like trusting someone enough to—"

Cindy looked at her, then laughed. "Loneliness? No! Come on. Are you lonely? If you're lonely it's your own fault! That's an easy fix. You go out one, two times, check loneliness off the list. Men aren't all that complicated.

"See . . . this is what I've realized," she leaned towards her, eyes widening. "Just because you might be lonely here and there, you don't have to get all hysterical about it. One night a week will probably take care of that problem, you don't have to go all 24/7. Men should be like pepper. You just need a little bit is all, you're not supposed to chug the whole bottle."

Cindy got up from the couch, and went to the foot of the stairs. "Jana?" She cocked her head, then rolled her eyes. "She's acting sort of . . . well you know teenagers."

"She seemed fine to me," said Cate. "Lovely. Remember what we were like?"

A car honked in the driveway.

"Jana," Cindy yelled, "your dad is here to pick you up! What are you doing up there for God's sake?"

"OK! OK!" said Jana flying down the stairs, putting on her sweater. "Had to go to the bathroom." She kissed Cindy on the cheek, then turned to Cate. "It was nice to meet you," she said, and ran out the door.

Cindy walked to the window. "Did you hear a toilet flush?" she asked.

"What?"

"A toilet flush. She said she was in the bathroom."

CHAPTER TWELVE

SEAMUS

"Reservations for three," he said to the hostess.

"Do you want to wait for your party or be seated?"

"I'll just go ahead and be seated, I'll see them when they come in."

He took his seat at the table, picked up his menu, then put it down, took a drink of water.

Oh, why had he agreed to this? After all, what did he owe her? They had gone out, what? Four, five times maximum, and the intimacy, thank God, had been avoided. But here he was having dinner with her and her friend like he was part of her family. It set up the wrong vibe. Shit.

He leaned back, wiped his forehead.

But what could he have said when she put it the way she did? He reached for his glass, finished off the water.

Thank God for the interruption that day in the bedroom! He'd be in much stickier shit if that had happened. Probably be getting invited to all sorts of things, like christenings and bar mitzvahs and graduations. Although lately her emails have tapered off, maybe she had sensed his waning interest.

He picked up his napkin, put it on his lap. Well he would be polite, but keep it short. He could say he had an early morning appointment, yes that was it! He'd do that and be done with it.

He looked at his watch. An hour, hour and a half max, then he could get home and change his clothes and maybe still catch that—

His thoughts were interrupted by the opening of the restaurant door.

A woman entered.

Jesus, Seamus thought, looking up. Jesus.

She had long, thick dark hair, just the perfect touch of messy. Slim body in dark jeans, a striking royal blue top. Dark, smoldering eyes. She looked around the restaurant with an inviting smile.

She looked, Seamus thought, like something slightly exotic but at the same time comfortably next-doorish. Like the love child of Marisa Tomei and oh, who was that new actress, the one who beguilingly fell down all the time? Jennifer Lawrence. Yes, that was it!

But she wasn't that young, she certainly had to be past her forties.

He sat back, smiled. Now *she* would be different, he thought. Earthy, low maintenance. And just when he thought that, Cindy entered the restaurant and spotted him. She said something to the woman and they headed straight to his table.

He stood up. Holy shit, he thought.

Cindy came over to him, kissed him on the cheek. "Seamus, this is my friend, Cate. Cate, Seamus."

He touched her outstretched hand, met her eyes. She glanced down for a moment, did a half laugh. "Nice to meet you," she said.

Cindy's eyed narrowed, or did he imagine that? They all sat down.

"I'm so happy to meet you," he said. "Cindy has told me so much about you."

Cindy raised an eyebrow, reached for a menu. "I have?"

"Well I mean, how you have been best friends forever." Seamus picked up his water glass to take a drink, but then realized it was empty. He softly put it down, then raised his hand to signal the waitress. "Can we get a round of drinks?" he asked as she came over.

"Hm. I'll just have an iced tea I think," Cate said.

"I'll have a seven and seven," said Cindy.

He ordered a scotch on the rocks, and the waitress moved off. "So when did you get in?" he asked.

"Oh this afternoon," Cate said.

"And you're from?"

"Akron," Cindy abruptly inserted, putting her menu down. "Remember?"

The waitress returned with their drinks.

"Oh yes. Yes, of course," said Seamus. "And you're here until . . .?"

"Sunday. Sunday morning," Cate said.

He glanced at her left hand to see if there was a ring. Why, oh why couldn't he remember anything Cindy had told him about her? His mind had turned to mush.

"She's not married," said Cindy, taking a long gulp of her drink.

"What?" Seamus asked.

"You were looking at her hand."

"Oh that? No, I was noticing her ring. The ankh. It's unusual."

"Not that unusual," said Cindy, holding up her right hand.

"Oh you've wearing yours!" said Cate. She turned to Seamus. "A mutual friend from college bought them for us as graduation gifts."

"A total queen," said Cindy.

"Cindy . . ." Cate said.

"What? He is a queen! He's sixty-five years old, wears a black cape and dyes his hair. What would you call him?"

"It's just . . . I don't know, a little dismissive." Cate reached for her purse on the floor.

"Doesn't mean anything bad," Cindy started, "just gives Seamus a better sense of who he is. Doesn't mean I don't appreciate the ring. Nothing about that. I even had a replica of the ring made for Jana. She admired it. She has a thing about me, things that I do, you know."

"Well that's a compliment," said Cate as she rummaged through her purse.

"Something wrong?" asked Seamus.

"Oh no, it's just—I thought I had something in my purse. I must have left it at home." She closed the purse, put it back on the floor.

"So Cate . . . what do you do?" Seamus asked.

"Do?"

"Work? Do you work?"

"Oh, I do some writing . . . freelance marketing stuff, some short articles. Before freelance, I worked in the marketing department of a prep school."

"Oh, so both of you guys sort of ended up at the same type of place."

"Same type of place?" Cate asked.

"Well I mean, Cindy working at The Colorado Day School and you at—"

Cate looked at Cindy. "You worked at a school?"

"Oh," Cindy said, turning to Seamus, "that was during a time when we sort of lost track of each other. You know how busy life gets with kids, marriages, work." She reached for the bread basket, pulled out a roll. "Oh good, they're warm! Don't you hate it when restaurants serve rolls that aren't warm? I do. It's insulting. What's the point of even eating them?" She tore the roll in half, lifted a piece to her mouth.

Cate glanced down at her purse, picked it back up. "Um . . . could you excuse me for a moment, I have to go to the rest room."

Seamus half-rose, then watched as she walked to the back of the restaurant. He sat down, reached for his glass, then noticed Cindy's expression. "Well thank you for inviting me," he offered.

"Oh, that. Well, at the time I thought you would enjoy meeting one of my friends," she said.

"Well yes, of course. I did—I mean, I do."

"Yeah. Although you know, even though we've been friends forever, Cate and I . . . we're really quite different." She reached for another roll with one hand, took a gulp of her drink with the other. "Love her to death, but she's so high maintenance."

"Really? She doesn't seem—"

"Oh not with women, just men. Men seem to throw her off. Not that she's ever without one, she just never sticks for long. There's always something wrong, even the ones who seem perfectly fine. It's so funny, so opposite from her schtick.

"And she's sort of unnaturally tied to her family. You know how Italians are, clannish. Never could really think for her—oh look, here she is," Cindy said, as Cate returned to the table. "You OK?" she asked.

"Sure," said Cate, placing her purse on the floor, then picking up the menu. She brushed her hair away from her face. "So . . . what is everyone having?"

⅄

Two hours later they walked out of the restaurant and stood at the front entrance.

"It was really nice meeting you," said Cate, extending her hand to Seamus. "And thank you for dinner, it was lovely."

"My pleasure," Seamus replied, taking her hand, then turning and kissing Cindy on the cheek. "Hey, I have an idea. Why don't you two come over to my place tomorrow night for dinner? I mean, if you don't have any other plans. I make a wicked lasagna."

"Oh," said Cate, looking at Cindy.

"Well, maybe," said Cindy. "Jana has a recital tomorrow afternoon, and I have to go to that. I thought Cate could explore downtown while I'm gone, check things out, do some shopping. I'm just not certain of when I'll be back." She looked away, jangled her keys.

"Oh," said Seamus, "well, it's no big deal. I'd just love to have you if it fits into your plans."

"OK," said Cindy. "I'll get back to you on that." She touched Cate's elbow, they turned and walked away.

Shopping tomorrow, he thought.

Yellow Springs wasn't Paris. Maybe tomorrow he would go shopping too.

CHAPTER THIRTEEN

CINDY

Typical, Cindy thought, as she drove home from the restaurant, listening to Cate babble on about everything besides that big white elephant in the room, Seamus. She shook her head.

"What?" asked Cate, stopping mid-sentence.

"He was really into you."

"What do you mean?" Cate asked.

"Seamus. I could tell. He was all into your vibe."

"You're crazy," Cate said.

"Why do you always do that?"

"What?"

"Refuse to talk about anything that might be uncomfortable," Cindy answered. "You were always like that. You'd think in forty-some years you would have grown a pair of balls."

"What? I'm just saying I didn't notice."

"Of course you did!" Cindy said. "And you're acting like it is some big deal to me. Didn't I tell you, he's just a good friend is all? Now a while ago, actually when I first set this thing up, I thought maybe things could be different. But now, come on? I like him and all, but can you really see me with him? Of course not. He's more your type."

She pulled into her driveway, stopped the car, and pulled the key out of the ignition. "He probably picked up on my feelings anyway," she said. "All I'm just saying is, if you want him, go at it, doesn't matter to me."

They got out of the car, silently walked to the house. "You want some tea or something?" Cindy asked as she opened the front door.

"Tea? Sure."

"Chamomile?"

"Sure, that's fine."

Cindy walked into the kitchen, pulled two mugs out of a cabinet and filled them with water. "Wouldn't this surprise Trey?" she asked, placing them into the microwave. "You and me coming back and having chamomile tea to top off a night? Well, he wouldn't be so surprised about you."

The timer sounded, Cindy dropped the bags into the steaming water, then handed a mug to Cate. "You were always more . . . I don't know, diligent? Reserved? Like you could have one or two drinks, stop, go back to the dorm and sleep like a baby, make it to class the next day. Me? I'd have a drink, then want five or six more and a line of cocaine, stay up all night, and blow off two days of classes."

They walked into the living room. Cindy took a seat on the couch, put her mug on a table. "Now that should have been a clue," she said, "but it wasn't. I thought it was all just good fun. How did I know that something so *fun* could morph into this huge albatross I'd have to carry around on my back for the next forty years? It's like the punkiest version of Russian roulette, isn't it?" she asked. "Who can walk away and who can't. Look at me! I just *now* got the strength to start casual drinking again. Just now!"

Cate sat down in an armchair, her eyes moved from Cindy to the picture over the fireplace. "That picture. It's melancholy, her smile. So . . . ironic." She pulled her legs up under her. "Ah, maybe everything now is striking me as melancholy, the kids, my parents." She laughed. "Oh you know, all the predictable reasons women our age are supposed to feel melancholy. A *Lifetime* cliché. That's me."

"Melancholy?" Cindy asked. "I never get melancholy over family stuff. Generally I just get pissed off. I guess I save melancholy for men. Yeah . . . now that's something worth crying for, not that bullshit stuff like the kids are gone, I don't have to do their laundry. Men. The way they used to be, the 'I can't wait to get into you' stuff. Now they're all—" she scrunched up her nose, "tender and sensitive, like little fricking girls. Yuck. What a turn-off. Like Seamus . . . he's that sensitive type."

"Well, I don't know about *that,* but hmmm . . ." Cate tilted her head. "Wait, are you saying you want sex the way we had it back in the day? The wham, bam, thanks ma'am type of stuff? You don't mean that, do you?"

Cindy leaned back. "Of course I do. That's exactly what I mean. Just like David Bowie said."

"But David Bowie meant it in a not so good way," Cate said. "And anyway, why should sex be the same as when we were twenty? We don't do anything the way we did when we were twenty, and thank God for that! Besides, all of the studies say—"

"Oh my God," Cindy said, standing up. "Oh my fricking God!" She walked over to Cate, knelt down. "See this is the problem, Cate . . . sex is not brain surgery, you don't need studies to figure it out, and by the way, reading a sex study is proof things have gone terribly wrong for you."

She sighed and stood up, "Let me break it down for you. What is the biggest turn-on for women?"

"They say clitoral—"

Cindy put her hands over her ears. "Oh please, don't say that. Oh Lord! You've bought that whole box of analytical garbage." She knelt back down, pulled herself close to Cate's face. "Desire, Cate. To be desired. That is what a woman wants, that's what gets the C thing going. Forget all that clinical sounding stuff with the step-by-step instructions that makes sex sound like an *Ikea* assembly manual. No. A woman has to feel . . . uncontrollably desired." She pushed herself up. "And it's the man's responsibility to do that. And if he can't do that one simple little thing, then what's his point?"

"But a man can show desire in lots of different ways. Doesn't have to be fast or—"

"Well of course it does!" Cindy said, walking back to the couch. "Otherwise you're just reminded of how old and hopelessly boring everyone has gotten." She held up her hands. "And who wants to fuck when you're thinking that?

"Anyway, I have proof that I'm right. Did we have sex clinics back in the day? At Woodstock? Did guys have to be counseled on what to do? Of course not." She closed her eyes. "God, it's a tragedy, what happened to the '70s. What was the point of saving the world if no one wants to fuck anymore?"

Cate looked at her for a moment, then shook her head and laughed. "Cindy, you are a trip." She disentangled her legs and got up, sat down on the floor next to her.

"You know I'm right," said Cindy, opening one eye, then the other. "I mean seriously, that was why Mark didn't stand a chance against Randy. Not a chance."

"But," Cate said, touching her arm, "Mark was so into you! So into you. I remember that day," she put her arms around her knees, "oh you know, right after graduation . . . you and Mark were going to D.C. in that big blue van. I remember him nuzzling your neck like you were some sort of goddess. I was so jealous! You having him, going off to the city, me packing up my car, schlepping off back to my parents' home, defeated. Remember?"

Cindy shook her head.

"Oh, come on. You have to remember. You asked me to come with you guys? Zeppelin was playing? *Stairway?*"

"Well," Cindy said, "I mean, it sounds like something that could have happened, I just don't remember it."

Cate put her hands on the floor, leaned back. "I remember everything about that day. I thought you were so strong and free and—"

Cindy turned towards her, laughing. "The day I left to go to D.C. with Mark? Oh my God, what was on your mind thinking that? I wasn't anything about strong and free then."

"But you said—"

"Oh honey," Cindy said, "how can you be so damn oblivious to the difference between what people say and what is really going on? I might have *acted* that way, but that's not how it was. I was going home to a job my dad had finagled at a neighborhood newspaper. And with *Mark*, Cate, not Robert Plant." She shook her head. "Now how in the world could you have romanticized that?"

CHAPTER FOURTEEN

CATE

She stayed in bed until she heard the front door close, then she turned over, and opened her eyes.

She had heard Cindy enter her room about an hour ago. Heard her say, "Cate?" but pretended she was still asleep. It was too early for even a short conversation. Not even a "see you then." She had underestimated how tiring socializing would be. It had been months really since she had been with people for unbroken stretches of time, and she hadn't slept at all last night. She had tossed and turned, finally getting up around 3:00 a.m. to take the last Ambien, and that had reminded her she'd have to call Kelly to ask for a refill when she got to Asheville.

Cate pushed off the bed covers, got up and went to the window. Kelly might balk, she thought, pulling a sheer drape aside, looking out at the sun-filled front yard. After all, she had cancelled her last two appointments, and Kelly had emphasized the prescription was only temporary.

Well, she would only ask for a small amount, just enough to tide her over until she got home. She'd make an appointment to verify her seriousness.

She turned around, appraised the room.

Yes, you could really tell this was Cindy's home. From the lavender colored walls, to the *Jefferson Starship* poster, and bright aqua bedspread with beaded pink pillows. So much color! No wonder she couldn't fall asleep.

She returned to the bed and picked up a pillow, watched its translucent beads reflect the morning sun. Yes, if you walked into this house and gave it a quick glance, you would know a lot about Cindy, she thought.

Her own apartment? She let the pillow drop.

Now, that would be a totally different thing. She had never really put her stamp on it, had treated it as a temporary holding ground on a road to somewhere else.

And now that she thought of it, all of her homes, even the ones with Tommy, had felt like that. The little ranch starter, the suburban split, the large colonial. None of them had that definitive, *this is who I am and this is where I will end up* feel.

She put her head on the bed pillow, closed her eyes.

Opposite from her parents. Their home was their first and only. Their lives didn't hold concepts of temporary stops or better somewhere elses. Their little brick bungalow was so intrinsically entwined with who they were, it was impossible for her to envision living there without them.

When her mother passed, she sold it to Joey, even though she knew it probably made her mother turn over in her grave, but he had so obviously wanted it, and selling it to him avoided all of the realtor hassles, the inevitable criticisms about things she couldn't, or wouldn't be able to see objectively.

But its sale hit her with unexpected emotional intensity. She hadn't anticipated what that last day would feel like, standing there in the kitchen, remembering the arguments, the laughter, the shouting, the kisses on the cheek. It felt like all of the sounds of her life were there as she waited for Joey to come for the keys.

His four year old daughter had followed him in, running through the front door, grasping his legs.

"I told you to stay at Grandpa's!" he said, looking down.

"I want to see my room," she answered with upturned eyes.

"Of course she wants to see her room," Cate said, taking her hand and leading her to the bedroom with its familiar slanted ceilings, to the window which overlooked the place in the yard where her father always planted his garden.

"See out there?" Cate asked, kneeling down. "You can plan a whole lot of wonderful things looking out that window." She patted her curly hair, and it felt so soft, so oblivious to a world of hair products.

That moment made things easier, but there was still a hesitation as Cate pulled out of the driveway. She kept the car moving, but tilted the rear view mirror so she could watch the house as it slowly diminished, then vanished from view.

It took a few days for her to see an upside. The sale of the house had offered her a freedom she had never previously known. Now she had a bona fide savings account, and that was not a little thing.

She opened her eyes, glanced around the room at the furniture, candles, the silky smooth bed linens.

Money, she thought. Now that was something Cindy always could take for granted. Sure, this wasn't a mansion, but it *was* a completely furnished and perfectly appointed home. How in the world could Cindy have done this *without* family money?

She certainly wasn't getting alimony from Mark anymore, and it didn't seem that she could have gotten anything from that second husband either. From what Cindy had said about him, he worked at a bar, and spent all of their money on drugs. Not the hallmarks of someone who could fund a huge divorce settlement.

And seriously, was Cindy the type of person who would deprive herself of anything in order to sock away a pension or savings? Until last night, and that odd mention of her working at, oh where was it . . . yes, The Colorado Day School, Cindy had never once mentioned working anywhere. Matter of fact, Cate was sure she remembered her saying in New Orleans that she hadn't worked since she had left D.C. for Dayton and that was what? Almost thirty-some years ago?

So it had to be family money, and that only made sense. Didn't Cindy always have money, even in college? Always had the newest clothes; always went to the best concerts; always seemed able to do exactly what she wanted. Every spring break, she could go to Florida; every fall, she would return to campus with stories of her European trips.

Crazy, Cate thought, how lucky she was with just that one little thing, being born into a family with money. No wonder she could be so free.

Cate pushed herself up off bed, picked up a candle on the dressing table. Jo Malone, Frosted Cherry and Clove.

Exactly, she thought. This candle wasn't anything like the twenty-dollar candles she let herself splurge on when one of the kids got a part-time job. This little candle cost well over one hundred dollars. People who bought candles like this didn't know what it was like to worry about money.

She looked up and caught her reflection in the dresser mirror. Furrowed forehead, narrowed eyes. She put the candle down and brushed the hair away from her face, then went into the bathroom where she found a note posted on the bathroom mirror.

Cate,

Something came up, have to go to my daughter's a little earlier than I thought. Will be home around dinner, late afternoon.

Apologize for change, but you can sleep late and then enjoy the town. To get there, turn left at the road and keep walking till you get to the main road, just a few blocks. You can't miss it and you'll love the shops! Later . . .

Cate pulled the note off, and placed it in the waste basket, then splashed some cold water on her face. She went back to the bedroom for her hairbrush, and as she was pulling it out of her purse, stopped. She put the brush down on the dresser, then took the purse to the bed, flipped it over. She sat down, sifted through its spilt contents, then shook her head.

That plastic bag that Danny left her? She had remembered it last night when they were at dinner, temporarily freaking out because she couldn't remember ever having removed it from the purse. She remembered *thinking* she should remove it, but couldn't remember actually doing it.

Well, she thought, she must have, because otherwise it would still be there! She dropped the items back into the purse, one by one.

Yes, she had obviously forgot. And wouldn't that make sense? Hadn't everything really been a blur ever since her mom's death? Granted, this would bring things to a whole different level, not remembering what she had done with a bag of cocaine, but things had been so scrambled!

She got up and went to her makeup bag, contemplated the eye shadow colors. She hadn't done this in weeks, she thought, grasping the bag, and returning to the bathroom. Oh, she had done rudimentary makeup, the necessities, but not this ritual of sifting and lingering over colors.

She applied the eye shadow, then lifted the eyeliner, *Black Night.* She wondered if they would take Seamus up on his dinner invitation. She leaned into the mirror, smudging the pencil close to her lashes.

Now that whole thing was awkward. Flattering, but immensely awkward.

Cindy's "go at it" comment—which she didn't buy, not for one moment.

Oh, she bought the part that Cindy might not be that interested in him, yes that was reasonable. After all, Seamus didn't seem anything like her type, not unless she needed something from him, like she sort of had with Mark.

But that did not mean that Seamus wanting Cate would be fine with her.

And that was sort of unfortunate, because Seamus had caught her attention from the moment she walked into the restaurant. She smiled, he smiled back. It was like—what? A few seconds is all, between that moment and the moment Cindy came up behind her, clarifying everything.

But in those seconds, Cate had a thought, a hope, that he was not the man Cindy wanted her to meet. Maybe he was just some random guy, someone Cindy might know, someone recently divorced, or better yet, widowed. And Cindy would introduce them, and then he would be fair game.

Because even at first glance, Seamus looked open, and kind, and interesting. Not anything like a Danny or Craig. His smile was warm and genuine, not player, not tight. Just the perfect temperature, like that sought-after porridge in the *Goldilocks* tale.

He looked like someone she would have sat with at the student union back in the day, because he looked . . . happy. She put the eyeliner down, shook her head.

Anyway, all of that ended with the clarification, which became even more unfortunate as Seamus talked, because her original impression, that *all sorts of possibilities* sense, wasn't chipped away piece by piece, which was usually what happened in her conversations with men. With Seamus, things worked in reverse. The more he talked, the stronger the possibilities became.

He *was* smart. And kind. And curious. Curious about her, her life, her thoughts.

Rare, that was rare. Almost like spotting Bigfoot.

But, she was very, very careful to project an air of obliviousness, an asexual friendliness. Anything else would have just been too unseemly. She knew women, and specifically, this woman. Any hint of flirting, regardless of Cindy's protestations, would have dangerously tread on Cindy's ego, and there was no need for that.

She pulled out her favorite lipstick, lifting the color to her lips, then stopped.

Oh that color was awful, she thought. Awful. How could she have worn it all these months? It looked like something you would wear to a funeral.

She swirled it down, replaced the top, and dropped it into her bag.

She sifted through the other tubes, grasping an old favorite, *Femme*. She took off its lid, twirling up the vibrant splash of coral.

Perfect, she thought, and lifted it to her mouth.

⅄

Cate entered the diner, and took a seat at a table near the door. She picked up a menu with *Breakfast All Day!!* in large, bold print across its top as a waitress came over. "Coffee?" she asked.

"Yes," said Cate, "thank you."

She returned with a pot, poured some coffee, drifts of steam rising. "Waiting for someone or do you just want to order?"

"Waiting for anyone? No. Just me." Cate glanced at the menu, then closed it up, handed it to her. "Two eggs over easy, whole wheat toast."

The waitress left, and Cate looked out the diner's front window, watching the people as they made their way in and out of the Main Street's stores and galleries. She took a sip of the coffee, then put the cup down.

Was that Seamus? Walking her way, a few stores down, hands in pockets, semi-smile.

Oh, her eyes were getting so bad! She squinted in his direction, then sat back.

For sure, it was him.

"Here you go," the waitress said, coming up in front of her, blocking her line of sight. "Anything else? More coffee?"

"Sure," Cate said, moving her eyes back to the cup. The waitress poured, then walked away. Cate lifted her eyes back to the street.

He was gone, replaced by mothers with strollers, a hipster, and an older man with long gray hair in a ponytail. She lifted a piece of toast to her mouth and took a bite.

Maybe she imagined it, she thought, putting the toast down, picking up a fork. She cut a piece of the egg, lifted it to her mouth.

But let's just say she didn't. What if it *was* him?

Hadn't she said she was going shopping in town last night? Or maybe it was Cindy. She couldn't remember who said it, but she was pretty sure someone did. Now, if that man was Seamus, and she ran into him on the streets of Yellow Springs, it could be a coincidence, but, most probably, it was not.

Men, Cate found, sometimes created this dance of coincidence at the very beginning, did an oblique approach to test the waters of interest.

Hadn't there had been all sorts of coincidences with Tommy at the beginning? Times he had shown up at various events she had to attend for work. And each time they would laugh, and he would say, "Gee, this is great running into you like this," or "We have to stop meeting like this," and buy her a drink. Yes, that was how everything started.

It was only later, right before they became engaged, that he confessed what she had already known, that none of those meetings were accidental, that he had shown up at the events specifically because he knew she would be there. She still remembered the look in his eyes when he told her that, the boyish look down, the slow and tentative backtrack to her eyes.

That's really when she had fallen in love with him, right at that moment.

She speared her fork into the last piece of egg.

"More coffee?" the waitress asked.

"No, just the check," Cate answered, picking up her purse.

The waitress handed it to her, and Cate got up and headed to the counter, handing the money to the cashier.

"Pretty top," she said.

"Oh, thank you," said Cate, looking down at the sunshine yellow.

"It's happy. A happy color. I get so sick of black. Like everyone's in perpetual mourning."

"Yes," said Cate. "Thanks."

She opened the diner door and felt the mid-day sun on her face, then scanned the street's store fronts and decided to go into a small art gallery a few doors down. She entered, and stood in front of one of the paintings closest to the door.

It was a sunny picture of Main Street with a Golden Retriever, who looked very happy, prominently featured in the foreground. She glanced at the other pictures and the groups of couples standing in front of them, then quickly decided to leave. She turned, and as she did, felt a tap on her shoulder.

"Hey," said Seamus. "Hi."

"Oh, hi," she said.

"Wow, this is crazy, running into you like this. I just had to stop in, drop something off for a pa—friend."

"Oh. Um, yeah." She shifted her feet. "Oh, again. Thanks for last night, it was great."

"My pleasure. Yeah. Hey, you like that painting?" he asked pointing to the picture of the happy Golden Retriever. "I know the artist."

"Oh, you do? Well it's um . . . yes, it's a good rendition. Happy."

"Yes."

"I just—" A couple came up from behind them, she moved to the side to let them pass. "It's sort of crowded."

"Yeah, it gets like this on weekends once the weather breaks. People come out of the woodwork. You want to go outside?"

"Sure. I'm just . . . well I'm not in the market for this type of art I guess. Street scenes I mean."

They walked out of the door, into the bright sunlight. "Wow, you were right, it's crowded everywhere," Cate said, reaching into the purse for her sunglasses.

"Are you looking for something special?"

"No, I'm not actually looking for anything."

"Coffee or lunch?"

"Oh, I just ate. Is there a park around here or something? It's such a beautiful day I feel like I should take advantage of it after last winter. God, I thought that would never end."

"Isn't that the truth! A park? Um . . ." he said, stopping. "I have an idea, I mean if it seems interesting to you. You want to go over to the college? Antioch? For all intents and purposes it's done for the year, but it's interesting and not all that far. Get away from all of this."

"Antioch? Sure, I'd love to see it."

Cate stood at the entrance sign at the front of the campus.

"So now there are only thirty students?"

"Yep. That's it."

"How in the world did that happen? I mean, back in the day—"

"I know," Seamus said, sitting down on a bench that overlooked the front campus lawn. "I was a student then, back in the day. Late '60s, early '70s. Three thousand students, an unmatched progressive history, national academic recognition. Was so excited when I got accepted, left Jersey, didn't look back. So much stuff was happening here.

"Met Lisa, my wife, our first year on campus, then later, after graduate school, we came back when she got offered a professorship. I had all these thoughts, here and there, about going somewhere else, but she wouldn't hear of it. Didn't ever want to leave, even after things started to change. I guess she had that imprinted vision in her mind of what it used to be . . . you know, like a familiar face you grow used to and then can't see objectively anymore? Anyway, in some karmic timing, around the time she got sick they finally closed the college down. By then there were only a few hundred students. The alumni got together, saved it in a manner, offered free tuition to the first class. Thirty-five of them just started back this year."

"Unbelievable," Cate said, sitting down next to him. "I never really heard of a college closing. I mean certainly not a college with Antioch's reputation and history. It was considered sub-Ivy League, no?"

"Yes, yes it was. Oh, everyone has their own version of who was to blame. Some people blamed the school for aligning too closely with radical causes, causing parents to freak out and prevent kids from enrolling. Some blame it on stupid financial decisions. In the end I guess the truth was a little bit this, a little bit that. Everyone guilty. Like an Agatha Christie novel."

"It sort of has a feel of going back to a boarded up amusement park. Sad," Cate said.

"Yes, yes, it is that. Of course I can't see it fresh, like you. Like what I said before with the familiar face, the memories mix in, creating a whole different thing. Not exactly what it was, but not exactly what it is either. Somewhere in between. Like, take that open space over there," he said, pointing in the direction of a small community park with rolling hills, just south of where they were sitting. "What do you see?"

"A park. Women with strollers. Joggers. Dogs."

"Yeah. I see that too, but it's mixed with other things, odd things, like Van Morrison and the Zippies." Seamus laughed, settled back in the bench. "Crazy huh? But to me, that scene is forever mixed with—when was it?" He lifted his eyes. "It must have been late summer, 1970, yeah, after Woodstock, just following Kent State . . . Van Morrison had just come out with *Moondance*, and he was on tour, well not like tours today, you know . . . caravans of painted up school buses.

"It was called the *Medicine Ball Caravan* . . . Van Morrison, Joni Mitchell, B. B. King, Alice Cooper. And there was going to be a concert slash festival at the old Antioch golf course, and not only that, a film crew was coming too, using the footage in a documentary about the whole counterculture movement. You can actually buy the DVD today on Amazon.

"Anyway," he continued, "a whole crew of Zippies—remember them?—come in with their cars painted with slogans like *Culture Rip Off* and *Sell Out Capitalist Pigs*, to lead an anti-*Medicine Ball Caravan* protest rally right in that place where you see the joggers and mothers and dogs."

"Protesting what?" Cate asked.

"Oh who knows!" Seamus threw up his hands. "You know what it was like then! All the passion, the anger. So overwhelming at the time." He shook his head. "Did you ever think about that? How it felt like raw nerves everywhere? How we really believed everything was just one little step away from a revolution? Today, just the word 'revolution' sounds silly, over the top. But then . . . well, I don't have to explain it to you.

"Anyway, I think the point of the protest was that the movie people shouldn't be filming rock stars and festivals, they should be filming ordinary working Joes in Dayton. That the counter-culture movement was about changing ordinary lives. I think there was a strike going on in Dayton that they were fired up about. Anyway, things got heated, the protesters started throwing rocks, and it ended with a guy in the film crew pulling a knife on one of the protesters, starting a small riot, like a poor man's Altamont."

He pointed to the park. "It happened right over there, where those dogs are catching Frisbees. So see, when I look at that, I see what's there but it's mixed with all that other stuff.

"Oh, I have so many stories about Antioch, don't get me started, I could hog the conversation for days. But enough about me, what about you? What was it like at Marietta?"

"Marietta?" Cate asked. "Oh, well I guess, compared to that, it was just Antioch *Lite*. Like I cannot imagine anyone there protesting a concert. Well . . . maybe Cindy. She was always a little edgier. You know, artistic, rebellious. A really good writer."

"Oh," he said, "I think she said the same thing about you."

"She did?" Cate asked.

"Yeah, back when she first told me about you. Actually I think what she said was you were a gifted writer."

"Cindy said that? No. That doesn't—" She moved in her seat. "Wait . . . Cindy! I need to call her. I totally forgot! What time is it? Three? Four? She should be home by now." She reached in her purse and pulled out her phone, then looked at it, and dropped it back down. "Oh figures," she said, "I forgot to charge it. I always do that. I'm hopeless with technology."

"Here, you can use mine," Seamus said, pulling his phone out of his pocket.

"Thanks," she said, taking it and entering Cindy's number. She listened to the ring, then the roll over to voice mail. "Hey, it's me," she started. "I'm just checking in. I ran into Seamus in town, and then we . . . well he directed me over to the college. I'm just about to leave and come back, should be there within the hour. See you then." She handed the phone back. "Thanks."

She stood up, smoothed down the front of her jeans. "I need to . . . I should probably get going."

"Oh, well, me too. Hey, I'll give you a ride," he said. "We pass my car on the way."

"Oh well . . . OK."

They turned and started down the street. "Thank you for today," said Cate. "I really enjoyed it. I love '60s stuff, college stuff. For years I thought it was all about the times. I just recently figured it out it was more about something else."

"And what's that?"

"Me!" She tilted her head back with a laugh. "Or anyway, the me I used to be. You know, that passion you were talking about? Sometimes I miss that, don't you? Age sort of numbs you down, that's what I think. You lose the terrible, wonderful. I think that's why people sort of gravitate to things that were popular when they were young, trying to recapture those feelings.

"Like music. The Greatest Generation has Sinatra; we have . . . well like a million different groups . . . the Beatles, Stones, Dead, Hendrix, Zeppelin and on and on." She stopped and looked at him. "Now you and I think that music was the best, right? But who knows? Maybe it wasn't, maybe we just feel that way because it's all entwined with who we were when we first heard it."

He shook his head. "Um. I don't know. I was following you until then. I think our music was the best. I couldn't even pick a favorite song, could you?"

"Favorite? That would be hard." She frowned. "Let me pick the one that most reminds me of the times. Yeah, that's easier. I'd pick Jefferson Airplane, *Volunteers* for that."

She stopped, pulled out a piece of paper and pen from her purse, and wrote *tell kids to listen to Volunteers,* then tucked the note inside her wallet. "Just to remind me if I forget," she said, resuming her gait.

He laughed. "Tell your kids?"

"Yes, of course. That stuff is important. Otherwise they have no idea who you are. You know . . ."

He shook his head. "Well, only in theory, I guess. I never had kids. Lisa never really wanted them, and I guess I never felt strongly enough about it to make it an issue. She had a sure sense of what she wanted, a very big personality. That's why . . . when she got sick . . ." his voice trailed off.

"I'm sorry about that. Her passing, I mean."

"Well, the hardest part was the year leading up to it. Yeah."

"I sort of understand that," Cate said. "Well not the way that you do, but I understand it a little. My mom passed a few months ago."

"Oh, I'm sorry," he replied.

"Oh, thanks. It's OK. She was eighty-seven, lived a full life. She didn't suffer or anything. She wasn't really ill, just had a little memory loss thing going on. But sometimes I'd, you know, lose patience. It makes me mad at myself. I wish that hadn't happened."

"Well, things are always easier in hindsight," he said, "and taking care of someone . . . if you ask me, what's appropriate or inappropriate is off the table. It's like walking through an emotional minefield. You can't understand it until you've lived it."

She stopped, looked at him.

"What?" he asked.

"Just . . . thank you." A breeze moved some of her hair in front of her eyes. He lifted his hand, gently brushed it away, then let his hand linger.

"Well—" Cate said, shifting.

He shook his head, brought his hand down, then pointed. "My car . . . it's right over there," he said.

They walked towards the car, and as they got in, he said, "Oh . . . we sort of left it open-ended about tonight. Getting together, I mean. I would like that if we could."

"Well that's sort of up to Cindy."

He turned the key in the ignition, and pulled the car out of the parking lot. "Right. And you're leaving—"

"Tomorrow morning. Early. It's about a seven-hour drive, I want to get started."

"Nashville?"

"No, Asheville," she said. "A totally different thing. In the mountains. I have read a lot about it, I have always wanted to go there."

"Why?" he asked.

"I don't know. It just seems like somewhere I should go. Old school vibe, arty, the mountains. It seems peaceful. I thought about it a lot over the years, I had this magazine." She paused, laughing. "Oh what do I know from that? Who knows? I might get there and hate it, but at least then I'll know for sure."

"Well, that's a very important thing," he said. "Knowing for sure I mean. Gets the imagination out of the way." He glanced at her, then back at the road, turning down Cindy's street, then into her driveway.

"Well thank you again for today," Cate said as she held out a hand.

He held it, then gave her an unexpected kiss on the cheek.

She hesitated, then opened the car door. When she got to the front porch, she turned around to offer a smile and a small wave goodbye.

CHAPTER FIFTEEN

CINDY

She sat at the kitchen table, plastic bag in front of her, and looked at the clock.

It was noon, Jana's recital would start in an hour. She pushed herself up off the chair, went to her albums, and pulled out *Let It Bleed.* She put it on the turntable, then stood back, waiting for the first note.

There it was, a salve. She floated to the music, moving back to a kitchen cabinet, pulling out a bottle of whiskey.

People today have no fucking clue about music, she thought, as she opened the bottle and poured herself a glass. Taylor Swift? Katie Perry? Fucking clueless.

Janis and Aretha, Gracie in her prime, Stevie. Yes. Now that was genius, feminine genius. The bleeding, deep guts of what it is to be a woman genius. Not the Girl 101 stuff.

She put her glass down, and went back to the albums, pulled out a new one.

Fuck you Mick Jagger, she thought as she replaced the old with the new, carefully dropping the stylus down.

Click, click, click, spoons, grave.

Better, she thought, feeling her body relax. She headed back to the table, sat down on a kitchen chair, and picked up the bag Layla had thrown at her that morning.

How funny, she thought, moving it, messaging its soft contents with her hands. Just proves sometimes you wake up in the morning, and before you even set your feet on the floor, you know exactly how the day is going to go.

Because this morning she had woken up with an overwhelming sense of deflation, the strength of which took her by surprise. The past few weeks things had felt so diametrically opposite. Getting the home had filled her early morning thoughts with happy possibilities, second chances. But this morning, as soon as her eyes opened, her first thought was *who am I kidding*?

And that feeling only strengthened when she faced the bathroom mirror and saw her reflection. It wasn't like the morning when she had first arrived at Layla's and was horrified by the creeping beige. No, on that day she felt things could all be corrected with a change in hair style or highlights around the face. No. This was much worse.

This morning when she looked at her reflection, all she saw was what was lost. The uplift in the eyes, the definition of the cheekbones. She touched her face, stepped away from the mirror, then sat down on the toilet.

What was on her mind thinking a house could change anything? She was almost sixty. You can't change a life at sixty; you can only come to terms with it.

And then, right then, her phone rang and she knew from the moment she heard Layla's voice something was up. The tightness of her voice, the paucity of words, *Come over now.*

And that was only confirmed when she got to the house and saw Layla sitting at the kitchen table, all tight-lipped. She knew then some sort of execution was just moments away, and she also knew that it was going to be issued at Layla's chosen pace, which, from the looks of it, would be in grinding slow motion.

So she said a soft hello, got a cup of coffee and took a seat at the table. Then she sat in silence, wondering.

Did Layla find out Jana wanted to quit ballet, move on to the hip hop studio? Was that what this whole drama about that? She shifted, then couldn't help it, ventured a move. "Where's Jana?" she asked.

"Luke took her to breakfast."

"Was she nervous?"

"Nervous?" Layla's black eyebrows raised like little half-moons.

"The recital?" Cindy asked.

"The recital is the last thing on our minds now."

Cindy sighed. "OK, Lee. I give up. What's this about? Is this about my taking Jana to that hip hop studio? She was going to talk to you about that today, after the recital—"

Layla's head snapped back. "You took Jana to a hip hop studio?"

"She just wanted to try—"

"Where?"

"In Dayton somewhere, you know how hopeless I am with directions. In the city. She wanted to try something new."

"Oh that's wonderful." Layla shook her head, put her hands around her mug, and took a sip. "Yes, I'm sure she did, and thanks for that by the way—the not telling me part I mean."

"I just told you."

"Yeah, weeks later."

"So this isn't about that?"

"No," Layla said.

"Then what?"

"You have no idea?" she asked.

"None, and to be honest Lee, can we cut to the chase here? I stayed up late last night, I have a friend visiting. I'm tired."

"Yes," she said, "I imagine you were up late with your quote friend." She got up from the table, went to pour some coffee into her mug, then turned around. "Funny, I'm tired too. But you know why? I was up all night too, but not because of a friend. Jana was in a car accident."

"What?" asked Cindy. "Is she OK?"

"Well, that's the question isn't it? She's not in the hospital if that's what you mean. But OK? Now that's a different story."

"Lee, please."

Layla slowly put her mug down. "After Luke picked her up at your house yesterday, Christopher came over, and Luke stupidly let him take her to the village ice cream store . . . only they never made it exactly, if they ever even tried. Chris ended up hitting another car."

"Oh my God, was anyone hurt?"

"Hurt?" Layla asked, raising her eyes. "No, basically the accident was just a fender bender, and luckily Joe, you know Joe, our friend from the Club? He was the cop who wrote it up. He followed the kids back to Chris's house, told his parents he gave him a speeding ticket, but had a hunch it might be a good idea, if they were his kids anyway, he would check out everything in their rooms because he had a sense that something else was off. That there was a sign of recklessness that's usually accompanied by well . . . something else.

"So they did that, went through Chris's room, his stuff, the car. And guess what they found, stuck under everything in the glove compartment?" She went to her purse on the kitchen counter, and pulled out a bag of white powder. "This. They found this." She threw it to Cindy; it fell on the floor.

"Oh geez," Cindy said, leaning down, picking it up. She opened the bag and licked her finger, put it into the white powder, brought it up to her tongue. She felt the immediate, familiar numbness. "Oh, yes. He *is* trouble."

"You didn't have to do that. I knew what it was," Layla said.

"I just wanted to be sure is all. You don't want to blame her if—"

"I'm not an idiot Mother!" Layla snapped, then took a breath, crossed her arms. "But anyway, yes, that is what I thought too, *he* was trouble. And I thought that until Jana told everyone, including, his parents, that it was hers."

"Hers?"

"Yes. She said that she had taken it from your house." She nodded her head. "Yep, that's just what she said. 'My grandmother's house.' My fifteen-year-old daughter said she got cocaine from her grandmother. The look on his parents' eyes!"

"Now wait a minute Layla, I mean Lee," Cindy said holding up an index finger. "Wait just one minute. *That* is impossible. I haven't done cocaine in thirty years . . . well at least twenty . . . a long time anyway. I don't have any cocaine in my house. As God is my witness."

Layla uncrossed her arms. "Oh really? Well, she said she got it there, said something about maybe that friend of yours had it?"

"Cate?" Cindy asked. "Cate?" She sat back with a laugh, then caught Layla's eyes, stopped. "Cate's straight as an arrow. So straight as an arrow you would like her." She shook her head. "No. I mean, I guess anything is possible, you never know the whole truth about anyone really, but Cate? No. No. Jana was covering for someone else."

"Of course she was!" Layla said. "She was covering for you! Of course, I know that. She thinks you're so ridiculously hip. Her comrade. And isn't that something? You of all people. Of all fucking people she picks *you* to admire?"

"Oh no, no, no . . . I need to talk to her because—" Cindy stopped, eyes widening. "Oh yes, of course! She was covering for Chris. Yes, of course, that's it! She is crazy about him. She would do that, take the fall. That has to be the truth, because I am telling you Lee, that cocaine did not come from my house. You'd have to be crazy to think that. The worst thing in my life was getting over that stuff."

"Sure."

"Lee! Look at me. *Look at me.* Can you not see me the way I am today? Do I look like I'm on cocaine? I look like what I am, an ordinary grandmother. Well maybe not ordinary, but you know what I mean. If I am on cocaine, don't you think you would have noticed it over the past few months? When I was picking up Jana, taking care of things? This whole thing is ridiculous, unfair!"

Layla laughed, shook her head. "Oh, that's a good one. You're talking to me about what's fair. That's really very funny."

"Oh my God, Lee," Cindy said, throwing up her hands. "Will you ever let me off that cross? You never listened to my side of the story, just your dad's and your grandmother's. I had a side of the story too! And anyway, you know I love Jana. You know—oh . . . that's it, isn't it?" Cindy asked, leaning back in the chair. "That is what this is really about. You *know* I love Jana."

Layla's lips tightened. "Don't get things twisted like you always do, manipulating the point. Who in the world do you think you're kidding with that *you know I love Jana!* If your money hadn't run out, you would never have seen her again, and that would have been fine with you. We would have gone on forever without hearing one word from you, not a question, or a birthday card or call. So I'm supposed to be jealous of Jana getting that kind of love? Please. I know more about that kind of love than anybody ever needs to know." She took a step forward. "Do you have any idea, any at all, what loving someone like you did to us? Dad, me, Grandma? Do you ever feel bad about that?"

"I did Lee, I mean I do," Cindy started, bringing her hands up to her head. "You have things, or me, so turned around—"

"Oh, please, stop!" Layla said. "The correct answer is *probably not.* You never gave our feelings two seconds of your time. You didn't even come to see your mother when she was dying. Who does that by the way? She asked about you, right at the end. I had to make stuff up, say you were on your way."

Cindy shook her head. "You don't know Lee. If she asked about me, it had to be the drugs because she had years to forgive me and never could. Never. She relished her role as moral executioner." She looked up. "Tell me Lee, what did I do that was so unforgivable? Fall in love with someone? What kind of mother turns her back on a daughter for that? Is that the great example of love you're talking about?

"You don't know the things I went through, the things she said to me. They didn't want me around. I swear. I kept a letter from her, it's at home." She stood up. "I can go get it, you can see for yourself. You can see—"

Layla held up her hand. "I don't need to see anything. I know everything I need to know. I thought this time things would be different, but I was wrong, and it's over.

"Oh stop looking so concerned! I'll make sure you get the money we agreed on. I am not sure why, maybe to prove that I am not you. I won't abandon *you.* But I swear, if you start maneuvering yourself into Jana's life again, the money stops. Because she is not going to become an updated version of you. So you can go now. I need you gone before they get back."

"But—"

Layla defiantly re-crossed her arms.

Cindy picked up her purse, started to the door, then turned back.

"The cocaine wasn't mine," she said. "And maybe the money was how things started, but that's not how it is now. If you could only forget the past for one moment Lee, one moment and listen. Why can't you do that?"

She walked over to her, started to lift a hand to wipe a tear from her cheek, but Layla turned away, walked to the kitchen table. "Go," she said, grabbing the plastic bag, lobbing it towards Cindy. "Here. We have no need for this, take it. I'm sure you'll find some use for it."

The bag fell at Cindy's feet. She looked at it for a moment, then stooped down and picked it up.

⅄

Cindy was asleep on the couch when she was startled awake by the ringing of her phone. She reluctantly pushed herself up, went to the kitchen table, and looked at the phone screen.

Seamus.

She reached for it just as the voice mail clicked on, then stopped mid-stretch. *Make him wait*, she thought. She sat down, waited for the message icon. When it appeared, she pressed playback, speaker, and Cate's voice filled the air.

Cate, she thought, *Cate*? What was Cate doing using Seamus's phone?

Cindy moved a hand to her aching head, listened.

Oh, wonderful. She had *run into* Seamus. Now wasn't that just fucking wonderful? Could this day get any worse?

Her eyes fell back to the bag of cocaine.

Oh, she needed time alone. She certainly did not need Cate coming into this house with her conversations about kids and her dead mom and Seamus and the endless blather of all that was good and right. No, she did not need that now, not today! She had to get rid of her.

She picked up the bag and walked upstairs to her bedroom, placed it in her top dresser drawer. Then she returned to the kitchen, poured herself another drink, and waited.

⅄

"So how was the recital?" Cate asked, coming up the front hallway, taking a seat next to Cindy at the kitchen table.

"Oh, that? Amazing! Really. Didn't see it coming at all, how amazing it would be." Cindy took a last drink from her glass of whiskey, and got up and went to the bottle on the kitchen counter. "You want one?"

"Um no, not now, but you go ahead."

"Thanks, I think I will." Cindy poured herself a generous amount, lifted the glass to her mouth. "And how was Seamus?"

"Seamus?" Cate asked. "Oh yeah, we ran into each other. He took me over to the college. It was interesting, yes."

"Oh he took you there did he? He talk much about that dead wife of his?"

"A little. He talked about how he took care of her at the end."

"Of course he did." Cindy got up and went into the living room, plopped down hard upon the couch. "Come here," she said, patting the seat next to her. Cate slowly got up, walked over and sat down.

"You took care of your mother? I mean, at the end?" Cindy asked.

Cate shifted. "Well no, she wasn't sick like that. She died suddenly."

Cindy took a sip from her glass. "I didn't even go to my mother's funeral." she said. "Now what do you think of that?"

"Oh Cindy . . . I don't know. I don't—I can't judge that, I don't know your life, really."

"No you don't," Cindy said, then laughed. "No, you sure don't. But you're probably lying about that not judging part. I mean, I just said I didn't even go to my mother's funeral, and even better, how's this? I didn't give a shit when she died. Not one little shit."

"Cindy . . ." Cate said, shifting awkwardly.

Cindy leaned closer, brushed Cate's hair to the side. "You ever do cocaine Cate?"

"Um . . . maybe . . . a long time ago. Once, twice, that's it," said Cate, moving back.

Cindy held her eyes for a moment, then nodded, turned back to her drink. "That's what I figured. You were never like that really. Always had that sure sense of right. Your mother, your ex—what was his name?"

"Tommy."

"Tommy. That's sort of a boyish name. You ever cheat on him?"

"No. No. I had three kids."

"And you love them all so much, your kids I mean."

"Yes. Yes, of course, I do."

"And I bet they love you."

"Well I hope so. Well no, I know so. Yes, I know my kids love me, as I'm sure Layla loves you."

"Oh you're sure of that, are you?" Cindy pushed herself up off the couch, went into the kitchen, and poured another glass. "Want a drink now?"

"No," said Cate.

Cindy put the top back on the bottle, then slowly walked back into the living room. "What are your holidays like with your kids?"

"Cindy, really. What a question. They're holidays. I mean, you have holidays."

"Oh yeah. Of course I do. But I bet mine are a totally different thing." She stood in front of Cate, took a drink.

"Look Cindy," Cate said, scratching the side of her neck, then put her hand down. "Um, what is going on here? Did I do something? Is it—"

"You? No of course not," Cindy said, going back to her seat on the couch. "We're just having a conversation is all, trying to get to the truth. You love the truth right? So now, here it is, all the stuff no one offers when they're glossing over all the bullshit of their lives. After all, I'm the courageous one, right? You said it yourself."

Cate moved in her seat. "You *are* upset. Maybe you need some time alone. I mean, that is fine with me, it's OK. I actually was thinking that drive tomorrow will be really long. I was thinking of breaking it up, getting a few hours in tonight."

"See, just like I said. You have no taste for discomfort." Cindy lifted her eyes to the ceiling, then brought them to Cate's. "That's probably why you had to go that easier way, that traditional bed of red roses. So tell me, how did all that work out for you *really?*"

Cate held her gaze, then dropped her eyes and shook her head. "I'm just going to go." She stood up, started to walk away, then stopped. "Why did you have to go there—red roses, Cindy? Easy? *I* took the *easy* way out? Raising three kids and working? And I don't mean picking up a job to waste idle time or to pay for a designer purse or a ski trip to Aspen. I mean working because you need x amount of money or everything blows. Everything. And being there for aging parents? Yeah, that's a real blast, that end of life stuff."

She picked her purse up off the floor. "And who in the world thinks that's the easy way out? No one Cindy. No one but you, and you know why? 'Cause you never did it.

"Now I don't know what happened to you today, if I did something or . . . I just think it's better for both of us if I go."

She turned to go upstairs. Cindy sighed, then stood up. "Shit," she said. "Cate. *Cate*?" She took a step forward. "Look, you're right. I've had too much to drink and you're right. Something did happen today, but it wasn't about you. Things with my daughter . . . they've never been good, but today was even worse than usual and I guess I just wanted to hear—I don't know what I wanted to hear actually, maybe I just wanted you to feel as bad as I did, maybe that was it.

"Look, I'm sorry. I am. You've done nothing. And you can go, but let's not end it like this." She turned and went over to her albums, pulled one out and put it on the stereo.

"Remember this Cate?" she asked, eyes lighting, as the first notes of the Allman Brother's *Ain't Wastin' Time No More* filtered into the air. "Remember us going to that concert? Ban Johnson Field House?" She returned to the couch, sank into its cushions. "Jesus, Cate. Duane Allman's second last concert, ten days later he'd be dead. A frickin' legend, and there we were, no frickin' idea, just figured it was a concert. And I was so messed up! The only thing I remember is how you helped me make it down the field house stairs. Do you remember that?"

"No, not really," Cate said, then slowly walked over. "I actually don't remember anything about that concert except the balloons. I told my kids I remembered, but that was only to impress them." She tilted her head. "Weren't there a lot of balloons at that concert?"

They looked at each other and laughed. Cate dropped her purse on the floor, sat down next to her.

"God it was fun," Cindy said.

"It was," said Cate.

"You know what I *do* remember?" Cindy asked, taking a drink. "I remember always feeling certain I was the luckiest person in any room. And I'm talking any sized rooms here, including cafeterias and auditoriums."

She laughed, leaned back. "Now? Now I probably couldn't even win this room. Yep, two people, you and me, and now I think the smart money's on you."

CHAPTER SIXTEEN

CATE

Cate got into the car and pulled out of the driveway.

What in the world, she thought.

She drove a few moments, then pulled the car into a town parking lot and stopped, sat back in her seat.

She knew something was off from the moment she entered the house. The whiskey bottle, Cindy's mannerisms, the prickly questions. And it wasn't only that she was drunk, or high, or maybe both. Yes, that was perfectly clear, but it seemed much more than that. Now Seamus could have been a part of it, there was that initial *dead wife* comment, but he couldn't have been the whole thing, could he?

Oh, she should have known better than to include that *running into Seamus* on the voice mail, but it came out so fast, and then there was no way to backtrack. But really, could Cindy's ego be that fragile?

She shifted in her seat.

It was probably just what she had said, she told herself. Something happened with her daughter. But whatever happened must have been huge to provoke that uncharacteristic *I think the smart money's on you.* That was not like Cindy.

Although couldn't that have been just a throwaway compliment, a make up for her prickliness? People do that all the time, try to smooth things over with nice. And maybe she had always underestimated Cindy's kindness. Hadn't Seamus just told her Cindy had given her that compliment, the *gifted writer*?

She tapped the steering wheel, looked out the window.

No, that was not how this felt.

Something turned in her stomach, she felt a reaction in her eyes. Damn, she thought, damn. She lifted a hand to the corner of her eye, brushed away a tear.

Maybe she should go back and check on her. After all, in twenty-four hours Cindy had gone from one drink and endless amounts of tea to an almost full bottle of whiskey. Hadn't she said she had only recently resumed "casual" drinking? Well, there was nothing casual about her drinking tonight! And her overly melancholy *I was always sure I was the luckiest person in any room*? People who suddenly resume drinking, then start getting melancholy . . .

She shook her head. Oh, she had to lighten up! She wasn't everyone's self-appointed savior, and Cindy had gotten through forty years of her life without any help from her. She was just letting her imagination get the best of her.

Anyway, returning would be so awkward! It would be proof she didn't believe her, or an implication she thought she needed her help. And hadn't she gotten the definite impression that Cindy wanted to be left alone? After all, *you can go,* is not a *stay*.

Yes, she had to stop her overreacting! She was always doing that. Making simple things complicated; inserting big meanings when there were none. Like that memory of the day in the college parking lot. Cindy didn't even remember that day, and for decades she—

That's it, she thought! That's exactly what she was doing now. Turning this into an allegorical turn-of-the-tables. Now she was the one going off, and Cindy was the one left behind.

She put the key back in the ignition, started the car. No, she thought, this stops today. New beginning, new habits.

Cindy had a family fight just like millions of people have every day. In a week, they're forgotten.

She pulled the car out of the lot, and tried to ignore the feeling that it sure didn't feel that way.

⅄

She had driven a short time when she noticed a recurrence of the noise she had heard on the ride down. She turned the volume of the CD player down to listen more closely when, all of a sudden, a yellow warning light appeared on the dashboard.

Oh Jesus, no, she thought. No. The noise got increasingly louder. She pulled the car off the road, put on her emergency blinkers, and opened the glove compartment to get the owner's manual. She was flipping through the pages when she saw a pickup truck slowly pass, then pull to the side of the road in front of her. A man with long mullet hair got out and walked towards her car.

Shit, she thought. Shit.

CHAPTER SEVENTEEN

JANA

Well, it couldn't *have been a worse two days. No it really couldn't.*

I don't know what was on my mind taking that bag of cocaine from Gma's house. When I saw it, I wasn't even one hundred percent sure what it was, but I was pretty sure cocaine was the logical guess. Who carries a plastic bag full of powdered sugar in a purse? So I took it on a whim, to show Christopher, impress him with my worldliness.

Lately he has been around Ashley, and she is older than me, more sophisticated. I knew she was offering more than I could, God knows half the time that crazy mother of mine has me in lockdown. So I saw the bag and took it, then texted him to come over. After we got in the car, I showed it to him to prove, I guess, that I was not as young as he thought, that I was worth hanging around for. Like, do not underestimate me.

To be honest, neither of us knew exactly what to do with it, not really, it was just the thought that we had it that was so exciting. And at first everything worked perfectly, his coming to the house so quickly, his excitement when I showed it to him. He wanted to go to the park to check it out further, experiment, but then he started driving so fast, he hit that stupid car, and the rest is now history.

Dumb, fat, policeman with nothing better to do comes back to the house and lectures his parents about vigilance and recklessness and then they do a whole house/car search and find the bag and all hell breaks loose. They call Mom and Dad and the four of them sit Chris and me down on the family couch and they stand over us, going all Gitmo, trying to find out the truth of the thing, how we got it. And Mom was all puffed up, I could see it on her face, she was sure it was Chris's so, I have to admit, I sort of enjoyed putting a needle in her balloon, which I did with the "it was mine" outburst.

Which really made her embarrassed and caused Chris's parents to turn on us. Chris's dad handed the bag to mom, as if it was hers, then acted like we had soiled their precious oriental rugs with all of our tainted family dirt. So we slunk out of there, and then, on the car ride home, it was all—where did you buy it? And what was on your mind buying drugs, we have prominent positions in the community! Don't you ever think of anyone but yourself, how will things look for us? So I listened until I finally couldn't take it anymore, and just to make them stop I said, I didn't buy it anywhere, I took it from Gma's!

Now, I didn't want to throw Gma under the bus. I told them I wasn't even sure I had taken it from her purse, it could have been her friend's, neither one looked familiar. But as soon as I said Gma, Mom was done. She confiscated my phone and told me all contact with Gma was done.

Dad took me to breakfast the next morning. We had a long conversation, unlike any conversation I have ever had with Mom. But in the end, he said it really didn't matter whose purse it was. The point was, either way, Gma was a bad influence. And, at least for the time being, she had to be out of our lives.

Then Grandpa Mark showed up. I do love Grandpa Mark, I do. There is a sort of sadness about him. He went into this long convoluted story about what he called the "toxic effects" of relationships with Gma. He said yes, she is interesting and entertaining and even exciting, but in the end relationships with her will always come to the same place because she only truly cares about herself. He says probably not her fault as she has an addict personality, can't help it.

That's when I said, how can she be an addict, because I have been around her every day for six months, and I have never once seen her do anything! And he said well unfortunately, using, not using, doesn't matter. You can take the drugs away from the addict, but you cannot take the addict out of the personality. And he said I have too much going for me to be tangled up in that—caring, really caring, about someone who can never reciprocate. It is what it is, he said, and it will never lead to anything good.

Then he started talking about Mom. Dad kept quiet during this part, awkwardly drinking his coffee.

Gpa Mark said he couldn't put into words how much Gma had hurt Mom, from the time she was little. How there were so many times he had to make up excuses, pick up the pieces.

He went into some story about a birthday party when Mom was five or six when Gma didn't show. Not even a card or a call. And no one knew exactly where she was, just where she wasn't. And even though there were like a million other people there, and even though Mom had received every gift she had asked for, her face kept moving to the window, the door.

You don't get over stuff like that, he said.

Now your mom, he said, leaning forward, your mom is trying to be the mother she never had. And sometimes, yes I know she can get too protective, but see, that is why.

It almost made me feel sorry for Mom, it did. So much that I almost thought of taking off that ring Gma gave me before I got back to the house, because I know it bothers Mom, like she interprets it as a big "f you." But in the end, I didn't.

Who knows why? I guess I am just not ready to, because even though I hear what they are saying about Crazy G, why do I have to be the one caught in the middle? All that stuff is from the past, way before I was even born! And can't they see how I hate to hear it, how it makes me feel? Gma has only been good to me, she isn't that person they talk about. She actually listens to me, to things that matter, like taking me to that hip hop place. Who else would have done that, and what was the harm? But now, even that is gone. I will be doing ballet for the rest of my life because even dance classes are overrun by this thing between Gma and Mom.

Why does it always have to be this never-ending battle, where Gma is the enemy and I have to prove my allegiance? Because of stuff that happened twenty years before I was born? And it all makes me wonder . . . doesn't Mom ever get tired of it, the energy it takes to continue this battle?

I did see Mom waver just a bit after the recital. It may have been my imagination, but I sensed a spot, not big enough for things to drastically change, but maybe big enough for a slight opening.

After the recital, crazy Barfield came over and told Mom how wonderful I was. Then she asked where Gma was, adding that "I was sure she would come after that conversation we had."

Then Mom said something like, oh she is sick and—what conversation?

And then crazy B said, "Oh didn't she tell you?" and then she laughed that annoying laugh of hers, cackling, head back, and replied, "When I was trying to motivate Jana, she came into my office and basically told me Jana didn't need any motivation or criticism from the likes of me!"

Then she leaned towards Mom and said in a stage whisper, "You know, Grandma talk. Grandmas should always talk like that about their granddaughters! I totally understood."

Mom didn't say anything back. She was quiet on the ride home.

So I am thinking, things might soften up after awhile, give it some time. But I'm not stupid. I know that even if that happens, something new will come up to take its place. And then I will once again be stuck in the middle where I can see both sides of things, each of their rights and wrongs, but can't do anything because both of them are entrenched in decades-old muck up to their elbows.

Yes, that's depressing enough, but there's even more.

Even if I never talk to Gma again, nothing really ends, not really, because Mom sees her in me. And I pay for that in her always-judging eyes; her inability to allow me to make one decision of my own; her refusal to consider the possibility something might have been just a teenage mistake instead of proof of an inherently bad seed.

And all because of how I look. I look like her enemy, untrustworthy, unreliable. And there the story begins and ends, on that one simple genetic fluke.

I have always wondered, what if I had been born looking like her or Dad? Would her assumptions have been different? Could we have been friends like they say some mothers and daughters are? Would she have listened to me about that hip hop class, about how the music made me feel? Or not freaked out when I, like twenty other kids, was busted at that holiday party?

Would I be able to look at her (outside of those moments after a good ballet performance) and instead of worrying about where I was failing, know, really know, that I made her happy just as I am? Doc said she was proud of being my mother, but then he messed it up by giving me all her reasons—the grades, the ballet. That was so like Mom, presenting a case.

If you love someone, really love them, you don't have to give reasons.

Now Christopher? Christopher understands. His parents are their own kind of crazy, all expecting this and that from him like he is some sort of performance puppet. Only with him, it's football instead of ballet.

But after the blowup with the car and cocaine, Mom won't hear anything about my seeing him. Said I needed to stay away, he was too old for me anyway, and she didn't appreciate the attitude of his parents. So if I want to see him, I have no other choice, I have to do it behind her back.

When Mom was talking to Barfield after the recital, Kelsey came up to me, said Christopher had texted her, asked if she could ask me to meet him tonight at the park. He said he was grounded, but would try to sneak out.

I told her to tell him I would try too.

There was a chance, after all, it could easily happen. On the way to the recital, Mom and Dad were discussing their evening's dinner reservations at the Club. Mom wanted to cancel, but Dad said it was too late, and anyway, it was something important to him, a possible job. He sounded unusually annoyed, saying they would only be gone, at the most, a couple of hours, and I had a feeling she would eventually give in, especially after I danced so well. And that was exactly what happened.

Before they left, Mom made me promise about fifty thousand times that I wouldn't get on the internet, or watch television. I solemnly agreed.

She never specifically said I couldn't walk to the park.

And really, how is it going to hurt anyone if I meet Christopher for a short time? Maybe it's technically not right, since I know it is not what she wanted, but tell me . . . what is right about anything in this family?

CHAPTER EIGHTEEN

CINDY

AS SOON AS Cate left, Cindy went back into the house, up to her room. She got the bag from the dresser drawer and took it downstairs, placing it on the kitchen table. Then she pulled up a chair, and sat down.

After all those years, she thought. Twenty years, that's what she had told Layla. But could it really have been twenty years? Maybe that was just an optimistic guess. Maybe it was more like ten, or five, or one.

Oh, what difference does it make now, she thought. It's all just a definite sometime in the past.

She slowly opened the bag, poured some of the powder out, then reached for her purse. She took a credit card from her wallet, tapped its flat edge against the counter. That familiar sound—firm, dependable. She moved the card on the counter, creating a tidy white line, taking time to ensure it was orderly, neat. Satisfied, she reached back into her wallet for a bill, and rolled it up tightly. Then she shook the hair away from her face, and after a slight hesitation, brought the bill up to her nostril, and leaned forward.

⅄

A half hour later, she decided to go to town. Why not, she thought. The night was young, and Jesus, what was she supposed to do, just sit in the house? She was passing the park, almost at Main Street, when she saw something, and hesitated.

Was that Jana? Sitting on a park bench next to that guy?

She looked away, then quickened her pace, but it was too late. Jana had spotted her, was running over. "Gma," she called, coming up to her, grabbing her sleeve.

Cindy stopped, lifted her shoulders.

Jana stepped back.

"What?" Cindy asked.

"Are you OK?"

"Of course I am. Why?"

"You look . . . I don't know." Jana shifted her feet. "Look Gma, I'm sorry. About what I told Mom, I mean. I'm sorry."

"Yeah, well that opened up quite the can of worms there Jana. But your mom was just looking for an excuse to unload on me anyway, it was just a matter of time. Although it looks like you got through everything fine." She nodded in the direction of the young man on the park bench. "They let you out?"

"Oh God, no. Mom and Dad had made plans for this Club dinner before everything blew, and they didn't want to cancel, so I promised . . . I just left for a short time while they were gone so I could meet Chris, but he didn't show. That guy? I don't really know him, we were just talking. I'm going home soon."

Jana took a step forward. "Grandma, I am pretty sure Mom will get over this. I really think so, because at the recital Mrs. Barfield told Mom—"

Cindy lifted her hands to her face and laughed, her purse fell to the ground. "Oh Lord!" she said. "Oh Lord, Jana! Do you really think it's as simple as that? That anything Mrs. Barfield says or doesn't say has the power to make everything right?" She leaned closer. "Come on Jana, you can't bullshit me. I know you're smarter than that. All this stuff in our family—me and your mother, you and your mother, me and my mother?

"It's not about anything that happened yesterday or today or thirty-some years ago. It certainly isn't about what anyone else in the world says or doesn't say, or what we say or do! No, it's nothing about that at all!"

She brought her eyes inches from Jana's. "You know what it is really about?" she asked.

Jana stepped back. "I'm not sure."

"Of course you are," Cindy said. She shook her head, then straightened her body. "It's because we are different. Different and . . . *special.* They know we don't want their boring, dull lives, and worse yet, they know we don't have to settle for them. See, that's what it's about, who we are, and who they are not. And you could dance with the Bolshoi Ballet, it won't change any of that.

"They look at you and me and wonder—why couldn't it have been them? Why do they have to be the drudges while we get to be butterflies? It really is unfair when you think of it, that quirky genetic fluke. We get the cheekbones, legs and freedom, and they get what? A book of rules to enforce, like they're God's Little Helpers. But I bet you've already figured that out—even if you won't admit it."

She bent over to pick up her purse, momentarily losing her balance. Her right hand steadied herself on the pavement. Jana leaned over, put a hand on her elbow.

"I'm fine," said Cindy, pushing her away, brushing off the soot from her hand. She nodded in the direction of the park bench. "Try to get home before they do. No point in making things hard on yourself, you've still got a few years to deal with it. But take it from me, nothing you can do will really make her happy. Nothing. So just go with what works for you."

She turned, and started to walk away.

"Grandma?" Jana called, running up to her. "Grandma, I think . . . I think you're wrong. Mom doesn't hate you. I think she loves you very much, it's just—" she began, then noticed the stiffening of her body, the quick turn away. She pulled on her sleeve. "OK, what about this? *I* love you Grandma. Me. I love you."

"Well," Cindy said, turning back, touching her cheek, "of course you do. Of course. We're exactly alike. How could you not?" Then she brought her hand down from her check, and turned and walked away.

CHAPTER NINETEEN

JANA

She watched as her grandmother slowly made her way down the street, then walked over to the park bench, slumped down, and covered her eyes with her hands.

"Wait, what happened here?" the guy sitting next to her asked, pushing the brown hair out of his eyes. "I just got you over the boyfriend who didn't show and now you talk to that old woman for five minutes and you're down again?"

Jana took her hands away from her face. "That old woman is my grandmother you asshole."

"Your grandmother? Wow," he said, leaning back. "I didn't mean anything about 'old,' 'cause she's sort of hot for a grandmother, just sayin.' But was she sick or something? Or wait, was she high? Was your grandmother high? She seemed sort of—"

"Shut up," said Jana, turning to him. "What's your name again?"

"Alex."

"Shut the fuck up Alex." She straightened her back. "You said you have some liquor in that bag?" she asked.

"Sure do!" he said, smiling, "cherry vodka."

"Good. Then shut up and give me a drink. I only have an hour before I have to be home."

CHAPTER TWENTY

CINDY

Cindy entered the first bar she came to on Main Street, sat down on the first barstool. She saw the man next to her eye her up and down, up and down, with familiar desire. He was younger, forty maybe? Not too bad looking. Maybe he was actually great looking.

She narrowed her eyes, looked closer.

He looked a little like Randy. The good Randy, the young Randy. Same black hair, same dark, smoldering eyes.

The bartender came over. "Manhattan, up," she said.

"Manhattan? I like that. Kicking it old school," the Randy guy said, leaning towards her. "And what brings you here on a Saturday night all alone?"

"I guess I'm here for the same reason you are. Trying to get lucky."

The bartender came over, handed her the drink. She laughed, lifted it up. "Used to be I never had to look for that. Luck, I mean. It followed me around like I was a magnet."

She took a long gulp, wiped her mouth with the back of her hand.

The man clicked his tongue. "Oh come on . . . things can't be that bad now can they? And anyway, you know what I always say?"

He put his hands around his drink and smiled. "No matter how bad things are, there's always one thing you can count on, they can always get worse! Um . . . what's your name?"

"Cate."

"Cate. That's a nice name Cate. Like that hot English chick. Well, this is what I say Cate. All you can do is enjoy the moment, right?"

She nodded. "That's exactly right, Randy. Right."

He took a drink from his glass; his forehead creased in a momentary frown. "Randy? I'm not—oh never mind. Not important. Just finish that drink and the next one's on me. See . . ." he added, raising a hand to the bartender, "how's that for jump starting your luck?"

CHAPTER TWENTY ONE

Dusk

Wow. What the fuck. I thought I was going the right way and then—what the fuck?

There was no way I should have taken that drink from him. And him pawing me like that. I didn't even know him, who was he to think he could do that? He had to have put something in that drink. How did I not think of that? Now my legs are so tired . . .

She stopped, tried to gather her thoughts. There. I need to go up there, cross that road, head back the other way.

Yes, of course. It is only a fricking five minute walk from there, I can do a five minute walk. How did I get so turned around? I've been walking for what? Ten, fifteen minutes? What time is it now anyway? It has to be getting late.

She reached for her purse, but it dropped to the ground, and she stumbled a little, steadied herself, hands on the ground.

Why in the world were things always so fucking difficult, she thought, pushing herself up, wiping her hands on her pants.

Walking, love, all that stuff. Should be so fucking simple.

She straightened herself, took a deep breath, then a tentative step forward.

You can do this. You *have* to do this, she thought, moving towards the bright lights.

Just cross that fucking road and be done with it.

It's just five minutes more.

Any idiot can do anything for five minutes more.

CHAPTER TWENTY TWO

SEAMUS

He walked over to his phone on the kitchen counter and picked it up, then put it back down. He opened the refrigerator door, looked inside, then shut the door, returned to the phone.

What would it hurt if he just called? Make it casual. It didn't have to be any big deal, she wasn't a mind reader. It was just something anyone with tentative plans would do. He would say *Cindy? Oh hi! I was just touching base to see if you guys still wanted to get together.*

Something like that. Harmless.

He just had to be certain to remember the *still. Still wanted.* Like he wasn't being stalker-ish, just giving things their due diligence.

He picked up the phone, put in Cindy's number, then listened as it rang, then clicked to voice mail. Shit. He thought about hanging up, but felt that would be worse, so he cleared his throat, and waited for the beep.

> *Oh hey Cindy, it's Seamus. Just touching base to see if you guys wanted to get together tonight. 'Cause we had sort of mentioned that, but I know you two are busy, so just double checking before I um—go out.*

But I mean, I'm not going far, just up to town. So um . . . OK . . . call me back if it works. Thanks. See ya, bye.

He pushed the end button.

How could he have not remembered the *still?* Just kept it short, like he had planned, the *still* covered everything, set the right tone. Why did he get into *oh I'm going to town.* Shit.

He went into the living room and sat on the couch, picked up the remote and turned on the TV. Oh, what did it matter, he thought. Most likely, Cindy saw the call coming in and just didn't pick up. That was probably the truth of it. She had been noncommittal from the start, even sort of prickly about the whole thing.

He tossed the remote onto the table.

Oh, why was he obsessing like a prepubescent boy over setting the right tone for a voice mail? What in the world was wrong with him? He had a couple of conversations with a woman—no, let's get real here. He *saw* a woman and decided before any words were spoken a whole lot of things, and then, he had two casual, friendly conversations with her that didn't go horribly wrong and what did he think? That he would marry her and they would go to San Francisco or Nashville or wherever and—what? His life would be perfect? He would die happy?

Jesus.

If someone came into his office and said, look Doc, I saw this woman and from the moment I saw her, I knew—

He would stop them right there, right fucking there because he would know, know without a doubt, it was not about the woman at all.

He tapped his feet, suddenly irritated by the television newscaster's voice. He reached back for the remote and turned the volume to mute. *Fricking stupid newscasters,* he thought. His eyes lifted from the television to the picture of Lisa on the bookshelf.

His eyes softly widened. God, she *was* beautiful, he thought. Sometimes he forgot.

He got up and walked to the picture, picked it up warily, gingerly, as if it were dangerous, then brought it back and set it on the coffee table in front of him.

He had taken the picture one beautiful fall day, about ten years ago, when the sun was out, and the leaves on the trees were those glorious colors of brilliant orange, deep maroon, and dark mustard yellow. It had been a Sunday morning, that was it. They had coffee on the deck and then she had said, let's go hiking in the park.

It was one of those days when ordinary mixed with glorious, when you got up in the morning and felt, for no tangible reason, everything was going to go perfectly right.

And it had. He found a parking space right by the park entrance. She wore the sweater he especially loved, its bright blue perfectly playing off the brilliance of the fall leaves.

She had gone slightly ahead of him, then turned around and asked, "See, wasn't I right all along? Aren't you glad we stayed?" and the sun danced off her long blonde hair, and her eyes were filled with an almost youthful exuberance.

It wasn't so much his "Yes, you were right" answer that took him by surprise, as much as the realization that it was true.

And that was when he snapped the picture.

Seamus closed his eyes, leaned into the couch's pillows.

After she passed, people told him, remember the good times, but the truth of it was, the good times were almost impossibly hard to remember.

Bad times, imperfect times, much easier.

He opened one eye, then the other.

Jesus, he thought, that was it.

Hadn't he spent the past three years reminding himself of everything that fell off the mark? The miss on San Francisco. The kids that never were. The personality that was so big, so enchanting, it sometimes had a tendency to steamroll.

The truth of it was, he had synthesized all that, weighed it against the leaving, and always came up firmly as a stay. Otherwise, he would have left her long before the diagnosis.

He stayed because he was happy. Why was that so hard to admit?

He picked the picture up and placed it back on the shelf, then returned to the couch.

She was there for forty years, and then she was gone, as if she had been a character in a beautiful fable set in an increasingly faraway time.

He closed his eyes.

It was much easier to think of all the things that had been wrong, but the truth of it was, most of it was very, unbearably right.

⅄

Seamus had gotten up early, decided to go into the office, clean some stuff up. He was thinking of taking some time off, heading back to Jersey for a while. He hadn't been there since his mother passed some five years ago. He hardly knew anyone there after all these years, some cousins, some old high school friends. But some might be enough.

He parked the car and headed into his office, draping his jacket over a chair, pulling out his cell phone. He was placing the phone on the desk when he noticed the two missed calls.

Oliver.

Oliver? On a Sunday morning? That could not be good. He quickly hit the call-back button.

"Oh Doc," Oliver said, picking up on the first ring, "Shit. Isn't this horrible? I mean, I hate to bother you on a Sunday morning and all, but I really need to see you."

"Jesus Oliver, what's wrong?"

"Didn't you get my voice mail?"

"I did, but didn't listen. Just called you back," Seamus said.

"Oh then Doc, oh, you need to listen to the voice mail . . . yeah, something is wrong. Seriously wrong, no *horribly* wrong. Not the 'I can't paint a good picture' stuff I usually talk about, the real thing. Can I come over now? I know it's Sunday but—"

"Sure Oliver. Actually I'm in my office now, cleaning some stuff out. Think I'm going to take a vaca—"

"Great. I'll be right there."

"OK."

Seamus sat back in his chair, then pressed the voice mail button on his phone, waited for it to cue up. Maybe Oliver had seriously relapsed, or maybe it was a new issue with Heather. There was always something with him.

He put the phone on speaker, and leaned back.

"Doc, this is Oliver. I mean . . . I hate to bother you on the weekend. Um maybe you know. I think it was in the paper, pretty sure anyway. I was in an accident last night. Like a horrible accident. I was in the truck and hit a woman. She ran in front of it. I mean, there was a witness and everything, the cops know it wasn't my fault. It's just . . . I can't get this out of my head. Can you call me at . . ."

Seamus turned to his computer, entered the *Yellow Springs Chronicle,* and waited for the online version to load.

He went down from the top stories. National stuff. End of school stuff. There. Accident, fatality. He clicked on the story.

He started to read and then stopped. Leaned forward and read again.

He read through it a third and fourth time, squinting his eyes, making sure he was reading correctly. And then he took off his glasses, and shrunk back into the chair.

CHAPTER TWENTY THREE

What Came After Cate

The morning sun filtered in through the hotel room drapes. Cate got out of bed and went to the window, held the drapes off to the side, and looked out at the mountains that encircled the city like peaceful emerald barricades.

How beautiful, she thought. She reluctantly stepped back, let the drapes fall from her hands. Now, what time was that appointment? She went to the phone to check her calendar. Monday, 4:00 p.m., Grove Park Spa.

She had made the appointment weeks ago, when the idea of the trip first came to her. Made it at the costliest, most exclusive spa in town, with a history of clients that included presidents and first ladies. At the time, the appointment had seemed a sort of personal accomplishment, her reward for those years when five minutes alone in the bathroom had to be negotiated with toddlers. What she would have given then for a day at a spa!

She put the phone down, and went into the bathroom, splashed some cold water on her face.

She hadn't slept the night before, tossed and turned.

The anxiety of that car problem had probably thrown her off, the guy in the truck. She had let him look into the car window at the warning light. He said he had a buddy in town who was a mechanic, he could call him and see if he could take care of it.

She said OK, and he pulled out a flip phone, punched in some numbers and talked for a few minutes. Then he closed it and leaned into the car. "Yeah, he can help. You have a GPS?"

"Um no."

"But you have a phone?"

"Oh sure." She reached for her phone, then remembered it wasn't charged. She started to say, "But it's dead," but instead said, "I'm terrible with technology. And directions and maps. I'm terrible with all that stuff."

"You know where Xenia Road is?" he asked.

"No. I'm just . . . I was visiting a friend. I'm from out of town."

"OK. I can lead you there, it's not too far. I can't stay though, the wife is expecting me back, birthday party for the grandkid, but he knows you're coming and you can trust him."

"OK. Thank you. I really appreciate it."

There, she thought, closing the car window and pulling out behind him. He couldn't be dangerous, *birthday party for my grandkid.* But she still had a general wariness (every single murderer she had watched on *48 Hours* and *Datelines* episodes, started out with a benign first impression and unusually bad haircut), but she felt there was no real harm if she just followed. If things started looking even remotely shady, she could turn the car around, find her way back to Cindy's, or at least back to town.

But that never happened because the guy turned out to be just as he seemed, someone helpful, no ulterior motive. And he did just what he said he was going to do, left her in the hands of his buddy who fixed the problem, and sent her on her way.

She only had to slow down once, just out of town, for a random traffic jam. She never saw the reason why, just a couple of police cars and a truck pulled off to the side, but after that, it was a clear, easy drive.

She drove four hours, stopped at a hotel, then finished the trip on Sunday, getting into Asheville by late afternoon. She checked into the hotel, then quickly headed out on a short walk to town. The easy-to-navigate city streets lived up to her preconceived notion of quirky mountain charm, with stores named *Chocolate Fetish* and *Waggers Dog Depot* interspersed between art galleries and boutiques that seemed to stock the mother lode of long, bohemian dresses. She purchased some phony ice cream, free of anything remotely harmful to animal or man, and watched as a drum circle developed in a small park.

Yes, it was just as she imagined—this mix of aging hippies, well scrubbed tourists and cool young hipsters—which was why she couldn't explain her general lack of enchantment. She decided she was probably just tired, and threw her barely eaten almost-ice cream into a garbage can, then headed for her hotel.

When she got ready for bed, she realized she had taken the last Ambien two nights before, and made a mental note to call Kelly in the morning for a new prescription. So this morning, right after she got out of bed, that is just what she did.

It was early, before office hours, which, Cate thought, was preferable in situations like this. She placed the call, heard the ring, then the expected transfer to voice mail. She waited for the beep, then began. *Hi Kelly! This is Cate. I hope you are well. I am doing great. I think I may have told you about this short trip to Asheville? Well I'm on it now, it is really helping! But I just realized I am at the end of my Ambien prescription, and was hoping, not that I need them, but just in case . . . If you could call a prescription into a pharmacy here. Just enough to get me by until I get home, say just two weeks or so? That would be perfect. I plan on making an appointment as soon as I come back. Oh, if you want, you can do that too, make the appointment I mean. That would be great. You can call me on this number. Thanks!*

Then she went to the bathroom and turned on the shower.

Oh, they had citrus scented soap! She unwrapped the bar, held it in her hand. Was there anything better than the scent of citrus, so fresh! She held it up to her nose, breathed in, then took it into the shower.

When she got out, she picked up the small bottle of body lotion. Vanilla! She opened its top, squeezed a generous amount on her legs, then her arms. She brushed her teeth, took the towel off her head, and shook her wet hair so it fell into its natural loose waves.

This was going to be a very good day, she thought. She walked out of the bathroom, towards her suitcase, and by habit, picked up her phone. A voice mail.

She clicked, held the phone up to her ear. "Hey Cate . . . this is Kelly. We got your message. OK this is the thing. I haven't seen you in a while, I think you had a couple of cancellations so really I cannot call in another prescription for Ambien. It really should only be used short term, six weeks at the most, and you're at that time already. But here's the good news . . . I have a good friend, a colleague in Asheville, you will love her. She has an office downtown and I have already talked to her. Her name is Naomi Kay. She said if you stop down around lunchtime she will fit you in, and after she meets with you, she might be able to give you a prescription to tide you over until you get home. Oh, and your appointment? Just call us when you get back, I will get you in, no problem. Anyway, I am happy to hear you are traveling, enjoying yourself. Be safe and oh yes, Naomi's number is . . ."

Shit, Cate thought, shit. What was so damn difficult about an Ambien prescription? It wasn't like she was asking for morphine! So stupid and inconvenient, making such a big deal about it, sending her to see Naomi what's-her-name.

She picked up her makeup bag and took it into the bathroom, leaned towards the mirror.

Well, maybe, if the office was downtown, she could stop, what would be the harm? It would take what, fifteen minutes? Kelly said around lunchtime, and she really didn't have anything to do until that spa appointment at four. She opened her foundation bottle, put a few drops on her hand, then smoothed it over her face.

Yes, she thought, I guess I could do that.

Not that I need to, but just in case.

⅄

She entered the office and walked into the small, empty waiting room.

No receptionist, no patients. For a moment she thought she was in the wrong place, and was just about to walk out when a gray-haired woman dressed in all black entered from an inside doorway.

"Cate?" the woman asked smiling, holding out her hand. "I'm Naomi, Kelly's friend. Or colleague, but that sounds cold doesn't it? She told me you would be here about noon, you're right on time."

Her maroon eyeglasses hung from a sparkly chain of little crescent moons. She was free of makeup and jewelry. Her short, spiky hair and loose fitting pants conveyed a disdain for anything that might imply a need for sexual attention.

Cate took her hand, "Oh yes. I appreciate this. I thought I might be in the wrong office."

"Oh, the receptionist doesn't come in until after lunch," Naomi said. "I try to keep my appointments to late afternoon, early evening. Semi-retirement, you know? Come on into my office."

Cate followed her in, then hesitated as Naomi took a seat in a small chair. "Come over, sit down," she said, patting the arm of the angular couch next to her.

Cate moved forward, took a reluctant seat.

"So, you're visiting Asheville?' Naomi asked. "Tell me, how do you like it?"

"Oh, what's not to like," Cate answered, crossing her arms. "I mean, I just got in Sunday, I've only walked around town, but it's very pretty, yes."

"But—"

"Oh there's no but. How could there be a 'but'? The mountains are beautiful, that is for sure. The city? I mean, it's interesting and who can argue with clean and pretty? Not one ounce of grit. Not even in the people. But. . . " she continued, lifting her hands in explanation. "I'm from Akron—well I was born in Cleveland, but actually there's no difference—and up there, we sort of expect a certain amount of grit with our cities. Like grit you can see. Pretty and clean are sort of—"

"You don't like that," Naomi said, nodding her head.

"Well no, I'm not saying I don't *like* it. I've always been a big fan of pretty and clean. I mean, who isn't? They're obviously great qualities. They're just a little too um Germanic maybe? I'm Italian. That might explain it."

Cate glanced at the books on top of the coffee table, *A Room of One's Own, Speak*. She felt Naomi's watchful eyes, pulled her hands close to her side. "Did Kelly tell you this was just about a prescription refill? Just a couple of weeks' worth? To get me through till I get home."

"Yes, Ambien. So you're still having trouble sleeping?"

"Well trouble—no, not trouble exactly. I mean it isn't a huge problem. I just . . . well sometimes it's just hard for me to get to sleep, here and there, and you know since I am traveling and all, I want to be sure to have some. Just in case."

"OK, well . . . that all sounds very good, but I don't write Ambien prescriptions for a 'just in case' thing," Naomi said. "Ambien is a short term solution to an underlying issue, and Kelly said you have been on it for what? Over a month?"

Cate shook her head. "Well, not over a month, well maybe just over, but look, if there is a problem, we can forget it. I just didn't think it was any big deal is all."

"Kelly also said you had cancelled some recent appointments, she had a concern about what might be going on?"

"Kelly said that?" Cate asked. "I can't imagine why she would say that. I was just busy, is all. My mother died, did she tell you that? It was hard to get to appointments. But me? I'm fine, probably the most resilient person you'll ever find." She picked a piece of lint from her blouse. "Yeah. I was a single mother for a long time. Did she tell you that? You get through that, you can get through anything."

"Hm, yes . . ." Naomi said. "I teach a class in writing at UNC Asheville, and I have some women in there, single mothers some twenty, thirty years ago, and the experience seems to be defining, the emotions of it I mean. It infiltrates almost everything they write. The anger, resentment, loneliness—"

"Look . . ." Cate said, moving to the edge of the couch, "I just wanted a short refill, that's all. It's really no big deal."

"OK," said Naomi, then with a momentary hesitation, pushed herself up off the chair, and walked to her desk. "So when you get home, I'm sure Kelly will be able to help you."

"Oh . . . OK," Cate replied, then slowly got up, and walked to the door. She put a hand on the knob, started to twist, then stopped, turned around.

"Go ahead," said Naomi, looking up over her glasses. "You've got nothing to lose. You'll probably never see me again."

Cate leaned back against the door. "I guess . . . I think I *am* having a little problem sleeping. It's a habit now I guess.

"Those women in your class—they're right, or you're right. It *is* defining, being a single mom. All the worries. If the job will hold; if you're missing something important in a kid because you're too busy or tired; the feeling that you're always only one step away from disaster. You can't turn it off, even when the kids are gone.

"The feeling stays. You start believing you weren't granted the luxury of fun. You're the one who always has to stand guard, pay attention."

Naomi walked back to the chair, and motioned to the couch. "Like I said, you have nothing to lose with me. Why don't you come and talk about it for a while?"

⅄

Cate sat at a picnic table in a place called Craggy Gardens, off the Blue Ridge Parkway, about a half hour drive from Asheville. She looked down at her shoes, the ugliest shoes she had probably ever worn in her life. Black, utilitarian and comfortable, even after the hike.

Now wasn't that crazy? Her buying those shoes? Her cancelling a spa appointment, at a world class spa nonetheless, because she suddenly felt it was something she really didn't want to do anymore, it was more like something she thought she wanted to do a long time ago.

After her meeting with Naomi, she had come out of the office, and looked up at the mountains, and decided that was where she really wanted to go. So she cancelled the appointment, and went to one of the many granola-ish stores and bought these ugly-ass shoes.

The day's whole string of events was amazing, unexpected. The hiking, the vista, the ugly shoes, the switch up of what she thought the day was going to be and what it actually became.

"Stop holding yourself to habit," Naomi had advised. "Surprise yourself. Do something different, not something you wanted to do in the past. Listen to the woman you are today, what she wants. It will shake the cobwebs away, and put you on a journey that fits, not one that would have fit some ten, twenty years ago. Who knows where it might lead?"

Cate reached in her pocket for her phone, put in her daughter's number.

"Hey."

"Sara, guess where I am?" Cate said, standing up. "You're not going to believe this, but remember that spa appointment I had? I cancelled and went hiking instead and now I am overlooking this beautiful place called Craggy Gardens, and it is amazing."

"You went hiking in what, your heels?"

"No. I bought these black hiking shoes. And they are ugly. Really ugly."

⅄

Each morning she would stop at a food stand and buy some fruit, then get back in the car and drive up to the mountains. Sometimes she would stay an hour, sometimes four. She timed her stay against *one really good idea.* When she had one really good idea, she knew she was ready to head back to town.

One day she had a thought that maybe, just maybe, when she got back to Akron, she should look for a home. A home as in "house." Something fresh and small, a '50s ranch, with hardwood floors and a fireplace. Close to the kids, but not too close. Maybe by the Metroparks somewhere.

She could fix it up, paint it happy colors. Yellow. Not a bright, garish yellow, a soft, promise yellow. And it would be cheaper than rent. Then she could travel more, different places. Maybe Santa Fe.

Her thoughts filled her with an unusual sense of sureness, and one afternoon, as she made her way through the town's little shops, her eyes were drawn to a beautiful writing journal, covered in bright pink and orange flowers, with the words *A May Queen's Spring Clean* in gold lettering on the front.

She picked it up and held it in her hands. It could be a perfect thank you gift for Cindy, she thought, a hopeful play on *Stairway* lyrics. So she bought it, and it was only the next morning, after her hike, when she was sitting on a park bench eating a pear, that she realized it wasn't an appropriate gift for Cindy at all.

Cindy didn't even write anymore. And those golden words on the journal's cover, the play on *Stairway* lyrics? They wouldn't mean anything to Cindy, not the way they did for her. Cindy didn't even remember that day, much less the lyrics of the song playing in the van.

Cate finished the pear, got up and threw the remains into the garbage, then returned to the bench and sat down.

No, Cindy liked immediate things like flowers and candy. Yes, that was better. She would buy her some bright sunny daffodils, or maybe yellow tulips. Then she would stop and surprise her with them on her way home. Find out how things had turned out; show her support.

And there it was, she thought, standing up. Her one good idea for the day.

She turned and walked to the car.

The journal? She would keep it for herself.

Or, the herself she had been before everything else happened.

CHAPTER TWENTY FOUR

SEAMUS

Seamus entered his office, turned on the lights, then went to the window. Ironic how beautiful the day was, he thought.

The memorial service had been grueling. He wanted to talk to Lee, but it just wasn't the time. He would wait, talk to her when he came back from Jersey. And Cindy? She had finally returned his call, said she would stop in sometime later this afternoon if she had the time. Said she was going somewhere?

God, who knew what was actually going on in that family. The body language, the vibe at the service was almost unbearable to watch it was so full of tension, stilted and uncomfortable.

But how could he have found that such a surprise? Hadn't he read all of her journal entries? He had just chosen to chalk everything up to teenage angst and exaggeration—even at that last appointment when he had a gut feeling something was terribly wrong.

He sat down at his desk, ran a hand through his hair.

Maybe his relationship with Cindy had distracted him, made him less diligent. Maybe he should have removed himself as Jana's counselor as soon as he knew of their connection.

He picked up a pen, tapped it on the desk.

But could he have prevented *this*? And anyway, wasn't there enough blame on this to go around before it landed on him? Didn't Oliver confess his own critical distraction, that fateful reach for the phone? And if Jana wrote truthfully, what about Lee? Her hands were certainly in the mix, as were Cindy's.

Seamus dropped the pen.

Stop, he told himself.

Maybe it's nobody. Maybe it's as simple as Jana did what most teenagers do when they're young and think they're invincible. Party, get high, end up in the wrong place at the exactly wrong time. Maybe it was as simple as that.

Or maybe—hadn't someone said they saw her with a guy in the park right before it happened? Maybe he had given her something.

He glanced up at the degrees on the wall, then went back to the pen, rolled it around in his hands. Well, the toxicology report might help, he thought, although really how much? If it confirmed Jana was high, it still wouldn't answer if it was just a party high, or her final response to a big something else. Things would always remain a pick 'em, a what do you prefer to believe.

There was a soft knock on the door. He reluctantly got up.

"Oh Oliver," he said, opening the door, keeping his hand on the knob. "You know this really isn't a good time."

"Yeah, I know Doc. The service was today, right? I wanted to go, but thought, I just didn't think it was appropriate. I was worried—"

"It's really better you didn't go. I mean, not that you are to blame. No one blames you. We've gone over that. It's just that this is not a good time for me. I am leaving next week for a trip and I need to finish some stuff up."

"Just five minutes is all," Oliver said.

"OK," said Seamus, taking his hand off the door knob. "But, I really have to make it short. I actually have to be somewhere else in a half an hour."

"I'm just . . . I've heard . . . well you know the talk, how she was sort of . . . well might have been hopped up on stuff."

"Well, people talk Oliver," Seamus said as he walked to his desk chair and sat down. "No one knows that for sure. People shouldn't be talking about it. I mean she was just buried today."

"Oh yeah, I know that," Oliver said. "But I heard someone saw her in town that night. Maybe with a guy or something? Maybe he had something to do with it."

Seamus opened, then closed a file on his desk. "Oliver, really. What's the point of all this? It's not the time, it really isn't. And it's getting obsessive, your constant going over *maybe this* or *maybe that.* We don't know what really happened. Maybe we'll never know."

"It's just . . . if I knew I would feel better."

Seamus held up his hands. "Of course you would. Everyone would! This is not just about you." He shook his head, then stood up and walked to Oliver, stood face to face. "Are you feeling OK?" he asked.

"I can't sleep."

"No. It's something else. Your eyes."

"My eyes?"

Seamus walked back to his desk, sat down. "I'm not an idiot Oliver."

"Doc," Oliver started, "things have been hard. I talked to you about it. When I leaned over in the car to get the phone, do you think . . ."

"Oliver please," Seamus sighed. "I just don't think I am the right person for you to talk to about this. Maybe I am too connected to her and the family. I'll refer you to—"

"You *knew* her?" Oliver asked.

"Well yes, I mean I didn't really *know* her, but yes, I knew her family from . . . the Club."

"What was she like?"

"I'm not getting into that," Seamus said. "I have a colleague, I can give you his name, he's right down the street. You're going to need someone else anyway—like I said, I'm going out of town." He pulled out a piece of paper and pen, started to write.

"But Doc . . . I can't do anything. I can't paint. Nothing."

Seamus looked up. "But you can get high."

"Doc—"

"Look, Oliver," Seamus said, dropping the pen. "You think I have a magic wand to take this away? I don't. I don't have a single thing. And I have been trying for years with you, but I've actually been no help at all. Even before this happened, when all you had were overblown everyday problems, stuff about newspaper columnists, demanding girlfriends, paintings that fell short. I couldn't help with that.

"Well now you've got *this*. And it's there and it's always going to be there, and no one will ever blame you for letting something like this ruin your life. I mean, this isn't just some wacky, forgettable newspaper column. This is the big leagues, someone died. Yeah, so you can do that—or you can take this guy's number and try to get on with things."

He picked up the pen, finished writing, then handed the paper to Oliver. "I'm not the right one to help you anymore, if I ever was," he said. "He's a great psychologist. Call him. He can help you if you let him."

CHAPTER TWENTY FIVE

CATE

She pulled the key out of the ignition, gathered the flowers (all yellow!), and walked up the stone pathway to the front door. She knocked, waited, then knocked again. Finally, she heard footsteps. A woman, in her mid-thirties with short brown hair opened the door, stood in front of her with a quizzical "Yes?"

"Oh," Cate said, "I was expecting Cindy. Is she here?"

"Cindy?"

"Cindy Allen? We're friends. Well, we were friends from college, like a million years ago. I just visited her week a couple of weeks ago. Thought I'd drop off these flowers as a thank you."

"Um, Margie?" the woman turned and called, as another woman came up. "She's here to see Miss Allen."

"Oh . . ." Margie said, as the first woman backed away, then walked out of view. "Miss Allen isn't here. We're just cleaning things out."

"Cleaning things out?" Cate asked.

"Well, you know . . . after the accident."

"Accident?" Cate asked.

"You don't know? Lord, I thought everyone knew."

"I'm not from here, I'm just traveling through."

"Oh please come in, you should sit down." She motioned to the kitchen table.

Cate walked into the foyer, stopped. "Was Cindy in an accident? Is she in a hospital or, oh no, is she—"

"Oh no, no, no. Not Cindy. It was her granddaughter. Jana. Was such a beautiful girl."

"Jana? *Was* such?"

"Oh I'm sorry, so sorry, yes," Margie said. "She's dea—has passed. There was a terrible accident, a truck. Oh, please sit down! I can't believe I had to tell you." She pulled out a kitchen chair.

Cate walked to the chair and sat down, set the flowers on the kitchen table. Margie went to the sink, filled a glass with water. "Such a horrible tragedy," she said. "The memorial service was packed. You know how it is when young people pass." She walked over to Cate, handed her the glass, then sat down next to her. "Did you know her?"

"Um, know her? No. I just met her briefly when I was here visiting last Friday—no, Friday before that."

"The Friday before that?" Margie asked. "That would have been the day before the accident. Yes, I remember because the accident was the next night, Saturday, and my son was coming over, and he was late because the traffic was—"

"Saturday night? I left Saturday night," said Cate. She took a sip of water, then set the glass on the table. "But Cindy . . . where is Cindy?"

"Now, I am not sure about that," Margie said, shaking her head. "Her daughter hired us to clean everything out. I got the impression she left and isn't coming back. Maybe things weren't so good between your friend and her daughter? Sad, isn't it? But I guess not so unusual, when things like this happen, these horrible tragedies, families go off, split apart. I think it's because they can't handle the weight of things. Crazy. You would think it would be just the opposite. Anyway, we're packing things up, getting them ready for a garage sale or donation."

"But what happened?" asked Cate. "The accident I mean."

"Well best as I know, Jana was trying to cross that highway going out of town early that Saturday night. I guess she ran in front of a truck, the driver couldn't stop. That's what the police say anyway. Just horrible."

"But why on earth was she crossing that highway?" asked Cate.

"Oh no one really knows. I mean, everyone knows it doesn't make sense. Some people say she might have been high, but you know how people talk. Nothing official or anything. And me, I don't like that kind of talk after someone passes, especially someone young. I'm just telling you what some people say. But who hasn't made a stupid mistake when they were young? *There but for the grace of God go I*, that's what I say." She looked at the flowers on the table. "Pretty," she said.

"Oh yes," Cate said. She sat for a moment, then pushed herself up. "Well . . . I really need to go, I need to find out. But, thank you, I appreciate."

"Oh, I'm so sorry I couldn't help. Do you want me to tell Lee you were here?"

"Lee?" Cate asked.

"Your friend's daughter. Jana's mom."

"Oh, I must be confused. I thought her name was Layla."

Margie shook her head. "I've always known her as Lee."

"Oh. Well no, she doesn't know me. I might send her a note—" Cate turned to walk to the door, then stopped, her eyes drawn to the items lining the hallway.

"Oh those things!" said Margie, standing up. "Those are some of the things we are getting ready to sell. Some of the stuff . . .well I guess you could say it's for a specific taste? Probably won't go for what's on the stickers, but you know how it is . . . you ask for something, you settle for something else."

Cate's eyes moved to the picture of the smiling woman. A red thirty five dollar sticker perched on her purple boa. "Yes," she said.

"Oh, wait!" said Margie, going back to the table. "Don't forget your flowers."

"Oh no, those were for—I'm traveling, they won't keep anyway." Cate said. "I think I'll just leave them. If you want them, feel free."

"Oh, thanks," Margie said, pulling one of the flowers up to her nose, then setting it back down. "I wish I could have been of more help with your friend, where she went. I really have no idea, and Lee is so overwhelmed, I hate to bother her with—"

"No, no, that's OK," Cate answered. "I think I know someone who will know. Thanks again, really." She turned and walked out of the house. Got into the car, and reached for her phone.

Yes, Seamus would know. But oh Lord, what was his last name? She hurriedly entered a search, *Seamus psychologist Yellow Springs.* There just couldn't be that many Seamus psychologists in Yellow Springs! And what day was this—Tuesday? Yes, Tuesday. Good, he would be working. Sometimes doctors take Wednesdays off or is it Mon—

A name popped up, *Seamus Callahan*, with the office location and number. That had to be him, she thought! She hit *call,* and a woman quickly answered.

"Oh hi," Cate said. "Can I talk to Seamus—um Dr. Callahan? Is he available?"

"The doctor is in a session right now."

"Oh, no. I need to talk to him. This is personal. Um. Cate, my name is Cate. I am a friend of Cindy's . . . Cindy Allen? I just found out her granddaughter died . . . Jana? And Cindy is gone and I need to find out where she is and—this is the right Dr. um Seamus isn't it? Friend of Cindy's? Cindy Allen?"

"Oh yes, yes, he is the right one . . . but like I said, he is in a session now, but it's ending soon. I can give him your number and he could probably get back to you within say, fifteen minutes?"

"Fifteen minutes?"

"Yes."

"OK. Tell him Cate called. Cindy's friend. Tell him to please call me back, I am in town and just found out and I need to talk to him as soon as possible. Can you tell him that please?"

"Of course."

"Thank you."

She put the phone down, then immediately picked it back up.

What was wrong with her? She would just call Cindy herself. She put in her number, then listened as the call immediately transferred to voice mail.

"Cindy. It's Cate. I want to tell you how sorry I am, how very, very sorry I am about Jana. I don't know where you are, I stopped at your home on the way back, and there were cleaning ladies there and they told me you left. Please call me when you can. Please. If there is anything I can do—" She was cut off there by a beep and a *voice mail full.*

She slowly put the phone down and put the car key into the ignition. She would go into town and wait for Seamus to return her call.

Cindy?

She tried to ignore the feeling that she would never talk to Cindy again.

⅄

"Cate," Seamus said coming out of an inner hallway into the reception area.

She rose. He put out his hand, and gave her a kiss on her cheek. "It's . . . well, I would say good to see you but—"

"Yes. And I apologize for the call, so spur of the moment on a work day and all, but I had decided to stop and see Cindy on the way home and then—"

"No, it's no problem at all. I understand, come in."

She followed him into his office, he closed the door behind her. "Have a seat," he said. "I have to apologize, this day is a little frantic. I am fitting in some last minute appointments, getting ready to leave for a trip back home."

"Oh . . . well I promise, I won't take much of your time. It's just . . . I called Cindy and left a voice mail, but I know her and I just don't think she'll call back and . . . do you know where she is?"

Seamus sat down on the chair next to the couch. "Not exactly. I mean, I saw her once after the memorial service, last Saturday actually. She stopped in. Said she was going to go see a friend down south? But I'm not sure of the exact place."

"Down south? Did she say New Orleans?" Cate asked.

"Gosh. I can't remember, there was a lot of other stuff . . . I would have thought maybe she would have called you."

"Me? No. I mean, we just recently reconnected, and this is something—I don't think she would talk about this. She was close to Jana, and she isn't like that with most people, she's usually guarded or . . . aloof? On emotional stuff, I mean." Cate lifted her hands, shook her head. "So what happened? And how was Cindy when she left?"

"Oh what happened exactly, I don't know. I don't know if we'll ever really know that for sure," Seamus said. "They are waiting for the toxicology reports on Jana, then they will know that part anyway. Witnesses said she seemed disoriented, was trying to cross that two-lane interstate, at dusk, Saturday before last."

"The night I left," Cate said.

"The night—I thought you were leaving Sunday morning?"

"I was, but things changed. I left that Saturday night."

"Oh . . . *oh*." He leaned back in the chair, smiled slightly. "Yes, then that was the night."

"But wait . . . did you say toxicology reports?" Cate asked. "Was Jana using drugs? I saw her the day before it happened, that Friday, she didn't look like she was on drugs! She was just this beautiful young thing, looked so much like Cindy when she was young."

"Well I would agree with that," Seamus said. "She may have dabbled, she definitely had a rebelliousness in her, but nothing serious, just a curiosity or adventurous nature. Overall, just normal teenager stuff. It would be hard for me to believe she was a regular drug user either, no matter what the report says.

"As I put the story together, her parents were at the Club at some dinner, and she was supposed to be home, but, I guess she got bored, and went to meet up with a boyfriend, who actually never made it. Anyway, that's what the boyfriend and his parents said. They said he was going to meet her, but they stopped him, kept him home all night. Now that didn't sound right to me, like I was missing part of the story, because this guy is older, seventeen, and what parents prevent a seventeen-year-old from going out on a Saturday night? Especially someone like him, he's a football star, his parents are movers and shakers. I don't see them as the type to ground him, my read is they are more the type to worship the ground he walks on . . . but anyway, that's what they said and I guess it's really beside the point. Point is, Jana went to the park to meet him and he never showed.

"There were a couple of people who saw her, said she was sitting with a guy on a park bench, drinking cokes or something, nothing out of the usual. No one had a really good description of the guy, just that he had brown hair. Everyone's attention was more on her I guess. The next thing anyone knows is the accident."

"And her mom? Layla? How is she?" Cate asked.

"You mean Lee," Seamus said.

"I must be confused on that," answered Cate. "I was sure Cindy said her name was Layla, but the woman at Cindy's house referred to her as Lee also."

"Well everyone here calls her Lee," Seamus said. "Well, she's . . . well you can imagine . . . Jana was an only child, so it's not good. But Lee's very hard to read, very contained, keeps things inside. I mean, to most people."

"Like Cindy."

Seamus started to laugh, then caught himself. "Well, I never saw a resemblance between them. No. To me, they're like fire and ice."

"Well I never met Lee, so I can't really say," Cate said. "I just . . . I don't understand Cindy picking up and leaving like that right after Jana's death."

"Um," Seamus started, moving his feet, "there were family issues I think—no, I know. Maybe you do too? Between Lee and Cindy? I think Lee was raised by her dad and Cindy's mom after the divorce. Cindy just recently came back into the picture. Up until then I got the impression she wasn't that involved. That's how it seemed to me anyway. Lots of resentment and blame on both sides."

"That could be," Cate said. "You know, the night I left . . . something had happened between Cindy and Lee. Cindy said an argument, but it felt much bigger to me."

"How so?" Seamus asked.

Cate lifted her eyes, then brought them back to his. "Well this is crazy, but it's how it felt. Cindy seemed defeated, like she had given up on something." She gave a small, nervous laugh. "Oh I know that sounds crazy. I have this tendency to exaggerate moments, but that's how it felt.

"It's just . . . it made me sad because over the years I've envisioned Cindy a million different ways, but never like that. It bothered me. It bothered me so much that I almost went back. I had to argue with myself not to do that."

"Hm, defeated?" Seamus asked. "Now that's interesting. I certainly didn't see that side of her when we talked the last time. When we talked she was more in warrior mode. But I think I tread on dangerous ice. I told her I thought she should tough things out, stick around for Lee, who needed her support. That after some time, maybe they could get to a place where they could resolve things. I said I hoped that could happen, because I felt they both needed it, but that whole approach was a huge failure.

"Cindy told me I shouldn't be offering advice on anything—that I was just some small town psychologist in bofunk Ohio who couldn't help teenagers deal with skin problems, much less offer advice on thirty-year-old adult matters I know nothing about. Then she said the only thing Lee said to her after the accident was, 'It should have been you.' And what did I think about that?

"From there, things went downhill fast. She said *she* was the one who lost the most when Jana died, not Lee! And if I wanted to know the truth, the truth was that Lee couldn't stand the sight of Jana, put her right in the path of that truck with all of her suspicions and judgments and ridiculous demands. So what in the world did she owe Lee?

"So that's how that went. And then she left, and I haven't seen or heard from her since. I have to tell you, that whole conversation got sort of dark."

There was a soft knock on the office door. Seamus looked up, "Come in," he said.

"Your next appointment is here," said his receptionist, leaning into the room.

"Oh, OK, I'll be right out," he said.

"Oh well, I have taken a lot of your time. I should go," Cate said, standing up.

"Hey, I wish . . . well obviously I wish we could have met again under different circumstances."

"Me too," she said.

"How was your trip by the way?" he asked.

"The trip? Oh yes. It was great. Great. I loved the mountains, yes, but I did miss home way more than I thought. And now you're going on a trip?"

"Yeah," he said, "just for a week or so. Going back to Jersey. That's where I'm originally from. My parents are gone now, and I haven't really been back for a long, long time. Going to reconnect with some high school friends I haven't seen since graduation. Forty-three years, can you imagine? Should be interesting."

"Yes, it will be."

She walked to the door, turned to leave. "Well thanks again, and have a great—"

He looked at her questioningly.

"What?" she asked.

"Nothing. Well . . . I was just thinking—when I come back, I think I go right by Akron. Maybe . . . if I do, could I give you a call?"

"Of course," Cate said. "Of course. Do that. I'll look forward to it."

⅄

Cate turned into a town parking lot, got out her phone, and put in Trey's number.

"Hey," he said.

"What's wrong?"

"Oh nothing."

"No, there's something," Cate said. "I can hear it."

"Well nothing that's important. And anyway, it was probably predictable."

"What?"

"Cindy—"

"Cindy's there? I was calling you about Cindy . . ."

"Well yeah . . . she showed up out of the blue a couple of days ago. Called from the airport, no warning. But all that's fine, you know me, I'm open to anyone coming in. She said she had some trouble with her daughter but it was all vague, you know, like she usually keeps things."

"She said she had some trouble with her daughter?" Cate asked. "It was a little more than that! But go on, tell me what she said."

"Well she was back into full party mode, you know, like back in the day, not like the time you were down here with her last year. 1973 party mode."

"Is she still there? Can I talk to her?" Cate asked.

"Not anymore."

"What do you mean? Where did she go?"

"Oh who knows!" Trey said. "She and Stretch left a note in my kitchen yesterday morning. They split. Decided to go somewhere else, Key West or something. Took the car. Stretch took some money. Done."

"Well I'll be God damned," Cate said.

"Yep, that's exactly what I said too."

CHAPTER TWENTY SIX

October 2013

Cate

Oh, why had she agreed to this? Now here she was, sitting on this panel of, let's get real, ten-years-past-middle-aged women, advising all these young, pie-in-the-sky coeds about life and the real world?

She shifted the papers in front of her, then immediately regretted the noise it created. She didn't want to draw any attention to herself. As far as she was concerned, the woman to her right, Dr. Lynn-fricking-Darton, could speak for the whole damn hour.

"When I started my work on my PhD in Women's Studies, it was unheard of, really . . ."

Cate reached for her glass of water. She felt like she was at a great aunt's house, listening to her rambling on about the good old days. How is it, Cate wondered, when everyone talks about their *good old days*, it's always so insufferably boring it makes everyone grateful they're over.

Well, she only had herself to blame for getting roped into this. When the alumni rep had called to ask her to participate, she had hesitated, but in the end, she acquiesced.

"We selected some alumnae from the '70s for a panel presentation for our coeds over Homecoming," the sales pitch began. "There is so much interest in the '70s! Such a romantic time! Kent State, Vietnam, the start of the women's movement! And additionally we have a lot of really successful women from those years . . . Dr. Lynn Darton, do you remember her? She has agreed to be on the panel. You must remember her! She was very active in student government back in the day, now she heads the Women's Studies program at Kentucky. And Andrea Garrison? She's retired now, but she was on the board of governors for the Federal Reserve. It will give the coeds great perspectives, not only on the times, but the real challenges ahead, the struggles of raising a family, starting a business or career. All that stuff."

"Well see, now you're intimidating me," Cate replied. "I mean, I'm not a PhD or governor of anything."

"Yes, but . . . we really have no one else in the arts, and I need one more panelist to round things out. And you have kids, right? And have sort of made a career in writing."

"Well yes, 'sort of made a career' pretty well captures it."

"Oh, I didn't mean that the way it sounded. We'd just love to have your perspective. And you're what? Only a few hours away? Have you checked the list of returning alums? We have quite a few from your class."

So Cate agreed, even though, yes, she had already checked the list and knew no one she really cared about was going.

Trey was holed up in his house in New Orleans. And Cindy? She hadn't heard from Cindy since the day she left Yellow Springs. As she suspected, she had never returned any of her calls.

Cate started to reach for her purse to check the time on her phone, when she realized Dr. Lynn had stopped her dissertation, and the perky moderator, along with everyone else in the room, was looking at her.

"Oh, I'm sorry," said Cate. "Did you ask me something?"

There were a few nervous laughs from the small audience; the young women moved in their seats.

"Well, we were just going down the panel to ask for any final words of wisdom," the moderator said.

Cate shifted in her seat. "Words of wisdom? Hm. I would say . . . well I guess I would say this. Beware of the past. Yes, that's what I would say.

"Because life after this gets very, very complicated. And it will get complicated for all of you. And totally unpredictable. Things that are supposed to happen won't, and things that aren't supposed to happen will. And at those times, especially at those times, that is when the past is at its most seductive, with all its set heroes and villains. You know, or think you know, what happened then.

"But you really don't know. And it's really not safe. It's actually deceivingly dangerous. So, yes, that's my best advice . . . try to avoid doing that."

The moderator looked at her blankly. "OK then." She shuffled the papers in her hands. "Now isn't that interesting? And Dr. Darton, your advice?"

"Well . . . I would say, and I am going to stick to practicalities here . . . the important points to remember as a young woman starting out today is that the opportunities are . . ."

⅄

Cate stood at the corner of Fifth and Putman, and pulled out her phone, entered his number.

"Oh Lord," she said when he picked up. "It was so stupid. And I was the worst! You know what I said when they asked for some final words of wisdom? Could I just have just said what everyone else says, 'Go into engineering?' No! Of course I couldn't do that. You know what I said? I said 'beware of the past!' Like I was Edgar Allen Poe. Shit. Where are you? Oh. Yeah. You're only about fifteen minutes away. I'm at the corner of Fifth and Putman, right outside of the campus. No. Let's just head back home, OK? I'm sort of excited to see it, the painters should be finished."

She put the phone back into her purse, sat down on a park bench that overlooked the entrance to campus. A young woman with long, brown hair walked towards her. She smiled. Cate smiled back. She passed, then turned around and came back. "I liked what you said back there," she said.

"Oh? In the panel discussion?" Cate laughed. "I think I sounded like Edgar Allen Poe, didn't I?"

"No. Oh, maybe a little. But it was better than the usual 'be fierce,' or 'go confidently into the future.'"

"Yeah. Well. It was the first and only thing that came to mind."

The young woman laughed. "No, really it was fine. Actually, most of the time, people aren't listening anyway. And what you said was light years ahead of hearing what a great life I would have if I just switched my major to engineering." She sat down next to her.

"Well," Cate said, "an engineering degree would have served me better than writing. I mean, if I could have just stayed awake in a math course. What's your major?"

"English Lit."

"Do you want to teach?"

"Oh God, no."

"Good. Then you will have to scramble. It will make your life interesting."

The young woman laughed. "Well, I guess I'll worry about that in a couple of years."

"You're a sophomore then?" Cate asked.

"Right."

"My sophomore year was the best. One of the best years of my life."

The young woman pointed to Cate's hand. "I love your ring," she said.

"The ankh?" Cate asked. "I actually got it when I was here. When I was about your age." She took it off her finger, handed it to her. "Here. Try it on," she said.

The woman slipped it on.

"It looks good on you," Cate said. "Keep it."

"Oh no!" the young woman said. "I couldn't."

"Of course you can," Cate laughed. "I *want* you to."

"Really?"

"Really," said Cate.

"Well then . . . *thank you.*"

A car pulled up to the side of the street. "Oh, there's my ride," Cate said, standing up. She turned to her, extended her hand. "Hey, best of luck to you."

"Oh," the young woman said, rising, "thank you. And thanks for the ring. Ill take good care of it."

"I think you will," Cate said.

Their hands entwined, then disengaged. Cate watched as she headed off in the opposite direction, her long brown hair glistening in the autumn sun.

Probably going downtown, she thought. Or maybe not.

But definitely, somewhere.

She glanced back up the hill to campus, then walked to the car, and opened the door.

About the Author

An award winning columnist and journalist, Sue Amari was born in Cleveland, Ohio and currently lives in Akron. Her articles have appeared in *The Plain Dealer*, and the *Cup of Comfort* and *Chicken Soup* series. A Calculated Guess is her first novel.

To contact the author, visit *acalculatedguess.com*

Made in the USA
Middletown, DE
13 August 2016